USA TOD

DAL

Vandals in the Vidalias

Lovely Lethal Gardens

REWIND 05

VANDALS IN THE VIDALIAS: LOVELY LETHAL GARDENS REWIND, BOOK 5
Beverly Dale Mayer
Valley Publishing Ltd.

ISBN-13: 978-1-834088-57-0
Print Edition

Books in This Series:

Zonked in the Zucchinis, Book 1

Yipped in the Yams, Book 2

X-Ray in the Xanth, Book 3

Weapon in the Watermelon, Book 4

Vandals in the Vidalias, Book 5

Undone in the Underbrush, Book 6

About This Book

Doreen eagerly anticipates her escape to the coast, leaving behind the wintery blues of Kelowna. However, the trip means returning to her old home—back when she was married to Mathew—stirring up a whirlwind of memories. She hopes for a peaceful journey, but, as soon as she steps into the conservatory, she realizes her hobby has unexpectedly followed her here.

Mack takes a few days off work to assist Doreen in sorting through Mathew's belongings, aware of the emotional challenges she faces when revisiting her former life. His curiosity about her past is piqued, yet what he discovers is both unsettling and intriguing.

Amid this visit, a perplexing mystery unfolds. Why is a victim in the Vidalia patch, Doreen's cherished garden bed? Could this be connected to Doreen herself? Or is she just unlucky again—or rather is she in the right place at the right time … again?

Sign up to be notified of all Dale's releases here!

https://geni.us/DaleNews

Prologue

NAN'S BIRTHDAY PARTY at Rosemoor the week before had been wonderful. Mack drove to Doreen's house to retrieve Nan's special birthday gift, placing it carefully in his truck bed before peeking under the wrapping. His expression had been wonderful to see. "Wow. She'll love this."

And Nan did. So did everyone else. Doreen felt so much joy to see her grandmother's face light up, as she and Nan both loved their furry and feathered family so much.

Now, however, the weekend and the party were already a warm memory, and the drive to Vancouver was almost over. Her animals had been very subdued, which made the travel time nice. Mack pulled up into the long fancy driveway, staring in shock at Doreen's former home.

"I know," Doreen muttered. "Even looking at it now, it's hard to believe I lived here for so many years."

"And yet it wasn't your *home*, but it should have been."

"Right," she agreed, giving him a bright smile. "It really wasn't. It was a cage, but it's still hard to go back in time and to face how long my marriage was and what my life was like here."

Mack just waited in the truck as she dealt with all these

memories, with all these emotions.

Finally she shrugged. "It's fine." She opened the passenger door and stepped out. "I can't believe we're here. It was a decently long drive."

"You were looking at flying down," he reminded her, "then changed your mind."

She nodded and smiled. "If we had flown down, then we couldn't have brought the animals." She let Mugs out. He raced around, sniffing.

Mack smiled. "I guess this was home for him too, wasn't it?"

"He certainly spent some years of his life here, yes," she agreed, "but it's not as if he cares. If he's with us, that's what's important."

Goliath got out, sitting right next to the truck tire, staring in disdain, as if not believing what kind of place they had brought him to. Yet he usually had that expression on his face regardless.

"What's the matter, Goliath?" she asked. "I would have thought this would be right up your alley," she said, with a snicker. "After all, it is fit for a king."

Mack shook his head. "It really is, isn't it? Good God."

Then a tall man in a security uniform stomped up to them, asking, "Who are you people, and why are you here? This is private property. This is a gated community. How did you get through?"

Doreen smiled at him. "The gate guard, Amos, checked our supporting paperwork and IDs and allowed us in. You can check with Amos to confirm. So do you work for the Parkers?" she asked, pointing in the direction from which he came.

He frowned. "No. I work for the Smithsons, the new owners next door."

Doreen nodded. "I'm the new owner of this property. My name is Doreen Montgomery. I was Mathew's estranged wife and now in charge of his estate." She pulled out her driver's license to share with him. "And your name?"

"Jefferson," he grumbled as he frowned, checked her ID, and then returned it to her. "Mrs. Smithson has seen a couple roaming around the property recently, and I attempted to speak with them, but they ran off instead."

Doreen frowned at that, turning to Mack. "Interesting," she muttered. Facing Jefferson again, she added, "This is my fiancé, Corporal Mack Moreau of the Kelowna RCMP."

Another vehicle pulled up behind them, and Mack turned and smiled as Nick Moreau got out.

"Hi, Nick," she greeted him. Turning to the guard again, she explained, "This is my attorney, if you wish to confirm these facts with him. Plus he can provide the name and contact info for the local probate attorney representing Mathew's estate."

The guard did take a moment to interrogate Nick and seemed satisfied with his answers. "Thank you for your time." And then he promptly left.

Nick frowned at them both. "What was that all about?"

Mack suggested, "Why don't we discuss this inside?"

Nick nodded. "Good idea." He took another look at the mansion before him and whistled.

"*Right*," she muttered, as she walked over and gave him a hug.

"Hey, my almost sister-in-law. How're you doing?"

"Since we stopped at Merritt and had brunch together," she teased, with a chuckle, "I think I'm doing just fine."

"Good." Nick nodded. "I wasn't sure how this trip would go for you."

"I'm fine. Besides, I brought Mack for support."

Mack chuckled. "That's me. I'm just here for support."

"That's a good thing too," Nick noted, "because, on the way down, I did get a call from the Vancouver police."

"Really?" she asked, turning to him. "What about?"

"Apparently you had some break-ins in the garden area. They couldn't find any damage to the house or any entry points, but the greenhouse was broken into."

She stopped and stared at him. "The private security man mentioned how those neighbors saw a couple, a man and a woman, walking around here recently. Drat. That was my little corner," she muttered, her heart sinking as the realization hit her. "Wow, I hadn't really expected to feel that."

"Hey, it's okay," Nick told her, patting her shoulder. "Let's get you into the house, and we can look around while we're here. The police do want me to contact them about it as soon as we have some answers for them."

"Answers for them?" she asked, turning to stare at Mack. "How are we supposed to have answers for them? We just got here."

Mack chuckled. "It's vandalism, and it's an unoccupied house. I'm pretty sure this is low on their list of crimes to investigate."

"Right," she muttered, raising both hands. "Why would they care?"

"You have to understand," Nick explained, "that Vancouver is a massive city and that you are in a very wealthy area to boot. So they do want to touch base at least."

She looked back at Mathew's palatial mansion. She slowly walked up to the front door. "It still doesn't feel real."

"Of course not," Nick agreed. "How long has it been?"

"I stayed nearby for just a month or two before I moved to Kelowna. That period is kind of a blur. It's just over a year as he kicked me out just before Thanksgiving," she muttered.

Nick nodded. "And look at how much your life has changed."

At that, Mack put a gentle hand on her shoulders. "Do you want to go in alone?"

She faced him and frowned. "Heck no," she muttered. "I still half expect Mathew to jump out of the woodwork at me."

"Even though he's dead and gone?"

"He may be dead and gone, but some things never die," she declared. "I was a ghost of the person you know now while I lived here, and I really don't want to go back to that timid existence."

"And you won't," he declared cheerfully. "We're here to take care of the business end of selling this house and its contents. That's it. And, if you want to keep anything, we brought the truck, so you can take whatever you may choose back with you."

Thaddeus poked his head out from under her hair and gave a massive whistle.

"*Right*," she quipped. "Could have been yours too, you know?" she told him and then laughed. "No, it couldn't. I refuse to live here. And, even in Mathew's lifetime, he would never have allowed a bird in the house. Poor Mugs had a hard-enough time here."

"Why?" Mack asked.

"He had to be perfectly groomed all the time. The maids were instructed to wash his feet each time he came inside from the yard. No jumping around or onto people. He was shut up in a room when we had guests over. No begging for food at the table, or he was shut up in a room again. No treats, except for those the staff and I snuck over to him. And, if he so much as passed wind, Mathew had him kicked out of the room immediately."

Mack chuckled. "Mugs is much better off where he is now. It's not as if a dog can control that."

"No, but I've got to tell you that it seemed as if Mugs had this instinctive knack for doing it on purpose, whenever Mathew showed up."

"Maybe it was his way of getting kicked out, so he didn't have to deal with Mathew," Nick suggested, chuckling. He handed over the keys. "I'll let you do the honors."

She stared down at them, made a face, and then turned to the front door. Putting the key in, she unlocked it. Pushing it open, she stepped in cautiously. Mugs raced past her, Goliath on his heels, both streaming down the hallway. Mugs knew exactly where to go. "He's heading for the kitchen," Doreen shared, "in case you are wondering."

"He's not really expecting there to be food, is he?" Nick asked.

"There was always a stash of treats for him in one of the bottom drawers," she explained, as she went in that direction.

She knew that the others were more or less following her, even as their shocked gazes stared around. She turned to them and admitted, "I know. It's a little over-the-top."

"A little?" Mack repeated, staring at her. "This is how you lived?"

"No, this is how I was caged, remember? Language is everything."

He smiled at her. "You do know …"

"Don't even say it," she muttered. "If I wanted this life, I would have stayed. I didn't want it even when I stayed for too many years. I certainly don't want it now, don't want anything to do with it."

In the kitchen, she walked to the drawer that had always been full of Mugs's treats. She opened it, expecting it to be empty, yet dog treats were right there. "I'm surprised they didn't get rid of these."

She pulled out a few and tossed a couple on the floor for him. He sat down and dug in. Goliath sat beside him, sniffing every once in a while, wondering what the heck he was chewing on but completely disinterested otherwise.

Catching sight of the attached greenhouse out the kitchen window, Doreen walked over to the ten-foot-tall double French doors, unlocked one, and pushed it open, stepping outside into the fresh air. She loved this place still. It was a mix of screen panels and glass windows, so she had a wonderful space to grow things.

Seeing the damage to one of the nearby glass panels, she cried out and raced over to it. "Why would they damage the greenhouse?" she asked in shock.

"Depending on who it was and why," Nick suggested, coming up behind her, "it could have just been maliciousness. A lot of people just want to destroy things."

Mack checked this side of the double French doors. "While they seemed to have entered this area, I don't see any forced entry into the main house itself."

"But destroying the greenhouse is just so sad," she whispered, as she stepped farther inside and looked around. "It's such a beautiful space."

"This is a greenhouse?" Mack asked from behind her. "No way. This is huge."

She sighed. "I guess most people here would call it a

conservatory."

"Yeah, ya *think*?" he muttered, clearly astonished.

It was obvious to Doreen that he was really struggling with what she had as her former home. She added, "Remember that none of this even matters to me."

"I'm working on remembering that," he conceded, "but I have to admit, … it's a shock. This exceeds anything I could imagine."

Still, it wasn't anything that she wanted him to feel bad about. As she walked through the greenhouse, conservatory, or whatever Mack wanted to call it, it broke her heart to see the damage. It was all fixable, yet it was senseless, and there was no need to hurt plants like this. She sighed. "We certainly have to put this to rights before we can sell it," she muttered.

Nick looked over at her. "Do you think it'll make a difference?"

"A conservatory like this should be in its prime," she stated, "and obviously it's not."

"That's true," he agreed. "Depending on how much it costs, it is something to take into consideration."

"I would like it brought back to the way that it was meant to be, no matter the costs," she explained. "This was my space, Nick. Can't you call the property manager who was hired by Mathew's probate attorney? Surely they can find someone with references and glowing reviews to properly restore this area."

Nick nodded. "Sure. I can do that. It was probably your only happy place amid all this … other."

Doreen nodded, giving another long sigh.

"And maybe that's why it was damaged," Mack suggested, turning to her.

She stared at him in surprise. "If it was, … that would imply it was done by somebody who knew me." She frowned. "I doubt anybody here even remembers me anymore. I have no friends here." She looked around again, shaking her head. "It is sad …" Then she walked over to where the worst of the damage was, planted her hands on her hips, and stared.

Mack came up behind her. "Problems?" he asked her.

She turned to him. "I had Vidalia onions here. I kept them growing all year-round, so we always had fresh onions. I know it sounds silly, … but it was just one thing that I could do myself, and it was always a fun hobby."

"Okay," Mack replied. "So, what's the problem?"

"This particular bed is where the worst damage is, and that makes no sense."

"Why not?" he asked.

"Because the broken glass window where they entered the greenhouse is on the other wall." She frowned, but then her eyes lit up, as a trickle of amusement slipped through her. "On the other hand," she began, "I get that this is not exactly a *case*-case, right?"

"No, not a case, just vandalism."

She chuckled again. "But maybe …"

"What is it that's making you laugh about this?" Mack asked, perplexed.

She snickered. "*Vandals in the Vidalias.*"

"Hopefully that's all that is going on here," Mack noted.

That comment made Doreen study the bed closer again, gasping as she pointed. "Maybe not."

He turned, and there—sticking out the far end of the garden bed—was something that didn't belong. He leaned forward to get a better look.

She whispered, "Is that a nose?"

He frowned, turned back to her, with his gaze finally going to Nick, and Mack nodded.

"Yes, it is."

Chapter 1

DOREEN SIGHED AND left the conservatory-turned-crime-scene as Nick called his local police contact to report this event. She led the way back through the main part of the house, Mack following closely behind her, with Nick trailing slowly along, as he made his call. Mugs seemed completely at home—even if Doreen wasn't. Goliath stayed nearby, and Thaddeus tucked closer into her neck.

The house remained the same and yet, in some ways, very different. When she mentioned that to Mack, he nodded.

"Is the house different, or are you different?"

She glanced at him and then quickly nodded. "You could be right," she muttered. "I hadn't thought of it in that way."

Nick faced her, pocketing his phone, and asked, "So, where do you want to start?"

"I don't know if we're staying here at night for the next few days," she began, with a bit of a grimace, "but, if not, we should probably find a place to stay."

Nick suggested, "It probably would be better if we stayed here, particularly since we have the police on the way."

"Oh my," she muttered and then shrugged. "That's fine then," she conceded, giving them both a smile.

"Why don't we start with the secret rooms," Mack suggested, a smile on his face.

She looked over at him and laughed. "What's this, just a treasure hunt for you? You're acting like a two-year-old at Christmas."

"Absolutely," he admitted. "Everybody wants to find hidden treasure. I am not so different than most."

She led the way into Mathew's home office, and there she stopped, looking around and frowning.

"Does it look different?" Nick asked.

"I'm not quite sure. *Something* is different." She turned around and pointed, "His desk and his chair still seem to be the same, but I'm not sure about this couch." She studied it keenly. "I thought a black leather couch was here, not this more modern one—not his usual taste."

"So could maybe Robin made this change?" Mack noted.

Doreen nodded. "That's possible. I really don't know. Mathew never let me decorate the house, claiming I didn't have good taste." She wandered over to his desk and sat down. It was hard to take it all in. She hadn't expected to come back here *ever*. Now that she was here, it all had such a foreign feeling, a heaviness that she hadn't expected. She looked over at Mack, catching him watching her, probably understanding what she was going through. Yet she could also see a little worry in his gaze. She smiled up at him. "I'm fine. Honestly."

"Good," he muttered, "because you don't look … comfortable."

She frowned and then chuckled. "That's just you being you." She got up from Mathew's desk and announced,

"We'll have to go through all the drawers because I know one of these opens funny."

"Funny?" Nick repeated, racing around to the side of the desk. "What do you mean by funny?"

"A secret drawer is in here," she replied, waving carelessly at the desk. "He used to taunt me about it, telling me how I would never get into it."

"Ooh, that's mine then," Nick stated, rubbing his hands together. "I love those."

Even Mack laughed at that. "He always loved puzzles when we were growing up, especially the kinds that nobody else could get. He was all over them."

"Then you've got your work cut out for you on this one," she declared. "I'm not sure what's in it. … I think he kept his gun in there."

At that, Nick stopped in horror and turned to her.

She shrugged. "A guy like Mathew is bound to have weapons around."

"Of course he would." He shook his head. "Let's figure out this puzzle."

She pointed to one drawer. "I know it had something to do with this drawer, but I don't know what the trick is." She left him to it, walking over to the painting on the far side of the wall. She waved Mack over and said, "I don't know whether this lifts off the wall or swings open. I don't want to damage it, so can you give it a try? You can reach it a little easier than I can."

He walked over and took a look and tried to swing it open. That didn't work. When he tried to lift it off the wall, it didn't lift either.

When he turned and frowned at her, she shrugged. "Another one of those things that he just loved. Anything that made everybody else feel stupid."

"I really don't like this guy."

"You don't have to. He's dead."

Mack snorted at that. "Even in death, I don't like this guy." He then returned his attention to the painting, running his fingers along the back of the frame. Suddenly came a *click*.

She eyed him in delight as he pulled the whole thing forward, as if opening a door, revealing a safe behind it. "Okay, so that's the main safe," she shared, staring at it. "I don't remember the combination though. I hope … it could be in one of his desk drawers."

"Which drawer?" Mack asked.

"The secret drawer. He used to keep stuff like that in there because nobody else could get into it."

Mack laughed, turned to his brother, and declared, "Okay, now back to you."

"Sure, no pressure," Nick muttered.

"But that's okay," she said, "because you're really good at this stuff."

He glared at her from his stooped position and stated, "If that was meant to be sarcastic, that's not fair. I haven't had very much time in here."

"Nope, you haven't," she agreed, and then she walked over to a picture closer to the window and looked back at Mack. "This one too."

"What about that one?" he asked curiously.

"I think another safe is in here."

"*Another* one?" He frowned at her.

"Yeah, I could be wrong, but I'm pretty sure. Another one is in here somewhere."

"Good enough," he replied. It took another minute or

two for him to figure it out, but soon he had that one swinging away from the wall too.

She looked at the safe found behind it and nodded. "I'm sure he changed the combination on this one, but at one time it was my birthday." Still she slowly and carefully entered her birthday, and unexpectedly the safe door popped open.

Mack crowded her to look inside. He whistled yet again. "Considering he used your birthday for the combination, I guess it's really not a surprise that it's full of jewelry boxes."

She stared at it and frowned. "I guess not. Yet, if Robin had any idea that the combo was *my* birthday, she would not have been happy."

"The good news is she apparently didn't know." Mack took out one of the many velvet boxes, opened it up, and stared. "Good God, these are what? Emeralds?"

"*Hmm*, I'm not sure," she admitted. "I can't remember the name, but he was working with some high-end jewels at one point. I don't know if they are emeralds, but what else looks like that?" She pulled out a couple more boxes, opened them, and noted, "These are yellow diamonds. I do know that." She rolled her eyes at Nick. "I've seen these necklaces before, a couple times."

"Did you ever wear them?" he asked.

"Of course not." She carelessly waved at one of the matching pairs of earrings. "*It's worth too much. You don't go out in public with this stuff.*" She snorted. "Mathew would never allow it. He would have high-quality imitations made so that nobody knew for sure. So, if they were stolen, the real piece was safe and secure."

"I guess that makes sense," Nick muttered, shaking his head, "but, good God, how much … I don't even want to ask how much money is tied up in this stuff."

"A lot," she declared, "and he used to deal in jewels all the time." She dug down to the bottom under the jewelry boxes and pulled out a bunch of paperwork. "If we're lucky, these documents will be the insurance riders, which should give us some idea of their value."

That caught Nick's attention, so he left the desk and grabbed the papers, flipped through them, and nodded. "That's exactly what these are," he confirmed, "so that's a boon." He shook his head when he glanced back at the docs again. "Pretty unbelievable." He carried the papers back to the desk, muttering to himself.

"Maybe so," she conceded, but she wasn't all that interested in them. "I know we're waiting for the police, but do we need to have them involved in any of this stuff?"

"They shouldn't have to be," Mack stated, standing beside her. "No reason to get them involved in all of this since it's your private property."

"And how the heck does that work?" she muttered, with a headshake.

Just then came a *whoop* as Nick popped up from behind the desk. "I think I got it."

She walked around the desk, saw the open drawer, and smiled. "Yeah, that looks like it."

Sure enough, Nick opened the secret drawer, and there was a small handgun.

She nodded. "I think the gun license is in there somewhere too." She stared at the weapon with revulsion. "It's nothing I ever wanted him to have. I'm not really a fan of a guy like him being armed."

Nick lifted it out gingerly with his handkerchief, frowning at it as he sniffed it. He told Mack, "I don't think it's been fired recently."

Using the handkerchief, Mack took it from him, looked it over, and sniffed it too. "No recent smell of firing. Seems it's been in this drawer for a while." He faced Doreen and added, "So, that's another good thing."

"I'll take any *good things*, considering we have a dead body in the greenhouse," she muttered, yet with a smile. "Plus anything that makes our job easier right now is good."

"And," Nick added, "the license is here. Seems in order. Oh, Doreen, you'll want this." He handed her some numbers written on a sticky note.

She smiled and walked over to the first safe. The numbers worked, and the safe door unlocked. Mack stood behind her as she checked it out. She snorted, pulled out one single sheet of paper. "This is so Mathew. *You're too late. I already moved these contents.*"

Just then the authorities arrived out front. Mugs alerted them the only way he knew how, by barking furiously. Nick looked out the window and nodded. "I'll deal with them, and you guys can stay here, if you like."

"Gladly," she muttered.

He disappeared from the office, while Doreen watched through the window to see some uniformed cops plus some forensic types in their white jumpsuits traipsing to the conservatory in the back. She realized it would be a bit of a circus now. She called Mugs back into the office and closed the door. She groaned and looked at Mack. "I didn't really expect to find a dead body here."

"Neither did I," he noted, watching the proceedings through the window.

"Do you feel out of the loop?" she asked him.

He turned to her and laughed. "No, I'm on holiday, remember?"

She rolled her eyes at that. "Which is why you're studying it all so intently. Did you honestly think I wouldn't notice that?"

"I notice even if I'm off work. I'm a detective. Once that gene turns on, there is no turning it off. It also makes me wonder who had access to the house. Yet, if you and I try to help solve this case, we'll piss off the local authorities."

She sighed. "Surely that's not a smart thing to do."

His lips twitched, and he murmured, "It's not a smart thing to do, as I've been telling you for a very long time. On the other hand," he began, giving her a side look, "will you let them investigate this all on their own and not have anything to do with it?"

"I can't do that," she admitted, staring at him intently. "It's my house, after all." Then she frowned. "God, that sounds weird."

"Right, it is your house," he stated. "I know for a fact you won't let this go on without your *assistance*."

"Correct," she confirmed, as she shook her head. "I can't."

"Of course not," he muttered. "So, as soon as they sort out what's going on out there, and they get the coroner involved, they'll need to talk to us."

"Of course," she replied, with a nod. "Yet we have alibis. So this should be easy."

Thaddeus poked his head out of Doreen's hair. "*He-he-he.*"

Doreen could only hope he was just being a smart aleck, not giving her advance warning of the mess they were in.

"We do have alibis, indeed," Mack declared, then did a double take. "Do you really expect them to look at you as a suspect?"

She frowned at him and shared, "You're the one who always tells me that the spouse is usually the first place anybody looks."

He smiled at her. "That's very true, but I don't think it'll be an issue in this case. Your spouse is dead. You aren't the spouse of the dead body in the garden. We don't live here. We can prove that we drove down today, stopping in Merritt, buying brunch and gas. Plus we found the body ourselves almost immediately upon our arrival. So, whoever has been in and out of this place, like caretakers or whatnot, that'll be a different story."

"And I need to find that information for the police, don't I?"

"Or Nick can share that. As you mentioned, Mathew's probate attorney had hired a property management company to get a caretaker on the property. I mean, the house was unoccupied, so that sounds like a good idea. The caretaker can mow the lawn and can watch for intruders. Probably cheaper than hiring a private security guard, the way your neighbors, the Smithsons, have."

"And what if the dead body *is* the caretaker?" she asked in horror. "What if it was somebody working for the estate?"

"Let's deal with that if it happens," Mack stated.

She pinched her lips together to avoid launching one million other questions that were all piling up and incredibly disturbing to her right now.

When Nick finally walked back inside, he smiled at her. "The coroner is on the way, and, yes, the police will need to talk to you."

"Of course," she said. "I didn't have anything to do with it though," she announced, staring at him.

He smiled at her and nodded. "I know that, and Mack

knows that. You just have to convince the police of that."

Mack groaned, chastising Nick, "Don't go sending her off so terrified that she'll be a suspect again."

"Right." Nick chuckled. "I forgot that you've already been through this once."

"Don't remind me," she muttered, with a nervous smile. "It wasn't much fun."

"Of course not," Nick said. "I've already explained that we three, in two separate cars, just drove here from Kelowna, and they can call the restaurant in Merritt, proving that we've only just arrived here, based on quite normal travel time. We've got the gas and brunch receipts from Merritt, and both of our vehicles are here. Heck, the car hoods may still be warm. Plus, Mack is a cop, which should help give us credibility, but they'll still need to check all our alibis to confirm that we literally did just come into town."

Mack added, "I was in at work early this morning in the station at Kelowna, with plenty of witnesses, including the captain. The drive takes about four and a half hours, without stopping for food and gas, and the talk with Jefferson too, so that should help. Plus, your being an attorney should make you an equally viable witness."

"Exactly, and I followed you both in my own vehicle," Nick pointed out. "So, if one of us will be looked at as a suspect, then all of us are."

"Oh dear," she muttered, staring at him in horror. "I would feel terrible to get you two involved in anything."

Nick gave her a smirk. "You can't get me involved in anything because I didn't do anything."

"Neither did I," she declared adamantly.

He rolled his eyes and nodded. "I know, and you don't need to worry."

Just then came a knock on the open office door.

She turned and found a man in a suit standing there, a detective no doubt. She frowned at him and asked, "Daniel? Daniel Sherwood?"

Chapter 2

DANIEL GAZED AT her in surprise. "Is that you, Doreen?"

"It is," she cried out, walking toward him with both hands out. Yet Mugs remained uncertain and sniffed Daniel's pant leg. Mugs wasn't barking but neither was he welcoming. "Daniel, it's so good to see you."

He tilted his head. "Yet not necessarily, at least in these circumstances."

She shook her head. "I don't know how, but I always seem to end up in trouble."

"I was talking to—" He turned to Nick and pointed. "Is this your lawyer?"

"So sorry, introductions are in order. This is Mack, my fiancé, and his brother Nick, who also happens to be my lawyer," she announced.

At the word *fiancé* Daniel raised his eyebrows at her, and she nodded.

"I know what you're thinking, and believe me that we can explain."

"Oh, I can't wait to hear this," he quipped. "I had heard that you and Mathew separated."

"Let's just say he replaced me, … with the proverbial younger model," she shared, with half a groan. "Not exactly an easy time."

"No, of course not, and therefore …"

"Right, and, therefore, you may think that jealousy or whatever would give me a motive to destroy Mathew's conservatory, but I wasn't even in town."

"I understand that you guys drove down this morning?"

Mack stepped forward, held out his hand, and introduced himself again. "I reported to work this morning in Kelowna, before we drove down. My captain and others will confirm."

"Okay, that should all be easy enough to check," Daniel noted, "possibly ruling you guys out right away."

"Absolutely," Mack agreed. "We didn't have anything to do with this."

"So, what are you here for?" he asked, turning to Doreen.

"I'm sure you've heard—or maybe not, I don't know—but Mathew was murdered in Kelowna some time ago," she began, then pointed at Mack. "I was cleared as a suspect, and Mack found Mathew's killer. However, since Mathew and I were still legally husband and wife at the time of Mathew's death, and I was still in his will, it turns out I'm the beneficiary of his estate. Nick's been working on the legal aspects of Mathew's estate all along, but we made this trip to begin to deal with the contents of this and other properties, so I can sell them."

"You are not coming back to live in the house?" Daniel asked.

"Oh no, we'll live in Kelowna. My grandmother is there."

"How is she?" he asked. "When last I spoke to you, you mentioned that she was the only family you had."

"Exactly," she confirmed. "She is doing great and really looking forward to the wedding."

"Have you set a date?"

"No, we sure haven't," she said, with a laugh. "We just recently got engaged. So I was hoping for a little more time to get adjusted to that, but some people don't want to give me much time before we set the date, like Nan and others."

Mack chuckled, wrapped an arm around her shoulders, and kissed the top of her head. "Regardless, I will give you as much time as you need."

"Yeah, you did promise me that," she agreed, smiling back at him, "but you know what Nan's like."

"I do know what your grandmother is like," Mack acknowledged, with a smirk and a shake of his head. "As far as she's concerned, she'll be dead if you don't get married soon, and she'll miss it all."

"I know, and your mother is no better." She groaned and looked over at a somewhat impatient Daniel. "It is really good to see you again. Are you handling the case then?"

"I am," he stated and then frowned. "You know, I did hear rumors about some crazy woman in Kelowna solving all kinds of murders and cases—cold cases. That wasn't you, right?"

Mack was already laughing. "It definitely was her."

Daniel noted, "I'm not sure how you ever got into that, but I can't have you messing with my case." When she frowned, he immediately shook his head. "I get that you're some amateur sleuth and that you've had some really good beginner's luck, but no way can I have you involved in my case."

"Of course not," she muttered, her shoulders slumping. "That would be way too easy, wouldn't it?"

He muttered, "I don't know about easy. Some of these cases never get solved, and we end up with an incredible backlog of cold cases," he muttered. "If we're lucky, we eventually solve them." He pulled out a notebook. "Right, so your husband was murdered. Any chance it would be connected to our dead body here?"

"To say a flat-out *no* wouldn't make a whole lot of sense," she replied, "so I guess the answer to that is a maybe."

Daniel groaned.

Mack quickly stepped in and explained about Mathew's murder. Hearing him, Daniel looked disturbed to say the least. "And your divorce lawyer was murdered too?" he asked Doreen.

"Yes, but I had nothing to do with any of it."

He stared at her for a long moment and muttered, "Good God."

"I know. It's been a rough year or so overall, especially the past several months for me," she muttered. "Thankfully I ended up at Nan's after Mathew kicked me out. Being with my husband as I was, I never even knew the basics about survival." She smiled over at Mack and added, "He's the one who taught me how to cook."

"Seriously?" Daniel asked, turning to Mack in astonishment.

Mack nodded. "She's a very special lady," he shared. "I also know that she had absolutely nothing to do with Mathew's murder."

"You may know that," Daniel pointed out, "so, from *your* perspective, … she's off the hook."

"Not just my perspective, as Mathew's murder has been

solved," he pointed out. "Again feel free to contact my captain in Kelowna, and he can give you the details, share a copy of the case files, if you feel that is pertinent to your case here."

"If this were your investigation," he asked, studying Mack, "wouldn't you check out this other murder?"

"I guess I would, yes."

"And wouldn't you also consider your own position in Mathew's case?" he asked Mack.

It took Doreen a moment, then she gasped. "Oh my, you can't possibly think that Mack had anything to do with this recent murder here or with the two prior murders. I mean, Mack works full-time in Kelowna, and he had nothing to do with Mathew's death. He had nothing to do with Robin's death either. He's been the cop trying to solve it on the other end."

"And you can defend me until you're blue in the face," Mack noted, crossing his arms as he stared at Daniel, "but Daniel must still do his job, and he'll find out all about that for himself."

"I prefer to think I would find it all out," Daniel clarified, "if people were honest and upfront."

"We have been," Mack stated. "As I already mentioned, feel free to contact my captain, and you can get any of the details you feel are pertinent."

Daniel nodded but his gaze didn't leave Mack.

Doreen was shocked. It never occurred to her that anybody would accuse Mack of having anything to do with it. "You do realize that we haven't even been down here before now, right? This is our first visit since I was unceremoniously booted out."

"That may well be true," Daniel conceded, "but this

guy's also come into your life fairly quickly, and I just don't want to see anything connected to him."

"Connected to this case?" Mack clarified, his tone settling into a hard line. "Or to make sure she isn't jumping into something she shouldn't too quickly?"

Daniel gave a wolfish grin. "You mentioned it, not me."

"Oh no, no, no, no, no." Doreen raised her hands, staring from Mack to Daniel. "This isn't happening. Mack is completely free and clear on all this. But, if I need to get him a lawyer, believe me that I will."

"I don't think a lawyer will be necessary," Mack declared, as he continued to stare at the detective in front of him. "Yet the grandstanding here has a very interesting side effect, especially considering that we are looking for a criminal here in the lower mainland right now, instead of somebody from Okanogan this time. Plus, we happen to have somebody right in front of us, who seems to know an awful lot about you and your ex." He turned to Doreen to make his point. "Somebody who knows you, maybe your love of gardening," he suggested.

Doreen frowned at Mack, reminded of his earlier comment about how this vandalism to her beloved greenhouse was somehow about getting back at her. She then turned to Daniel. She knew what Mack was trying to do, and it didn't take Daniel very long to connect the dots. His face turned bright red, his expression muddled, but it was more fury than anything.

Mack nodded. "So, just a little advice from one cop to the other. I suggest you take good care on how you approach this case," he began. "I didn't have anything to do with it, and the case in my corner of the world is all closed up, while the one in your corner is still wide open."

At that, Nick stepped in. "Hang on a minute. Let's keep everything nice and friendly," he suggested. "Daniel, if you have some questions to ask Doreen, maybe we can get to those right now, with her attorney present. We've been traveling, and we're tired, and this wasn't exactly the easiest arrival we could have asked for. Plus, we haven't eaten lately and are in need of some food."

Doreen shrugged. "If any of the old staff were still around, I could ask them to prepare something. Yet you told me that everybody had been let go. Is that correct?" she asked, turning to Nick.

"Yes, all but the caretaker, and he was keeping an eye on the property."

She frowned at Nick and asked, "And we haven't seen any sign of him?"

"No."

She nodded. "So, then that's suspicious, isn't it?"

"That potentially could be his body out in the greenhouse." Mack pointed out, with a nod, completing her thought.

She winced, but it was definitely possible.

Daniel frowned, silently watching their interactions and intently listening.

"And could you identify him?" Mack asked her.

"I don't think so," she replied, "unless it's Philip. He used to work here when I lived here, but I haven't seen or heard anything from him—or even about him in a very long time."

"Okay, so Daniel will ID the dead body in the greenhouse and will get back to us to share that info, can't you?" Mack asked.

Daniel gave him a very stern look, not saying a word.

Nick interjected, "As I understand it, the current caretaker was originally your husband's hire. The property management company hired by Mathew's probate attorney kept him on to look after the property, just until we got the details sorted out and transferred to you, Doreen," Nick explained. "So it should not be anybody you know, but we'll see. Daniel, if and when you're ready to remove the body, we'll take a look to see if she can ID the body."

"I don't think she should do that," Daniel argued. "I don't know how long the body's been there, but I can't imagine it's a pretty sight."

Doreen snorted, finding it funny to hear somebody concerned about her sensibilities because she was a completely different person now than she had been so many months ago. She turned to him and explained, "I've done a lot of work with the coroner in Okanogan." She gave Daniel a wry smile. "She's become a good friend now." She glanced down at her phone and frowned. "Oh shoot, we forgot to tell her that we were leaving."

"I can send her a message," Mack offered. "Weren't you supposed to meet her for tea or something?"

She nodded. "I was. I forgot."

"It's fine. I'm sure she's more than busy."

"More than busy?" she repeated, turning to him. "Did a new case come in or something?"

He laughed. "I'm certain the cases will keep coming, even while we're away," he told her, "but we took this trip to get things settled in Vancouver. So we need to keep our eye on the ball right here."

"Right," she muttered, "that is why we came after all." She again addressed Daniel. "It'll be fine, Daniel. I don't know what the situation is with the body in the greenhouse, but I can't imagine it would be worse than what I've already seen."

He frowned, but Nick intervened. "She'll be fine," he told the detective. "After all, she's dealt with many dead bodies in Kelowna since moving there. You can also confirm that with Mack's captain as well."

Mack nodded. "Now, if you have any questions, it would be great if we can get through that process. We're planning on staying here in the house, and the greenhouse is accessible from its own back entryway. So your people can access the crime scene that way. I understand that you'll need time to go through things out there, but obviously we want you to get it done before too long. We were hoping to be back home in just three days or so." Mack shifted as if done with the conversation.

Daniel straightened his stance. "As you all seem to have some level of experience with law enforcement, you know perfectly well it will take however long it takes. So, let's dig in, shall we?" Daniel turned to face each of them, and he did not look happy at all. "But first, … what is on your neck?" he asked Doreen.

Thaddeus poked his head out and squawked. "Thaddeus is here. Thaddeus is here."

Doreen smiled. "This is Thaddeus, and I still have Mugs, but you've seen him before, and Goliath, my Maine coon, is right behind you."

"You drove down with them?" Daniel asked in astonishment.

"Always," she answered quietly. "Where I go, they go. Now about your questions …"

Chapter 3

DANIEL THEN PLUNGED into a series of questions that they could all answer easily enough. Once he had checked all his boxes, he turned to Doreen. "We'll have to come into the main house."

"Even though it was not broken into?" she asked.

He nodded.

Mack stepped in closer, staring him down. "On what grounds?"

"That the murder most likely happened in the house. For all we know, the murderer had a key and got in on their own."

Mack shook his head. "But the break-in clearly happened in the greenhouse, where the body is buried. However, we'll walk you around for sure," Mack noted, "just to alleviate any concerns. As it happens, we haven't had a chance to get through all of the house yet ourselves."

"And that is why we came here," Doreen stated. "Let's do the walk-through with Daniel, and hopefully I can see if anything is out of sorts."

"When were you last here?" Daniel asked.

"Over a year ago, and then Robin moved in after I was

forced out. So she had been living here in the meantime. I don't know what changes she may have made that will look different to me."

"Coming back after all this time must be hard," he noted, giving her a hard look.

Doreen shrugged, and they got started and walked toward the kitchen. Goliath now joined Mugs, and both stayed close but out of the way. Thaddeus snoozed in the fall of her hair. "It is difficult in some ways, but in other ways it's very freeing. This place wasn't a home as much as it was a cage for me," she murmured. "A gilded cage perhaps, but a cage just the same."

"You never looked very happy whenever I saw you."

"I didn't know happiness with Mathew." Then she laughed. "I do know happiness now. And you're right. I wasn't very happy back then because this whole place just wasn't *me*. I wasn't allowed to be myself at all. I was a copy of whatever Mathew wanted me to be," she shared, with a smile. "That's all changed now."

"You definitely seem different," Daniel conceded, eyeing her thoughtfully.

She nodded. "Freer, happier, more me," she confirmed, with a bright smile.

"And you think it's all because of him?" Daniel asked, with a nod toward Mack, who was walking ahead of them.

"A substantial part of it, yes," she agreed, "but then a large part of it is just because I've been free of Mathew. That was the biggest change in my life when I left Vancouver and moved to Kelowna. With my grandmother close by, I was reminded about what love really is and what love could do for a person. That has been the best gift ever."

"You certainly look as if the change has been good for

you. You do realize, of course, that, if we'd had anything to do with Mathew's death investigation, we would have looked at your partner here."

"You could have looked at him but still found nothing," she replied. "He's a moral man, a good man, one who lives by his ethics. Believe me that we were both interrogated over Mathew's death and Robin's, particularly since I am the one who found Mathew's body."

"You did?" Daniel asked.

She nodded. "That added so much stress to my life at the time. Since they determined I didn't have anything to do with it, I've gotten over that issue." Daniel eyed Mack suspiciously, and she smiled. "He's not the bad guy here, Daniel."

"Maybe not," he replied, "but I don't know him."

"Nope, you don't. And I guess, for the sake of this investigation, you probably don't really know me either."

"No, I don't," he agreed, "and that will be something we have to deal with."

"Of course," she murmured.

A full tour of the house didn't find anything amiss per Doreen, and Daniel didn't find any evidence of a break-in. Mack confirmed that too. Daniel told her, "As you continue to go through things in more detail, let us know if anything is missing because that could definitely be a connection we didn't see right away."

"Of course." She didn't bother saying that she probably wouldn't know if anything was missing or not, which also made the timing of her visit interesting. Thus, if she couldn't tell whether or not anything was missing, maybe nobody could tell if something had gone missing before either.

Either way, something was definitely here for her to consider in another light. As soon as Daniel returned to the greenhouse, she looked over at Mack and Nick, both standing at and staring out the window.

"I don't believe anyone has a key to this house," Doreen declared. "Seems like a diversion to me."

Mack considered that. "We did check the inside of the house, all exit doors, even the windows—and there are a lot of windows—and I found no evidence of tampering. I'll confirm by doing an external search of the residence once Daniel is gone. I also noted, and didn't share with him, that the security system seems offline."

Doreen grimaced, shaking her head. "Mathew would have it on permanently. Can you find out when it was shut down?"

"Theoretically," Mack replied. "I'll give a call to the monitoring people."

Doreen sighed. "So, do you think we're off the hook?"

"Nothing to be off the hook about," Mack declared, turning to smile at her.

"Good, I'm getting hungry though. Thoughts on food?" she asked.

Nick agreed. "I'm starved. Let's order in?"

Mack concurred. "Sure. That sounds more reasonable than trying to find a place and leaving the animals alone."

"Also, I don't want to leave the animals alone in the house while the greenhouse is full of strangers, so ordering in is best."

Mack turned to her and asked, "What would you like?"

She frowned, then shrugged. "Just food, I'm really not too fussy. We did stop for brunch on the drive down, but we didn't eat a whole lot there."

It didn't take long for them to just order pizza. She

laughed. "That would be a first. I don't think a pizza delivery has ever been made to this house. … I wonder what happened to all the staff that Mathew had," she muttered, looking over at Nick.

"The local probate attorney dealt with that," he replied, "and I'm sure they were all given their final paychecks."

"What are the chances that one of them decided they hadn't been paid quite enough and, knowing something about what Mathew may or may not have been up to, decided to help themselves?" she asked, turning to view her surroundings.

"I noticed you didn't tell Daniel that you may or may not have known about anything missing," Nick pointed out to her.

"That's because a part of me is not sure what might be missing versus what might not be missing."

"What do you mean?"

"Robin lived here for a few months, right? So there is that. Otherwise I think I just need to be here for a bit while I figure out where things are again and just what Mathew might have done with various bits and pieces." The two men just stared at her, and she shrugged. "I know how that sounds, but he was paranoid, so he had other options for where he could have hidden things. I have to walk around and figure it out."

"You do that," Mack stated, with a nod, "and, if you think of anything else or of any other secret places, we will help you open things up." He and his brother chuckled.

She smiled. "You guys are just plain enjoying this, aren't you?"

"It is interesting. I'll give you that," Mack conceded. "I am enjoying being on the outside in an investigation."

Doreen noted no frustration in his tone and perhaps even a sense of relief that he wasn't on tap for this one. "It's also a good thing because you need a holiday."

He smirked at her. "Because it's Mathew's house and Mathew's headache—but in your name now—we don't want anything to put us in a bad light, which just ends up causing us trouble," Mack explained. "We don't need all that while we're here for just a few days, with plenty other issues to take care of."

"But we didn't do anything," she said.

"No, we didn't. So, let's just stay out of everybody's way, and hopefully they'll come to that same conclusion."

"Do you think they'll make life difficult for us?"

"We weren't here when the murder happened. The house had been unoccupied for a while, and it got broken into," he summarized, with a shrug. "Not a whole lot more we can say to that."

"And chances are, they're already trying to figure it out," Nick added.

"Yeah, I would think so," Mack muttered. "Any detective worth his salt would be on it."

They watched the forensic guys for a little bit longer, and then Mack turned to her. "Even more reason for us to stay here now. Unless … you have a problem with that."

"No, I think it's for the best," she agreed, "particularly considering we had the break-in. And remember how Jefferson said that a man and a woman were found walking around the property? Maybe casing out the place?"

He nodded. "Exactly what I thought. Maybe the street cams can give us more info. I'll check with Daniel, see if he'll share that with us, once we've been cleared of murdering the man in the Vidalia bed. Shall we go to the bedrooms and stake out one for each of us?"

"Sure," she replied, with a shrug.

They grabbed their bags from the front entranceway and headed upstairs. She went to the guest rooms, making assignments to each of them. "These are the nicer bedrooms."

"You don't want to sleep in the master?" Nick asked.

She screwed up her face, wrinkled up her nose, and declared, "Nope, I sure don't, but we should take a closer look at it."

Chapter 4

As the trio walked into the master suite, Doreen stopped and raised her eyebrows. "This was definitely redone." The tufted chairs and bench seat and draperies all matched. The really dark blood-red-colored brocade with gold thread accents was over-the-top in her opinion. "How very oppressive," she muttered, with a shudder. "This is not my style at all."

Mugs growled his own displeasure. Goliath always seemed to view his world with disdain, so nothing was new here. Thaddeus was quiet, which concerned Doreen a bit. Maybe it would take a day or two for her animals to acclimate to a new location. Especially this one.

"Do you think this was Robin's doing?" Mack asked.

"I don't know," she admitted. "I wouldn't have thought Mathew would have gone for this, but you never really know." She shrugged. "I'm just glad I don't have to sleep or live here anymore."

He smiled at that and nodded. "I'm glad too."

She looked over at him and chuckled.

"Anything else in here you want to share with the class?" Nick asked, giving the room a critical eye.

She stopped and scanned the room a bit, frowning. "A safe is in this room too."

Immediately the men stepped farther into the suite.

"Where?" Mack asked.

"*Hmm.*" She pondered that as she looked around. "It looks so different."

"That's okay," Mack noted, taking her hand. "Just close your eyes and think about it back when you were still here. If he asked you to get something from the safe …"

She rolled her eyes at that. "Nobody would get into the safe if Mathew had his way, but he did leave it open sometimes," she muttered, as she stared around. "Oh, I think it's over here." She headed to one of the walls. She stopped, frowned at it, and added, "I think it's in here, but no painting is here anymore."

Mack started tapping the wall and, sure enough, one spot sounded very different. He chuckled, and it didn't take him long to find the paneling that opened up under his fingers. "This safe?" he asked, pointing to it.

She looked at it and nodded. "That looks about right. Of course, for all I know, he could have put another one in here when they remodeled this room." That was the thing about Mathew. He was paranoid and way too into hiding stuff. So, if she were to get into his head, she knew there would always be one safe nobody else knew about.

Nick asked, "Meaning that he didn't always let you know about everything?"

"No, gosh no," she declared. "So, another one is around here somewhere." She turned slowly. "I don't know where. As soon as I find it, I'll show you." In the meantime, she pondered the rest of the master bedroom.

The men searched, tapping the walls, as she entered the

en suite, frowning when she saw all his personal stuff just sitting on the counter. That was so not Mathew either.

She groaned, and Mack walked in. "Problems?"

"Mathew wouldn't have left stuff out like this. He was a clean freak in a way. This right here," she pointed out, "this mess before us wasn't his style at all."

"So, do you think somebody else has been here? Or maybe that somebody else has been living here?"

"No, I think, when he came to Kelowna the last time, he was probably not planning on staying, and would be back home very quickly. Instead he never came home." She frowned at Mack.

Mack opened his arms, and she walked into them, as he quickly wrapped his arms around her and held her tight.

Thaddeus took the opportunity to walk up to Mack's shoulder.

"I'm not upset," she whispered, "but it is an uncomfortable feeling."

"Of course. This was your home."

"And yet, in a way, it doesn't feel like home at all."

Mugs woofed at her side, and she leaned down to pat him. "I know, buddy. This was your home too."

"He seems to be quite comfortable," Mack noted.

"I'm not so sure," she countered, looking down at Mugs. "He hasn't left my side at all. None of the animals have left my side in all this time. They all seem to be so … subdued. Either they're not comfortable in this house or they're just really not relaxed enough yet."

"And it could be either, I suppose," he pointed out.

She smiled and nodded. "You're right, but we'll get there." She scrubbed Mugs on the chin and added, "I know Mathew had another secret safe somewhere in this suite, but

I don't remember where it was."

Mugs wandered deeper into the bathroom, taking a few drinks out of the toilet bowl. She groaned. "He used to do that all the time, and it would drive Mathew nuts."

"But it's clean water," Mack noted. "So, from Mugs's perspective, it's good."

"Oh my goodness." Doreen lifted the lid off the toilet tank and smiled. "This was one of Mathew's hiding places."

Mack frowned and leaned forward and pulled out a small waterproof black case. "Do you know what's in this?"

"Probably cash," she replied, "but I don't know."

He took a towel, dried off the black bag, and pulled out another small black zippered case. He opened it up just as Nick walked in.

Nick whistled. "Good God, that's a lot of cash."

Doreen snorted. "Yeah, I hadn't really thought about that. Mathew kept it there, but I don't think I was supposed to know about it."

Mack stared at her and shook his head. "And you never mentioned it to him?"

"No, I never did. It didn't matter to me," she shared, with a shrug. The smile on Mack's face made her flush. "What?"

He stared at her intently. "Even when you left, forced out by Mathew, you … didn't try to take any of this?"

"No," she declared, waving her hand in a careless wave. "It was his. In my mind, it was always his."

"Guess what?" Nick asked her.

"What?" she asked, turning to Nick.

"It's all yours now."

She stared at him and then snorted. "I bet Mathew would *not* be happy to hear you say that."

He burst out laughing at that.

She added, "Yet I really hope he's listening in." Then she groaned. "I shouldn't be mean. He met an unpleasant end."

Mack interjected, "And yet you know that Mathew chose a lifestyle that could very easily have ended his life early at any time in some *unpleasant* way."

"True," she murmured. "Still, it's a hard thing to accept. He was a big part of my life for a long time."

"Of course," he noted.

She shook her head. "I was so unhappy here. I don't know how I made it through those years. I was here over a decade." She looked up at Mack. "I should have left him long before he kicked me out."

Just then the doorbell rang, and Mugs lost it. She turned, startled.

Nick shook his head. "Don't worry about it. It'll be the pizza." He pulled out his wallet and shared, "I have enough cash on me, I think."

Mack snorted and held out the wad of Mathew's secret stash, still in his hand.

Nick chuckled. "Yes, we are all well aware of Mathew's cash. We'll keep it intact for a proper inventory. I'll cover this meal. The sooner we can sort out all this, the better. It's best to keep any cash together as we found it. That way we know exactly what's been unearthed, down to the serial numbers on each bill—probably consecutive would be my guess."

"Exactly. Could be dirty money, attached to some bank robbery for all we know," Mack replied. He raised the stash again and added, frowning at Doreen, "Hard to imagine people having money that just sits here, hidden in a toilet tank of all places, and nobody was the wiser."

She nodded. "Mathew called it his running money."

"By why?" Mack asked. "He could easily hide in this mansion of his. Plus, he had at least one gun on the premises. I just don't understand the mentality of hiding money. He could have done so much good with that. Why hide it instead?" he asked again.

Nick replied, as he reentered the room, "Maybe because Mathew made more enemies than friends."

"He really did," she confirmed. "And again, that's his problem."

Mack smiled. "Let's go grab some pizza while it's still hot."

Suddenly Mugs raced out of the en suite bathroom and stood before her, barking at her.

Startled, she looked around. "What is your problem?"

"Are you kidding?" Mack asked, as he joined them. "He heard the word *pizza*."

She frowned at Mack, not so sure it was that simple. Yet Mugs started barking and barking again. Laughing, she nodded. "It does seem to be one of the magical words in a dog's life, doesn't it?"

As she headed downstairs, she called out for Goliath but got no answer. She frowned and muttered, "I don't want him getting lost in this big house."

"Not to worry," Nick called out from downstairs. "He's here where the pizza is." And, sure enough, as Nick carried the pizza in his arms to the kitchen table, Goliath was trying to climb his legs.

"Good thing you wore jeans today. Sorry, Nick," she said. "We need to get some cat food. We brought a few days' worth for each of them, but we could always use more."

"It's in the truck bed, along with the other pet food,"

Mack said. "We can retrieve that as soon as we're done eating."

They quickly ate a hearty dinner, and then Mack turned to Doreen. "I suppose you want to go get pet food now."

"It wouldn't hurt. Plus, we could use some fresh milk for tea and maybe a bit of fresh fruit."

Leaving Nick in place to guard the rest of the property and to satisfy the police—just in case anybody needed something—they unpacked the rest of the truck. Then they popped down to the corner store. She was actually struggling to remember where it was.

"It's as if I've never been here," she noted in frustration. "I've completely forgotten everything I went through here, including where anything is."

"And that's good for your health," Mack noted. "You can forget about it forever. Even though you'll be here for a little while, it won't be for long." He grinned at her. "I'm sure there's a song in that somewhere."

She laughed. "And, if there isn't, there should be."

Back at the house, they put away the milk and the other items, and they now made their way back to Nick, who was talking with Daniel in the greenhouse.

Nick turned to them and nodded, walking over to meet them, his face serious. "They've got the body excavated. So, Doreen, take a look and see if you can identify him."

She winced and muttered to Mack, "Good thing I've had dinner already."

"Just keep it down," he whispered. "Otherwise you'll belie your smooth *I can handle anything* expression."

She shot him a look as she headed over. Daniel nodded to her, a forensic tech at his side. The tech unzipped the body bag so that she could take a look. She stared at it and shook her head. "I don't know this person at all." She stepped back, looked over at Mack, and asked, "Do you?"

He raised both eyebrows and asked, "Why would I know him?"

"I don't know," she admitted. "I guess it's just a natural question on my part."

He stepped forward, checked out the body, and shook his head. "No, I don't know him either." He turned to Nick. "You?"

"No, I've already taken a look," he shared. "I'm not sure why he was even here—unless he was the property manager's caretaker."

Doreen agreed. "In which case we need to send him a photo and ask him."

Daniel quietly watched.

Nick quickly took a photo of the dead man's face and phoned Mathew's probate attorney, who had handled Doreen's husband's estate, and asked about the caretaker.

Mack and Doreen couldn't hear the whole conversation, which was half-a-dozen questions posed by Nick. When he finally ended the call, he told them, "He didn't know the guy personally but will see what he can find out from the property management company."

Within a few minutes, the probate lawyer called him back and shared, "All I have is a name, a *Pete Singer*. May not be his real one. These caretakers are known to bounce from property to property as needed, with no real homes to go back to. I don't even know if the property management companies do proper background checks on these guys. So the one we used here is checking for further details. What is going on down there?"

"Not sure," Nick conceded. "As soon as we find out,

we'll be in touch." Nick ended the call.

"Good God," Daniel muttered. "I'm the point man on this murder investigation, if you three have any further information."

"One more thing, Daniel," Doreen added, "our neighbors, the Smithsons, have made complaints to the police about strangers on the property when the house was clearly unoccupied. I don't know how often this happened but I would like to see those police reports."

Daniel stared at her. "I can look, but why concern yourself with any such neighborhood reports?"

She frowned at him. "Because we had a break-in and a dead person on the premises."

Daniel shook his head. "Stay out of my investigation, Doreen."

"I am the legal property owner, Daniel, so I must insist that I see any reports of mischief filed with the police in relation to my new property, especially since the house was unoccupied after Mathew's death."

Daniel glared at her, avoiding giving her any answer either way. Meanwhile, everybody exchanged information, and Daniel quickly turned to Doreen. "You be careful now. We don't know why or how this guy was knocked off but presumably because the house was unoccupied, it made for a good dumping ground."

"It wasn't my choice to leave, Daniel, so remember that," she told him defensively. "Mathew kicked me out, moved Robin in. Since then, his murder investigation has been completed, as has Robin's, and now a quite lengthy and complicated estate process has ensued for both. Everything takes time to sort out. Thus an unoccupied house."

He nodded. "It does take time. I'll talk to you as needed—but, please, if you're leaving town, let me know."

"Will do," Mack agreed. "Regardless we'll be here until we get to the bottom of it."

"The bottom of what?" Daniel asked, now on the defensive.

Mack gave him a one-arm shrug. "I didn't mean your job on the murder investigation. I just meant that we have a house here to sell, including all the furnishings."

At that, the detective looked around the property and nodded. "Better you than me. I would just get a Dumpster and ditch it all."

Mack nodded. "None of this is what you want to sit on."

"That's true, and I wasn't allowed to sit on much of it either," she replied, with a knowing smirk. "On the other hand, it's all very expensive."

"Figures," Mack muttered, staring around the house. "So expensive that you can't sit on it, yet so uncomfortable you don't even want to."

With a snort, Daniel turned and walked out.

Chapter 5

DOREEN WOKE THE next morning, happy to have her animals with her. Mugs and Goliath were on the bed with her, on opposite sides, and she hugged them both. Thaddeus had designated a valet stand as his new roost. She had to laugh at his ingenuity. All her animals made this place feel more like a real home. She stroked Thaddeus as she got up to get dressed.

They all trooped downstairs, and she was surprised to find Mack and Nick already downstairs in the kitchen, drinking coffee. "At least you figured out how to make coffee," she noted, yawning as she walked in. Thaddeus walked behind Mugs and her. Goliath now stretched out on the floor, looking hopeful.

"Good morning to you too," Nick quipped.

"Is it a good morning?" She huffed. "I'm just glad to have coffee."

"It would take a lot for the two of us *not* to figure out a coffeepot," Nick noted, with a shrug.

Mack smiled at her and asked, "How did you sleep?"

She shook her head. "Not great. Tons of memories. I wasn't expecting that," she muttered, as she poured her coffee and came over to join them and sat down. She looked around and groaned. "Plus, we have to deal with this house. I mean, this kitchen alone is huge."

"Yeah, something like that," Mack clarified, with a laugh. "Nick and I were just discussing it. It emphasizes the absolute excesses all around us, and it's so not needed."

"Not needed, sure. However, in their minds, not even excessive."

"Also," Nick interjected, "I got an email from Scott."

"Right, when's he coming?"

"He's in Vancouver for the next few days and wants to know if he can come over."

"He can come, but we won't even be finished just looking for Mathew's hidey-holes," she pointed out. "Mathew owned four houses here and I believe one in France. Although most local ones were rentals and not of this caliber."

Nick nodded. "I checked out this address on Google Maps. Still, even with the satellite image, I hadn't really considered how big this place was or just what a job this would be," he admitted.

"I didn't either," Mack shared, looking at his brother. "I had no idea whatsoever. I don't think anybody could if you weren't part of this whole … *shenanigan*."

"You mean, the whole over-the-top situation?" she asked in a dry tone.

He turned to her. "Not trying to insult you, honey, but this is incredibly far out of the norm, at least our norm."

She nodded. "It might be far out of your norm, but you've got to remember it's not exactly my norm either."

"But you lived here."

"No," she corrected. "I was a long-term guest in Mathew's house. I wasn't even allowed to sit down on a lot of the furniture. I wasn't allowed to do anything that you guys would consider normal. So don't associate me with this place. It just isn't me and never was. This is all *Mathew.*"

"Sorry, I didn't mean it that way." Mack studied her, obviously worried.

She nodded. "I know you didn't. I need to remember that myself. Just because I spent time here doesn't mean I really lived here. I'm a very different person now than I was back then. Here, I was a person who just existed."

On that note, Nick got up and announced, "I did find some unexpired foodstuff in the kitchen we can use. So either we can make pancakes or we can go out to breakfast."

Doreen voted for pancakes.

He looked at her. "Are you okay to eat here?"

She shrugged. "The food is here, so we might as well put it to good use. I'm not sure what else we're supposed to do with food just left here. It's not as if we can sell it, and it seems wasteful to throw it away."

"Right, but we can also take some of it back with us," Mack pointed out. "If you think it's still good, no reason not to. Presumably the products Mathew chose to have in his house were good quality."

"The very best, I assure you," she noted.

"In that case, we might as well take advantage of it and take home whatever we think we would use."

"That's true," she replied, "but there's just so much stuff here that it's overwhelming to even consider food as well. I was floundering to deal with Nan's house and her furniture."

He laughed. "I know. I remember. Nick and I were already discussing that. Just how many bedrooms are here?"

"Ten." She frowned, shaking her head. "Yet, as with Nan's stuff, I don't plan to take anything here. If we do happen to choose some stuff to bring back to Kelowna, we are limited by the size of your truck." She laughed. "Regardless I hope that Scott can again help us here."

She turned to Mack, adding, "I know many freezers and fridges are here—possibly with all kinds of high-end foodstuff—but how much would even fit in your truck?" she asked. "Not to mention all the pantries and such."

"Correct. A lot may be here, but I'm also not into waste. So, if we can make *good* use of it," Mack suggested in a firm tone, "then we will. If we can't, we'll do the best we can with everything else. Maybe there's a nearby food bank."

"But they surely won't take anything opened," she noted, pointing out that obvious fact.

"True, and they may not take anything from the freezer if it's been repackaged because it'll be unidentified. So, we'll take back as much food as we can and want, then sort out the rest from there," he shared, with a shrug.

Doreen nodded. "Hopefully some food bank will be happy to pack up all this and use it."

"Let's not get ahead of ourselves," Nick reminded them. "Let's see what Scott can deal with, but we may well have to stay down here a little bit longer than planned."

Mack frowned. "My captain won't like that."

"I could also stay without you," she offered, "and maybe Nick can work from down here as a possible option."

"That's something we can look at too," Nick agreed. "Again, let's not get ahead of ourselves."

She laughed. "You mean, more than we already are?"

"Yes," Nick confirmed. With that, he got up and made pancakes.

She asked him, "Are you ready to move to Kelowna yet?"

Nick snorted. "Closer but not yet. Still considering my

options. I might buy a condo so I have a place to live up here as I'm here so much but no decision on that as of yet. Someone is keeping me busy."

She watched him with curiosity and shared, "I guess your mom would prefer if you stayed with her but I can see wanting your own space."

Mack and Nick both nodded, sharing a knowing look.

Doreen added, "And she really did teach both of you to cook, didn't she?"

"Of course," Nick stated. "It's a wonder to me that any mother wouldn't teach her children to cook."

"Right. I don't know what mine ever taught anybody," she muttered. "She wasn't into anything home-oriented."

"That doesn't mean it was wrong necessarily," he pointed out. "You had a different childhood and a different adulthood, but you're in a very different stage of life now."

She chuckled. "That is certainly true."

"So, it's all good," Nick said, with a glance back at her.

She smiled and nodded. "It's all good. I'm not worried. I'm not coming apart at the seams."

"I can't imagine you ever doing that."

She looked at him, beaming. "I think that's a compliment. I'll take it as such at least."

"It was a compliment," Nick confirmed, smirking at her. "Now, why don't you fry up some eggs to go with these pancakes?"

"I think I can manage that," she replied.

But the big gas stove stumped her, until Nick pointed out how to turn it on. And, with that, Mack got into the fray, and very quickly all three of them were busy in the kitchen, getting breakfast ready to eat. They had just barely finished eating and were loading the dishwasher and wrangling about what to do next, when the doorbell rang.

Of course Mugs went crazy, barking like a madman.

Doreen and Mugs walked over to the front door, and there was Scott.

He grinned at her. "Hopefully I'm not too early." He bent down to pet Mugs, who gave him a tail wag.

"A little excited by any chance?" she asked, a teasing grin on her face.

"You could say that," he admitted. "Besides, I hear time is of the essence."

"We only have so many days here too."

As he walked inside the entryway, he stopped and stared, something akin to reverence crossing his face. He gingerly stepped forward to a painting hanging on the wall. "Oh my God, Doreen, this is a Rembrandt," he whispered in awe.

"Is that the real one though?" she asked, coming to stand beside him. "I'm not sure. … It's probably the copy."

"*The* copy?" he asked, turning to her.

"Oh," she gasped, her hand involuntarily covering her mouth.

"Oh what?" Mack asked, now behind her.

She turned, grimacing, and said, "I forgot about the room downstairs."

"The room downstairs?" Mack repeated.

"Yeah, a temperature-controlled art gallery in the basement," she muttered. "I guess we need to get down there too."

Scott looked at her with rapture. Mack just rolled his eyes, and Nick started to laugh uproariously.

Chapter 6

IT TOOK DOREEN a bit to find the way to the gallery room, but, by the time she got all four of them down there, Scott crowed in delight. Her pets followed along too, yet seemed on alert. As soon as they all stepped into the room, he froze in complete silence as he stared around, a hint of tears in his eyes.

Turning to her, he asked, "Do you want to keep these or some of them?"

She looked at him and shook her head. "No, not at all. I don't want to keep any of them." A look of absolute joy overtook his face. She smiled and told him the words he wanted to hear. "So, I would appreciate it very much if you could sell them for me."

"Absolutely." He rubbed his hands together in joy as he turned to look at the one directly in front of him. "You have a complete array here. It's almost as if Mathew didn't know what he liked, so he just had a bit of everything."

"He was a collector but not for the love of art," she explained. "He was a collector because he thought it was something that would elevate him from being the slumlord—or within the slumlord lifestyle that he used to live—

somehow making him bigger and better." She shook her head. "He was not a great person, but I do understand a lot of why he did what he did."

"Of course," Scott muttered, staring about. He stopped for another moment, and the look of absolute joy spreading across his face was almost intoxicating.

She smiled at him. "I presume this collection is substantial."

He nodded. "Yes, absolutely, and *substantial* hardly seems to be the correct word. You're truly blessed."

She shrugged. "And yet, to me, … they're just paintings."

"And I get that," he cried out, "but …"

She looked over at the two brothers, each with big grins on their faces, agreeing with her all the way on this issue. "I get it," she told Scott, "and that's why I brought you in to handle the job."

"It'll be a big job just to move these," he muttered, staring around, his hands in prayer mode as he contemplated that. "We'll have everything flown privately."

"Rather than commercially?" she asked.

"Yes, of course. We can't risk having anything damaged. Some of these are the great masterpieces," he murmured, as he stared at several of them.

"That's for you to figure out," she stated cheerfully. "And I know that this is where you want to stay, that this is where your heart is desperate to live for the next little while, and I promise I'll let you back in here again, but we do have a bunch of probably lesser-known pieces of furniture and whatnot that I really don't know anything about. So I'm hoping you can tell us if they're something we should sell or just give away as a donation."

He faced her, a smile on his lips, and he whispered, "I can't imagine anything coming out of this house being that level. Then again, depending on the furniture, some of it can be quite valuable, as you already discovered with your grandmother's collection."

"I know, but this isn't Nan's collection. This is … my ex's collection."

He shook his head. "And a fascinating collection it is too," he muttered, as he was reluctantly led out of the gallery room.

Doreen suggested, "Let's go upstairs and walk through the house, room by room, and you can tell me yes or no."

They started with the bedrooms on the second floor. By the time they had gotten through all the guest bedrooms, he had yet to say no to anything, except for some small decor pieces and unmatched lamps. When they got to the master suite, he stopped and stared. "This has got to be the most incredible bedroom collection," he muttered. "These are all very old designers, very rare antiques," he noted, gently touching the items. "This is absolutely incredible."

Once he had looked at the frame of the king-size bed and the matching set of wardrobes and dressers and nightstands and sitting room pieces, he finally turned to her and said, "I'll just ask for form. Do you want to keep any of this?"

She shook her head. "No, none of it."

He gave a small nod, then pulled out his phone and started texting. "So, we need to get in the furniture experts, and we've got to arrange for shipping of all the paintings and almost all the second-floor bedroom sets." He looked around the master suite again, noting artwork on the walls. "The artwork is not just in the basement, is it?"

She replied, "These wouldn't be as valuable."

He nodded. "True, but they're still worth tens if not hundreds of thousands of dollars."

She heard Mack choke behind her. She watched as his gaze went from the paintings on the wall and back to her. "Poor Mack," she pointed out to Scott. "He's really struggling with the idea that anybody had this kind of money for any of this stuff."

Scott turned and smiled, informing Mack, "Some of the paintings in this house will go for millions."

Even Doreen was shocked to hear that.

Nick just stared at him, then told Doreen, "I need to raise my rates."

She laughed. "Yeah, when *this* job is done."

He groaned and asked, "Are you kidding me? I should be doing this job on a percentage basis."

"*Ha*," she replied. "You are regretting initially offering to help me *pro bono* with my stalled divorce. You just want to be part of the wedding party, right?"

"I already am, as the best man to the groom," he muttered.

She turned to fully take in the master bedroom. "We need to get as much of this removed as quickly as possible," she said to Scott. "We don't have a ton of time to just sit around."

"Sit around?" he repeated, then shook his head and laughed. "You are such a joy to work with."

Doreen sighed. "Nothing here we are too worried about keeping. We may find bits and pieces. If so, we'll let you know. Otherwise take it all away."

"Good enough," Scott replied, with a huge grin. "And where will you stay while you're here?"

"We're sleeping in several of the beds here," she shared. "Unless … are you telling me we can't sleep on the beds either?"

Scott winced and turned to the brothers. "They are worth a lot of money."

"That's fine," Mack replied. "We can go buy some sleeping bags."

Doreen held up one hand. "I think a bunch of camping gear is in the storage room downstairs in the basement," Doreen announced, pointing in the direction of the gallery.

"Camping?" Mack repeated. "Seems totally unlike Mathew."

She sighed. "He thought glamping would be chic. He instantly didn't like it. Anyway all that should still be in that big storage area. So, Scott, if you want us to abandon the beds, we certainly can."

At that, Scott chuckled. "Perfect. You guys do whatever you want to do with alternate bed setups, and I'll arrange to get a transport team here as fast as I can."

"Good enough," she muttered.

Doreen frowned. "I just thought of something else."

"Something else?" Nick looked over at her warily.

She shrugged. "Yeah, something else."

"Something else for me?" Scott asked, turning to her with avid interest.

"I need jewelry evaluated."

Scott chuckled with interest. "Of course you do."

"Yeah, there's quite a bit in that safe." She looked at Mack and asked, "That's probably the best answer, isn't it?"

"I would think so," he agreed, nodding at Scott. "I'm no judge, but some pretty high-end pieces are in there."

Scott looked back at her and asked, "You don't want to keep any?"

"No."

He grinned. "I won't say anything against that," he muttered. "You certainly seem to know your own mind when it comes to these things."

"I don't know that I do," she argued, chuckling. "However, I do know that we're on the clock for this one."

"And you're okay if I organize to get things moved?"

"Yes, absolutely. … I just need receipts, please."

"Of course," he agreed. "You can't even imagine the amount of paperwork that some of these things will generate. May I see the collection?" he asked with delighted anticipation.

Doreen nodded, giving him a smirk. "Of course."

"I'll come with you," Nick added. "I'm not sure I saw any of this."

She led the way to the safe that held all the jewelry. She keyed in her birthday, got it open, and smiled. She brought out the first couple small boxes and handed them to Scott.

With a reverence that she appreciated, even though she had absolutely zero interest in the contents, both Scott and Nick went through the first two boxes with gasps of admiration, surprise. Nick brought out the rest, and, in a couple of cases, both were shocked at the contents.

When Scott gleefully looked over at her, she muttered, "I know. I know. It's just too much. And there are good copies of a bunch of these as well."

"And the good copies are also important," Scott noted.

"Why the need for good copies?" Nick asked her.

"Because in many cases these pieces are far too valuable to wear out, so extremely high-quality copies were made so that nobody would know."

He stared at her, but she shrugged. "I was never allowed

to wear the real thing. What if I somehow damaged it, broke it, lost it, I don't know," she explained, "so, yes, the copies are important."

She walked over to where she knew most of them were—in a lockbox behind a secret wall panel—and brought them to Scott as well. "An awful lot is here too."

"And did you want to save anything?" Scott asked her again.

"No, the answer remains no."

"Not one piece?"

"No," she repeated, "no to my future daughter, if I have any, no to any other family I may have, no to friends, et cetera. If I am blessed with a daughter at some point in time, I would like for her to have something a whole lot more meaningful than a piece of jewelry from some guy who dumped me like garbage."

Scott winced at that and then nodded. "An unbelievable amount of money is here, Doreen."

"I don't care," she replied, as she stared at it, then shrugged. "It was such a Mathew thing to do."

"What was that?" Nick asked her, as he stared around at the sparkling jewels in this room.

Doreen snorted. "Just like me, these are showpieces, something to show off, trying to tell everybody how big and powerful he was, and how much money he had."

"And yet you didn't get to wear the originals," Nick noted.

"No, but everybody would know that, if we had the copies, we would have the originals."

"On the other hand, maybe it was also a case of showing off for the sake of showing off, and he didn't have the originals at all," Nick pointed out.

"True, but that would be a matter of pride for him. Every time I was strutted out in a new piece, people would know he had just bought that piece," she stated, with a shrug. "There was no making him understand that it didn't matter to me, and, if I tried, he would say something about me not being classy enough to wear such things or smart enough to know how important it was or one of any number of other insults he came up with regularly."

Scott opened up each of the boxes atop Mathew's desk, completely covering it, now revealing the beauty inside. He sighed happily. "This is incredible."

"It might be incredible," she conceded, "but I don't want any of it."

"Understood," he confirmed, with a careful look from the fine pieces back to her. "You do realize how much of an anomaly you are, right?"

Nick chuckled. "I don't think she gets it."

Then Mack spoke from the doorway. "No, she doesn't get it at all. On the other hand, I wouldn't have her any other way."

She smiled up at her fiancé. "Scott will take pictures so we have that stash documented and, of course, will write it all up as well."

"And then hopefully you can arrange for a secured transport?" Mack asked.

Scott nodded. "I'll contact my colleagues over this haul as well," he explained, "and I think we'll get an armed security guard in here." When she looked at him in surprise, he shrugged. "Unless I can get it out really quickly and quietly. I don't want to risk it."

Just then his gaze on her was interrupted by uniformed cops out in the backyard area. He eyed her quizzically.

She frowned and explained, "When we arrived, true to form, I found a man buried in the greenhouse with the onions." His jaw dropped. She nodded. "Yes, my *luck* continues."

"Good God," Scott muttered, as he stared at her in shock. "That's not normal, Doreen. You know that, right?"

She snorted. "*Ya* think?" She rolled her eyes. "I don't know that there's anything called *normal* anymore."

With Scott firmly refocused on making his phone calls and arranging everything that he needed to accomplish, she waved at Mack and Nick, leading them outside to the garage—not the front garage but the back garage.

Mack looked around and asked, "What are we doing? What's back here? Why does he need a second garage anyway?"

Nick got it first. "Oh no, you've got to be kidding me."

She shrugged. "I figured these might be something you guys would want to see first."

Mack frowned at her, then at the garage. "*Uh-oh.*"

"Yeah, *uh-oh* is right," she muttered. "Mathew did have a thing about Jags, but he also had a thing about a few other cars." She walked up to the touchscreen keypad on the outside of the door and frowned as she tried to open it.

"Did you ever know the entry code for this one?" Mack asked.

"I think so," she muttered, as she tried again. Then she held up one hand. "Oh, hang on a second." She tried one more number, and, sure enough, the first of the doors opened. And, with that one open, she quickly opened up the other two beside it. With the lights now on, they could see Mathew's car collection. She muttered, "Oh, it got bigger."

"What do you mean it's bigger?" Mack asked, his voice rising.

"It used to be ten vehicles," she noted. "Seems to be what? Twelve now?"

"More like thirteen," Nick corrected.

As she expected, the two men froze in place, staring. Nick looked over at his brother, tapped Mack on the shoulder, and mentioned, "If she asks you if you want to keep one of these …"

Mack stared and shook his head. "A new truck is one thing, but what does someone do with all these?"

"You could take them out for a Sunday drive, maybe. We need to get Scott back here," Nick pointed out. "He'll think he's died and gone to heaven."

Doreen snorted. "Maybe. These were another part of Mathew's many various collections, but I don't know if they're valuable. I just figured because you guys are guys"—then she stopped and laughed—"you might be more interested in this." They just stared at her in shock, and she shrugged. "I mean, it doesn't matter to me."

"You're getting a new vehicle, a reliable one, a safe one," Mack declared. "If you don't want one of these, then we'll make sure you get something once we get home."

Just then Nick added, "I'll grab Scott and bring him out here. He's probably already lost in the house." With a chuckle, Nick left.

Doreen turned to Mack. "We also have to go through the dower house."

"What do you mean, the dower house?" Mack asked, turning to look at her.

"The second house on the property. Although it's likely minimally furnished. It was never used in all the years I lived here."

He shook his head. "Jeez, and Mathew owns how many

other homes? Even one month won't be enough time."

"With Scott's expert help, I'm pretty sure we can get this property ready to sell in no time," she explained, "but it'll still leave a lot of Mathew's other homes to deal with."

Mack groaned at the thought.

While she was talking to him, Scott arrived, took one look, and started to laugh in sheer joy. "Oh my. … For many people this may not be their happy place, but, for a lot of others, *this* most definitely qualifies." He looked over at her and asked, "Do you want any of these?"

She looked over at Mack, who shook his head in horror. When Nick shook his head with a bit of indignation, she frowned. "Mack says I have to get a new vehicle."

"Yes, you do," Mack confirmed. He turned to Scott. "What's the cheapest vehicle in this garage, right now?"

"Ooh, I don't know," he said, as he considered them all. "Maybe that McLaren, but it's got a number two on it."

"Oh, I think that's number two because he crashed number one," she shared. "I'm pretty sure it was part of a deal he did, and then he took it out and crashed it. So you would have to talk to him about that."

He stared at her for a long second.

She groaned. "But you can't talk to him about it, so what would you say is the cheapest?"

He shrugged. "Nothing here is under half a million."

She gasped at that. "Fine." She turned back to Mack. "Can't we just get a normal car at home?"

"Yes, we can just get a normal car at home," he stated, staring at her. "Unless you want something here that has a special memory for you. This is your house, and these are all your things now."

"No, they're not," she corrected, with a wave of her

hand. "These were important to Mathew. To me, these are just *his* things, and nothing here matters to me."

Scott was almost in a swoon by the time they got through inspecting all the vehicles.

She added, "Don't forget the side garage."

At that, the men groaned. Mack asked, "What's over there?"

She shrugged. "The motorcycles." They walked over and opened it. By now, she could see that Mack was in the same state she was, blinded by it all.

Mack muttered, "There is just so … *much*."

She agreed. "It's just too much all the time, and that was always one of the arguments I had with him. He never really did anything except … collect. He didn't drive these. He didn't take them out. He didn't do anything with any of his collections. I didn't understand the point of having them, and he told me that I was just too dense to understand. While I won't say I was dense, I definitely didn't understand."

"Oh, Nick—before I forget," she began. "Can the estate manager give us an update on the other properties in the lower mainland? Give us a status if they are rented, furnished, empty, and in need of repairs or any other details. They won't be full of treasures like this one as Mathew would never have trusted others with his special items."

"Let's focus on selling this property first. As for the others, we have a property management company already hired by Mathew's probate lawyer to watch over Mathew's main residence. Why don't we hire them to also lease out or rent Mathew's other Vancouver homes? That would bring Doreen some monthly income, as well as advertise these homes. Even as rentals, you always get some inspired couple who wants to buy it outright, before the public sees too much of it." He turned to Dorren and Mack, asking, "What do you two think?"

She glanced at Mack, who nodded, and she confirmed their agreement. "Sell this first. Rent the rest, if they aren't already, with the plan to sell eventually, with Christie's auctioning off the furniture and whatnot, then donating the rest."

"That's sound in general," he replied. "I'll work something up."

Doreen sighed. "Sounds good to me. I just want this *done*. … Now can we eat?" she asked as she led the way back to the house. "I'm starving."

"There's leftover pizza," Nick suggested.

"Is there?" she asked, turning to him. "I thought you finished it all."

"*I* finished it," Mack admitted, "so there aren't any leftovers." When his brother looked at him, he shrugged. "I snagged it for breakfast, long before you guys were discussing pancakes." Then Mack laughed. "So, do you want to go out and get something?"

"We'll need more perishable goods if we're staying here for a few more days." Nick glanced between the two of them.

"I picked up milk for tea," she muttered, "and we have coffee. A few bananas too but, yes, we need more."

"There's lots of coffee. Plus, we need to use up groceries in the freezer anyway," Mack suggested. "So why don't I rustle up something for food?" And that's what they did.

By the time they had a meal ready, she suggested, "Let's go track down Scott and invite him to join us."

They found him out in the garage, still taking inventory of the cars and the motorcycles, while excitedly talking to people on the phone.

When he noticed them, he shared, "Eight specialists are coming in over the next twenty-four hours. Two will be here this afternoon, and the rest will be here tomorrow."

"Good enough," she replied. "We rustled up some groceries, if you want to come inside and eat with us."

He smiled at her with gratitude. "I really could use some food," he muttered. "It's been a pretty exciting day." Over lunch they talked about the logistics of what would be required to get everything out of this place.

Scott added, "You'll need to stay for at least a few more days, give or take, so we can start packing, shipping, and sorting. You'll need to be here so we only pack up and sell what you want to sell."

She looked around and shook her head. "I can't think of anything that I want to keep."

"What about the jewelry?" Mack asked. "Are you sure you don't want to keep anything?" He paused and noted, "And I know that we're pushing the line here, but, if we do have kids one day"—he waggled his eyebrows at her—"would you want a piece for your daughter?"

She immediately shook her head. "No way. As I said earlier, I would rather pick out something for her that had meaning to me, rather than a super-expensive showpiece that came from someone who discarded me like garbage."

Silence came at her remark. Nick looked over at his brother and said, "Too bad she doesn't have a sister."

"Why?" she asked, staring at him curiously.

"Because I would like to meet her."

"Okay," she muttered, not sure exactly what that meant. Yet Scott was grinning broadly, so she would take it as a good thing. Just when they finished eating and were about to get back to work, the doorbell rang.

And, just in case they didn't hear that, Mugs commenced barking nonstop.

It was Daniel.

Doreen sighed, then looked over at Nick. "You want to escort him to the greenhouse?" she asked Nick.

Surprised but willing, he pointed in that direction.

The detective narrowed his gaze and asked, "Trying to get rid of me?"

"We have work to do that doesn't involve you," she declared. "You may not be against us, but you're obviously definitely not for us."

"I'm not for anybody," he replied coolly. "We have a victim who needs to be taken care of."

"Exactly," she agreed, "so please, go take care of him."

And, with that, Nick led Daniel to the greenhouse.

Chapter 7

AS SOON AS Nick and Daniel left, Goliath appeared from nowhere to wind around her legs. Then Thaddeus poked his head out, rubbing his beak against her cheek. She reached up and stroked his head. Mack studied her and asked, "You seem to have a problem with him. Want to explain?"

"It's funny," she began. "When we had met before in my other lifetime here—and I don't remember in what capacity—but my ex knew Daniel. I also knew him as a young and sweet guy back then." She frowned as she thought about that. "Is he allowed to work on a case if he knows the victim?"

"Yes," Mack told her, "just as I worked on some cases where I knew the victim as well. As long as the victim is not family, it's all good."

She nodded. "I'm not trying to cause any problems," she murmured, "but I just get the feeling that I went from being an old acquaintance to a suspect."

"No," Mack argued, "you were always a suspect. When first on the scene, there will be some doubts."

She groaned. "Fine. I'm a suspect, whatever." She looked

over at Scott and asked, "Shall we proceed?"

"I've already got somebody coming in from the airport," he shared.

"Right, good."

And, before long, multiple people arrived, Mugs alerting everyone with his frantic barking. So she was busy, going from one room to another to guide people throughout the house. Packers came in behind them, and, in an efficient way that she had never seen before, Scott was already organizing the shipments of a lot of the furniture and was in major discussions about the paintings now.

When he rejoined her, he explained, "The paintings will take a little bit. I must get the proper transport for them."

"Now that you've had a closer look at all of them, are they in good shape?"

"They absolutely are. Mathew did look after everything well." She nodded, as Scott went on. "These possessions were more than just things to him. For many collectors, they are status symbols, somehow replacing something they didn't have within themselves," he explained. "Very few collectors do so because they absolutely love the artwork. They're collectors because of the value they represent."

"And that would have been Mathew too," she agreed.

Scott asked her, "Is it cathartic being here, or painful?"

"In a way, it's cathartic," she shared, with a small smile. "It's also helping me to understand who he was."

"And maybe that's good—or not," he told her, with a smile. "You seem to have landed on your feet very, very well."

"If you're talking financially, yes," she agreed. "That would be a mild way to put it."

They went on to discuss the paintings, arranging time

frames and the logistics of getting them moved properly.

Doreen asked Scott, "What about the status on the furniture?"

He looked at his watch and nodded. "I have a particular specialist coming in for just that, and he should be here in about twenty minutes. As I mentioned, they'll be coming in all day."

And he was true to his word. They came one after the other. As they each surveyed all the furniture individually, Mack trailed beside Doreen as she did her own individual inspection of each piece of furniture. She murmured to Mack, "I don't know why, but, probably because of Nan, I feel as if we need to check every piece."

His eyebrows shot up, and he eyed her in question.

"Just for, … you know, hidden treasure."

"Oh no," he muttered, as he looked around. "That's an awful lot to check."

"Yes, and I am not sure of another way to address this."

Scott looked over at her and asked, "Is there a problem?"

"I just feel we need to check for hidden treasures in every one of these pieces."

At that, he studied her with interest and asked, "Was your husband in the habit of hiding things?"

She snorted. "Absolutely. We've already found some of his hidden safes and one hidden drawer," she shared, "but I know there was more."

"I do love hidden drawers," Scott replied in absolute delight.

"I think there's more than one in the desk in his office."

"I could take a look," Soctt offered. "I certainly have seen an awful lot of desks with hidden drawers."

She led the way to the office, and Scott sighed happily as

he stared at the desk. Then he turned to her and asked, "Are you okay to sell this one?"

"Sure, but I have to empty it and deal with the contents first," she noted. He nodded, his gaze fixated on the desk. She laughed and said, "Go for it."

Mack frowned at her, obviously worried that Daniel would not approve of this. She smirked. "Can you check in on the detective?" He nodded and quickly disappeared.

She stayed with Scott while he went through the desk with a fine-tooth comb. Disappointed, he straightened up and shook his head. "Are you sure a hidden drawer is in here?"

"I'm pretty sure there are two. We found the one with the gun in it and some related paperwork. The reason I think there is another one is because Mathew told me a long time ago that the one was almost a camouflage for the other."

At that, Scott's face lit up, and he went back around to the other side and pulled out the secret drawer Nick and Mack had found earlier. With that out of the way, he checked deeper inside, and, sure enough, a second drawer opened up. "And there you go," he exclaimed, with a happy crow of delight.

She walked around to see paperwork upon paperwork. "Now, this is interesting," she muttered.

"You don't know what this could be?" Scott asked.

"No, of course not," she declared. She opened up the paperwork, but she didn't understand it.

Scott raised his eyebrows when he glanced at the docs over her shoulder.

When Mack returned, she handed the stack over to him and asked, "Do you recognize what these are?"

He looked at them, and his face paled.

She noticed right away. "*Uh-oh*, not good news?"

"For you," he replied. "I mean, … technically these could represent very good news. We'll have to get Nick in here."

"What are they?" she asked.

"Cash bonds, bearer bonds, plus some original stock certificates."

She stared at them and then nodded. "Mathew always talked about having a getaway bag or a getaway fund—like the large sum of cash hidden away in the toilet tank."

"*This* would be one hell of a getaway fund," he noted, pointing to the paperwork, shaking his head.

Scott grimaced as he looked over at him. "It takes a bit to get used to, doesn't it?"

"More than a little bit," Mack clarified. "I never really considered how different it would be to have large sums of money. Yet, every time I turn around, she keeps falling into more and more."

"Oh, I love that phrase," Scott said, truly fascinated as he stared at him. "*Falls into* fits because that's really what she's doing. If she believes in all that stuff about manifesting and whatnot, I would have to say she's doing one heck of a job."

"I would say she is too," Mack countered as he turned to her. She just silently shrugged. He noted, "Whatever she is doing is certainly working."

"I'm hardly doing anything," she muttered. "This was all Mathew. He was always so very paranoid."

"And do you know why?" Mack asked her.

"Not specifically," she replied, "but I would guess an awful lot of people were probably very unhappy with him."

"You're thinking about the Pete Singer, our dead man buried in the greenhouse?"

"Yes, and I'm afraid that poor man was probably killed because of something that Mathew did."

After hearing that, Scott jumped when his phone buzzed. He checked it and smiled. "We've got more people on the road," he told Doreen. "I've also got trucks coming." When she frowned at him, he shrugged. "We really need to get moving what has been packed to date. As we all know, an awful lot of stuff is here."

"And what are you moving first?" she asked him.

"The bedroom furniture."

"Which one? Mack and I will get a head start, checking to see if anything's hidden."

"Oh, that's a good point," Scott noted, eyeing her anxiously. "You told me that you wanted me to get started, and I didn't even consider that, not until you just brought it up today."

"That's understandable, but this is, … well, not a normal situation."

"That's an understatement." Mack chortled.

Ignoring him, she turned back to Scott. "Just give us a few minutes, and hopefully we can clear a couple bedrooms. So confirm with us before they're okayed to pack stuff. Which bedrooms are being done today?"

"I was hoping to get all the guest bedrooms done today."

She rolled her eyes and sighed. "Then we need to get moving."

With that, they roped in Nick to help them. Gathering the animals, Doreen and Mack and Nick all raced up to the second floor, checking the guest bedrooms, starting with all the bedding, all the drawers, and everywhere else they could think to look for secret places.

In the first bedroom they found nothing. In the second

bedroom they found nothing. In the third bedroom they found nothing.

Nick asked her, "Are you sure there's a point to this?" She just shrugged and continued her search.

In the fourth guest bedroom, she found a safe behind the wall.

"Oh no," Nick muttered. "Any idea what's in there?"

"Nope," she replied, staring at it. "And I don't know where we'll find the code."

"We can always get somebody in to crack the safe," Mack interjected, "but, if we can do without that, it would be better. Right, Nick?"

Nick agreed.

She didn't say anything more but went to work on the rest of the room. By the time they were more or less done, she looked around and muttered, "It still feels as if we're missing something here."

The two men frowned at her. Mack asked, "What do you mean?"

"I don't know exactly. … I don't know how to explain it. Yet, if Mathew put a safe in this room, then it should be an important room to him."

"But the safe could be empty, as he had the other safes as well," Mack pointed out.

She considered that and then nodded. "That's a valid point."

"Thank you," he quipped, taking a mock bow.

She rolled her eyes at him. "It's really irritating when you're always right."

He snorted. "I am never right, and, just for the record, you end up being the one who's always right. And you always being right … is extremely irritating." She stared at him, but he just waved a hand. "No worries. I'm fine."

"Good," she muttered. Just then her phone rang, and it was Scott.

"Hey, the car expert is here."

"Good," she muttered.

"How are you doing with the bedrooms? The transport trucks aren't very far away."

"We have three cleared," she shared, "and we're working on the fourth but just found a hidden safe." She frowned and added, "I'll see if Mack wants to go give you a hand with the vehicles." With that, she ended the call from Scott and waved a hand at Mack. "The car expert, whoever he is, is apparently here."

"I'll go," Mack offered. Then he faced his brother, a bit of a guilty expression on his face. Still, Nick just laughed and shooed him away. "Go on. I'll stay here and help out Doreen."

And, with that, Mack disappeared.

Nick turned to her and explained, "You know, it's bound to be a little hard on him, … exposed to all this money."

"Why?" she asked, frowning at him. "Isn't money supposed to make life easier?" she asked in confusion.

He chuckled, smiling at her. "Absolutely. At least it's supposed to, but, in many cases, it also makes life more complicated."

"I'm not into making life complicated," she muttered. "I'll need help setting up some donations to charities and all that, but I don't plan on making any life changes that will affect Mack."

Nick's lips twitched. "Are you telling me that the money won't affect Mack?"

She took a moment to consider that, then groaned.

Nick reminded her, "You'll have *so* much money now. So much more than before."

She glared at him, protesting, "That's not an issue."

"Good. So, you might want to tell Mack that. Otherwise he may worry that it'll be a problem between you two."

"How can it possibly be a problem?" she asked, staring at him. "We can do an awful lot of good with this money, as you know. I was hoping that, with your help, we could get that rolling."

"And I'm willing to do that," Nick confirmed. "I just don't want my brother to feel as if he's not important, or that ..." He frowned. "I guess I'm more concerned that he'll feel he has nothing to offer you because he doesn't have this kind of money, the same as you do."

She snorted. "Nobody does," she declared, with a dramatic wave of her hand. "This money issue is ridiculous. I mean, look at him. ... He spent all that time and energy amassing all this wealth, and where is he?"

Nick stared at her in confusion. "Where's who?"

"*Mathew*," she cried out. "He spent all that time creating these various collections of whatever, paranoid every moment, stashing away good money that he refused to spend, and now he's dead. He's not here to enjoy any of it. I would say that he *never* enjoyed any of it."

"That's a lesson for you then," he noted, with a smile, "because I think you will also be one who never spends it."

"I haven't spent it," she pointed out, "because I don't have it yet."

"You have a pocketful of it now," he stated.

She frowned at him. "I do?"

He chuckled. "Remember the wad of cash we found in

the toilet tank earlier?"

"Oh, yeah, right," she muttered, with a headshake. "However, you told Mack—and I'll remind you now of this—how we can't spend this money. It needs to be properly logged in and serial numbers documented, et cetera. So, yet again, I don't have any money to spend."

"Yes, and we should probably be checking the rest of the toilet tanks in this mansion as well. The bottom line of all of this is that you just have to keep being you. Don't let the money get to your head or change who you are."

"I can't imagine that'll happen," she muttered. "It never mattered to me when I was married to Mathew, and it certainly won't matter to me now that he's gone. I'm very happy with the life I have these days."

"Good."

They went back to searching through the guest bedrooms, in a bit of a panic as they realized how much time they didn't have.

By the time they had finished another two bedrooms, they had completed six of the guest rooms. That left the master en suite and three more guest rooms—the ones each of them were sleeping in. She was well aware that Scott had movers coming right now to remove all the bedroom furniture. Still, she headed back to the fourth guest bedroom where she'd found the hidden safe.

"We haven't found anything, but it still bothers you, right?" Nick asked.

"Yes," she declared, "I don't know whether it's the safe that bothers me or something else about this room."

She walked over to the picture, moved it aside, and stared at the safe for a long moment. Then she suddenly turned around, her back against the safe, facing the opposite wall, and studied it for a long moment, now smiling. "There it is," she declared. She walked carefully forward, her gaze glued to the one spot on the far side wall, Nick walking every step with her, not seeing a thing, just making sure she was okay. She reached out and pressed the heel of her hand against the wall, and out popped a section of it.

"Good God," Nick muttered, as she opened the hidden cubbyhole.

"I remember something Mathew mentioned one time," she shared, as she stared at the numerous cloth bags inside there. "I think this is more of his running money."

"*This* is … *more* running money?" he asked, whistling. He pulled out the nearest bag and opened it up, and, sure enough, a lot of cash was stuffed inside. Same for the next three bags. Still more were inside this deep cubbyhole.

"Yeah, that may be the last of it here," she muttered. "He told me once, if he had to run, he would leave and not have to worry about paying for anything for the rest of his life. So I assumed that meant he had stashed aside a fair bit of money."

"That would make sense," Nick noted.

She looked around and added, "If we look in the closets, we should find a bag, maybe a duffel bag."

Nick headed over to the closet, which was empty except for a couple duffel bags on the bottom, also empty.

"And that would be how he knew which bedroom, if he ever forgot," she stated, with a laugh.

Nick brought them both over and they removed the contents of the hidden compartment into the duffel bags.

She looked down at these and asked, "Now what will we do with this?"

Nick shrugged. "Technically it needs to go in the bank,

but we don't really have time today."

"You're making me really nervous," Doreen shared. "Let's put it all in the master, before anybody knows it's here," she suggested. With that, Nick picked up the duffel bags, and she closed the secret cubbyhole, then looked back at the safe on the other wall and nodded. She added, "I think that's a dummy. And it was meant to draw our attention, but the real treasure was right here."

Nick noted, "We might have to get a safecracker in, just to be sure."

She frowned and walked back over to it and pressed on all the corners. She heard a little *click*, and the safe popped open. She smiled as she peeked inside, picked up an envelope left there, and told Nick, "This is what's in here."

As they opened the envelope, they found a big happy face, with a handwritten note under it. *Try again.*

She laughed, showing him the note. "That's so Mathew."

"Sorry, but the guy sounds like an absolute jerk," Nick muttered.

She nodded. "Absolutely. Are you just figuring that out?"

He laughed. "I'm just figuring out the depth of it because I had nothing to do with him personally. However, his home reveals so much about him."

"He was all about money, all about power, all about esteem," she stated. "And, when he couldn't get that, everything in his life was focused on making sure he did."

"Got it."

And, with that, they carried the duffel bags to the master bedroom. She sighed. "We still have four more rooms to check. This master and the three we're using."

"Let's go search mine first," Nick suggested. "It doesn't seem to have all the furniture that the others do. The movers can take the furniture in mine, while we search the remaining bedrooms."

They quickly searched his and found nothing.

Doreen sighed. "I don't feel anything else is in here."

"Are you relatively secure about this?" Nick asked her.

"I am," she replied.

Nick added, "I think we'll still get them to sign a doc, stipulating that anything they find inside the furniture is yours."

She shrugged. "I feel as if that should go without saying, particularly in this situation."

"Maybe," he conceded, "but let's just make sure that we reinforce it by documenting that thought."

Next, they went through the room where Mack was staying. Since she had chosen to have a separate room herself, they went through that guest bedroom too.

"So, all these are fine," she noted. "I'll definitely need more time to go through the master."

"That's okay. We'll tell Scott to do that bedroom last."

Scott came up the stairs just then and had four men with him. He asked her, "Well?"

Nick stepped up and shared, "We've gone through the nine guest bedrooms, so you can start with those, leaving the master for last." He pointed out the master. "Given that the owner of this house was a person who absolutely loved to hide things, we'll need some reassurances."

"What kind?" Scott asked.

"Simple and easy. If you find anything inside any of the pieces taken from this house or its garage, it belongs to Doreen and has to be returned at the earliest opportunity."

"Of course, of course," Scott agreed. "Let me take a look at the master, if you don't mind. I mean, I do know some of the pieces, but I don't think these styles typically have hidden drawers." He pointed at the crew gathering behind him. "Let me just get them started, and I'll come right back."

Scott walked with the packing crew to the farthest guest bedroom, telling them to work toward the master. The head guy nodded, and they stepped inside the first of ten bedrooms and started making plans to move this as efficiently as possible.

Chapter 8

MEANWHILE SCOTT QUICKLY did a pass through each of the nine guest bedrooms and rejoined them in the master suite, shaking his head. "I don't think anything in those nine bedrooms falls into the *secret drawer* category—not like your grandmother's antiques, where hidden compartments were more the norm."

"Probably not," she replied, "but, as paranoid as Mathew was …"

"I understand fully," Scott confirmed. "I get it, and your request will not be an issue. They are moving things as we speak. The sooner we can get all the bedroom furniture moved, the better. Because of the value involved, everything will be taken apart to move, wrapped in protective coverings, and then reassembled. We can't take a chance of damaging anything."

Mugs came up to Scott, expecting a hug or a pat on the head or the scrub of an ear. Scott smiled and was more than happy to give some attention to Mugs. Doreen smiled at their interplay.

"In other words, they'll be at this for days," Doreen noted.

He laughed and nodded. "Sadly they may well be at this for days. So, you have time to go through anything else."

"Good enough," she replied. Then her phone rang. It was Nan.

"How is it going?" she cried out in a cheery tone. "I've got you on Speaker because I have the whole gang here. We're all eager to hear what's going on down there."

"You won't believe it," Doreen began and described what had happened since they had arrived.

After a moment of shock and then absolute cries of joy, Nan exclaimed to all, "Oh my gosh, how could that be? Trust Doreen to find a dead body."

She sighed. "Honestly, I didn't do anything. You know that, … right?"

"Of course not," Maisie stated. "But, my, you do find trouble, don't you?"

"Unfortunately I find it everywhere apparently," Doreen acknowledged, "and here I sit, going through Mathew's things. We've definitely found some hidden treasure here too."

"I'm taking it off Speakerphone," Nan announced, and her voice dropped into a half whisper. "Is there *treasure*, real treasure, child?"

"Yes," she whispered right back, "treasure, real treasure."

"Oh my." Then she chortled. "I think you should enjoy spending every penny that comes from that house," she told her granddaughter, with glee.

"I was thinking about giving most of it away."

First came silence, then her grandmother sighed. "As much as I approve of that sentiment, I think you should take time to do something you will absolutely love, knowing Mathew's precious money bought you some happiness. Too bad he didn't make you happy while you were married to him."

Doreen chuckled. "You just want me to have revenge on him."

"You don't need any revenge. He's dead, child, but thankfully you're the one who's still kicking."

"I am," she said, "and it's a … strange feeling in a way."

"Of course it is, in many ways, no doubt. He was all you knew for a long time. Just let Mack know that you love him, that the life you had with Mathew was a very unhappy time for you."

"I have. Yet with each find of more treasure here, he seems to need further reassurance. Yet I'm not trying to make him feel insecure."

"Not sure you can. Mack's a pretty stable guy, you know?" Nan replied.

"He usually is, but an awful lot of money is involved here, which seems to be multiplying by the millions," she shared.

Nan laughed as if it were the best joke ever. "You know that I didn't like Mathew," she began, "but this really is a nice send-off."

"He didn't need to die though," Doreen added.

"And you think and say these things because you're such a lovely, sweet girl," Nan replied. "For all his abuse and greed and hate, Mathew couldn't kill off the real Doreen in hiding. … Enough about that. We can talk about options for the money when you get home."

"Yes, and that won't be right away because this will take a bit longer than I thought. Oh, I didn't tell you about the local detective on the case."

"Oh my," And then she muttered, "*Daniel, Daniel.*

Someone you knew when married to Mathew?"

"Yeah, except he is now *Detective* Daniel Sherwood."

Nan snorted. "If he knows Mathew, he shouldn't be on the case."

"I asked Mack about that, and he explained how definitely it is allowed under some circumstances, just like me with the cold cases, working that one with his mother and the jewels," she pointed out. "At times information from somebody who knows them can be very helpful."

"And Daniel's there now?"

"Yeah, he's here now."

"Is he with … a whole team?"

"No." She frowned as she thought about that. "He's always alone, unless forensics is here or the coroner. He doesn't seem to have a partner who he works with on this investigation. I guess that's a problem too, isn't it?"

"Don't know how you might take this, but I wouldn't let that man run loose anywhere."

"He's supposed to only be in the greenhouse, but you're right. I don't know where he is." She turned and looked around. "I was looking for Mack too."

"Go find Mack," Nan stated, "and keep an eye on that detective."

"Just because we don't necessarily like detectives?" she asked her grandmother, eyeing Nick who rolled his eyes at her.

"True, we don't like them," Nan declared. "Only the ones we know and trust. This Daniel is guilty by association with Mathew. Too bad I'm not up on the art scene down there, but I still have quite a few friends there."

That came as a surprise to Doreen. "You do?" she asked.

"Yes, I was big in the art scene down there for a long time, remember?"

"Yes, of course," Doreen muttered, "but I hadn't realized you might still be in touch with people."

"Of course I am," she snapped, with a certain amount of indignation. "You certainly haven't seen the last of me in all of this."

"Of course not," Doreen murmured, ending the call. She turned to Nick and whispered, "Nan doesn't like anything about Daniel."

"I thought you knew him."

"I met him through Mathew." Nick frowned at her, and she nodded. "So, I knew his name, and face as an acquaintance but certainly not as a close friend. Honestly, I can't place when and how I even first knew him."

"So him as part of this investigation may not be completely legit?"

"Right, and I asked Mack about that, but he told me that it can happen. It's just—" She asked him, "When you took Daniel to the greenhouse, where did he go?"

"He went over to where the body was found."

"And you left him there?"

"I did leave him there," he confirmed, "but now you're making me question my judgment."

"None of us have answers to that just yet. Nan remembers him somehow too. She's digging deeper and will get back to me. It's just a little …" She frowned and continued, "It feels a little suspicious."

Nick nodded, glancing down the hallway at the movers. "Maybe we should go find Daniel."

"That's a good idea," she agreed.

The two of them walked back down to the kitchen, where they saw Mack talking to the detective.

Mack smiled at her and asked, "How is the visit with the

antiquities people going?"

She replied, "Fine. The movers are already emptying bedrooms, as we speak."

"That's good." Mack motioned to Daniel. "He's finished here for the day, so he'll head back."

She nodded at Daniel. "Thanks."

"For what?" he asked, staring at her.

She shrugged. "Just thanks. I'm glad to see that you're getting somewhere."

"But I'm not getting anywhere," he pointed out. "So far, there hasn't been any place to get."

Not knowing what to say, she turned to Mack. "If you're done here, I have a couple things I want to show you."

"Sure enough."

She looked over at Nick, who nodded back at her. Nick swung out an arm and told Daniel, "I'll escort you to the front door."

"I really don't need an escort." Daniel snorted. "Seems you're just trying to get rid of me."

"We have work to do," Doreen added in exasperation. "I can't leave what I'm doing to babysit you all day."

Mack stiffened. Daniel glared at her.

Obviously that was the wrong thing to say. She shrugged. "If you're done here, you're done. So thank you, Detective Daniel Sherwood," she said primly. "If you're not done here, tell us what else you need."

"I'm done," he snapped. And, with that, he turned and stormed off, the front door slamming behind him.

Doreen couldn't help herself as she walked to the window and watched as he drove away.

Mack came up behind her. "So, does that mean things are not going well?"

"Things are going just fine," she declared, with a scoff, "but he's getting on my nerves."

"Apparently," Mack noted. "Still, you must remember that he's a cop and is just doing his job."

She shook her head. "Is he though? He just told us that he isn't getting anywhere. How come we don't have copies of those neighbor reports of trespassers on this property days before we arrived? Did he *ever* tell you that he has confirmed each of our alibis? Because he sure hasn't told me anything about anything. Has he shared anything about our dead body from the greenhouse? Even given us some background on Pete Singer? Also, we asked for a list of Mathew's former employees, which is a pretty basic element of a murder investigation. But, for whatever reason, he's not telling us squat. I am the legal owner of this property. Aren't I entitled to findings from his supposed investigation? His attitude toward me and this investigation triggers something in me. Yet his failure to conduct a proper investigation really angers me. I'm so on edge around him."

Mack nodded. "I've seen you edgy but never quite like this." He watched as Mugs and Goliath circled around her, aware that she was upset. "I'll call my captain and see if Daniel touched base with him."

Doreen muttered, "That would at least be something we learn."

Mack raised one finger and stepped out of the room, already making the call.

Doreen refused to listen in. She trusted Mack and his captain. She made coffee, yet warm brewed coffee was already there. Shaking her head, she looked out the window but saw the greenhouse, which just made her even angrier, not less.

Mack wasn't gone long and soon approached her.

"*Uh-oh*, I know that expression. Tell me."

Mack grimaced. "Daniel never called my captain. He's checking around to see if anybody in the department got a call from Vancouver, checking on my alibi."

"I knew it. Daniel can't be trusted."

Mack added, "Let's not jump the gun, but this isn't a good start."

Doreen snorted. "Speaking of guns, can we find out more about the weapon that killed Pete Singer, if it was registered, some background on Singer? Or do we confront Daniel to his face? I vote that we take on this investigation as our own."

Mack sighed. "We will wait for confirmation from my captain."

Doreen nodded. "Then?"

"Then," Mack added, "maybe it's time I spoke to *his* captain."

"Yes, please," she whispered, her gaze downcast. "I don't know what it is about Daniel, but he's pushing all my buttons," she muttered, bending down to hug her animals. "Anyway, how did you make out with the garage?"

He shrugged. "That is an incredible hoard of cars down there, and I still can't envision why anybody would own them all."

"That's the thing. Mathew didn't even drive them. Maybe it was because he wrecked that first McLaren. If you have one that you love, and you want to drive it all the time, or even on certain occasions, I get that. Yet to have all those vehicles that you never, ever drive makes no sense to me at all. I mean, aren't you supposed to recharge the engine or whatever by driving each car for ten minutes or so a week or whatever?"

Mack chuckled. "Some things with Mathew never really add up."

At that, Mugs barked at her several times. "I know, buddy. I get it. Shall we go out to the garden and forget about this for a while?"

So, with Mack in tow, the three of them stepped out into the backyard. Mugs immediately raced around the yard.

She looked around and asked, "Where's Goliath? He was just with us."

"I have no idea," Mack replied. "And where's Thaddeus?"

"I left him on the roost in the master bedroom, which is just the valet chair," she shared, scrubbing her face.

"Are you okay, honey?" He massaged the back of her neck.

"It's all been more exhausting than I thought," she admitted. "I shouldn't have come down here."

"Oh, you definitely should have," he corrected, still massaging her neck. "You're finding all kinds of stuff."

"Yes, but some of it? … I'm not sure I wanted to find."

Just then the captain returned Mack's call. "Captain?" Mack answered, then listened intently for less than a minute.

Doreen stared at him and knew immediately. "Daniel never called anyone, did he?"

Mack grimaced and nodded. "You call Nan and prod her memories on Daniel. Meanwhile, I will call Daniel's captain, asking for some professional courtesies from him in lieu of Daniel's inaction on this investigation."

Nick joined them, asking, "Did you tell him?"

"No, I didn't."

At that, Mack handed Nick the paperwork they'd found earlier in the second secret drawer in Mathew's office. Nick read over the paperwork, while she told Mack about what she and Nick had found in the one guest bedroom with the safe in it.

He stared at her. "Duffel bags of cash?" he whispered.

She nodded. "Yeah, I filled duffel bags with cash. So, maybe I could ask for your help later."

"And what help would that be?" Mack asked, staring down at her.

She shrugged. "Charities that need help."

He asked her, "Is that all the cash means to you?"

"Of course. It means more charities get help," she replied, staring at him. "What else will I do with it all?"

A smile started at the corner of his mouth, and, by the time it was fully developed, it had crossed his entire face. He was smiling at her in a way she'd really never seen before.

"That makes you happy?" she asked in a questioning tone.

"It makes me very happy," he whispered. "I have to admit it's a little daunting to think that you could have all this, and now … you do have all this. Yet you seem happy enough to … just be with me."

She stared at him. "I'm totally happy to be with you," she declared. "None of this means anything to me, not now, not before. Even worse, it's Mathew's money, and I wonder how he got it. So please, don't ever, *ever* compare the two of you or the cost of his *things* or the amount of money he hid everywhere. Everything with Mathew is dirty, tainted."

From behind them Nick snorted. "Good thing you said that because I just checked the current stock prices of one of these companies, and it has soared. It's a social media company, and Mathew has had these stock shares for a very long time," he muttered. "You can sell them, get cash," Nick pointed out. "Those alone amount to hundreds of thousands of dollars."

She nodded. "So, we need to go to a bank. We have to close out Mathew's accounts and put them in my name anyway, right? So we can also deposit all this cash we have found so far. Plus, do whatever with the cash bonds so we get the cash, not somebody else."

"Do you want to cash it all in, even the stock?" Mack asked her, just to be sure.

"I don't know. Do I?" she asked. "It seems to be the safest solution, right? Because Nick said these were the same as cash, correct? As for the stocks, I defer to you, Nick." She turned and looked from one brother to the other.

"Sounds good to me, but, in the meantime, all of these," Nick said, holding up the paperwork, "need to be in a safe place."

"*Yeah,*" she quipped, adding an eye roll. "Along with the duffel bags."

"Good God." Nick shook his head. "Just seeing that much cash makes me rethink my life."

"Not a whole lot of rethinking needed," she said, as she turned to face him. "I was just explaining that to Mack. Absolutely nothing in all this matters to me more than people and my animals," she shared. "So, if you can help me put together a list of charities that need help, it would mean a lot more to me than anything we found here."

"Then we'll set it up as investments," Nick shared, "so we're not just handing over straight cash to them. We'll invest the cash instead, and the interest is what goes to the charities."

"You must have a reason for that. Why?" Doreen asked.

"Plenty of reasons," he began, "but, for one thing, you

will never run out of money, and, for a second thing, you will always have money to give to the charities."

She blinked at that and then nodded. "I like that idea."

He smiled. "I thought you would. But then again, you've forgotten that we'd already discussed this option before."

"I do remember that vaguely."

Nick turned to his brother and shook his head. "Filling those duffel bags was unbelievable."

Mack nodded. "And that's what my life will be like now?"

"We won't keep coming up with duffel bags," she clarified, staring at him.

"Are you sure?" Mack asked, giving her a wry smile.

She winced. "No, I'm really not sure, but we're just fine as we are."

Together they trouped up to the master bedroom where the duffel bags were stashed in the closet. Mack took one look and whistled as he opened one of the bags. "Good God," he muttered. "We'll have to find a way to get all this into the bank … and fast."

"I know and maybe sort the stuff in the safe deposit boxes too."

Both men froze.

Chapter 9

DOREEN'S EYEBROWS SHOT up at their reaction. Mugs noticed a change in the mood and sat down at her feet.

Nick, in a very odd tone, repeated, "Safe deposit boxes?"

She frowned at him. "Yeah. I thought … everybody had those. Don't you?"

"Do you have one in Kelowna?"

"No, I don't have anything there."

"Right, so did you have one here?"

"He did. I don't know that I did." She shook her head at that. "I don't think I did, but he might have used my name for one or two of them." The men visibly swallowed. She stared at them and asked, "Is that a big deal?"

"We need to get the location of all of them, change the name on any we keep to yours and yours alone," Nick began, "preferably before anybody else finds out."

She nodded. "So, is that something you can handle, or do we need to contact Mathew's probate attorney?"

"I will contact the estate attorney right now because there should be a record of those safe deposit boxes." He handed the paperwork to Mack. "You keep track of these, please. You may want to move those duffel bags under your bed too."

"Under my bed that I'm not supposed to sleep in, per Scott? Under my bed that will soon be dismantled and hauled off today?" Mack reminded Nick.

"Right," Nick grumbled. "Forget I said that. Or maybe you *should* sleep on that money, under your sleeping bag, until we get it to some bank and it's properly deposited in Doreen's name alone."

Mack stared at the big master bedroom. "By the time the movers start taking apart all the bedroom furniture, it'll be that much harder to keep anything hidden."

Doreen suggested, "We need to check this room now for any hidden drawers. It's the only one we haven't gone through."

"You've been through all the others?" Mack asked them.

"Yes, the others are done." She turned around to look at the master suite. "We really need to do this one because they may load up all this furniture today. Scott seemed to think this bedroom suite was very valuable."

Mack nodded. "The more furniture they take, the less we are left to deal with."

"But we need to figure out if any more stuff is hidden in here, waiting to be found."

"Was he really that paranoid?" Mack asked, shaking his head.

"Yes," she declared, as she slowly studied the bedroom. "You would think that he would have had a safe in here," she muttered.

"Why?" Mack asked, stepping up beside her.

"Because he didn't like the idea of ever getting pinned in one place."

"So, you're thinking that, if he couldn't have reached the other safes in the other bedroom or in the office, then having a safe in the master makes sense?"

"Something like that." She nodded. "I know it makes him seem paranoid."

He snorted. "Definitely. Doesn't all this money make you a little paranoid too?"

She turned to him and declared, "Not my money."

"It is now," he instantly corrected her.

She thought about it and nodded. "Good thing we've got people who can help us deal with it."

"Right."

"And I will feel better when the cash is in the bank and in my name." She asked him, "Did you get receipts for all the cars?"

He nodded. "Yes. Plus, I've got photographs of them, and we did an itemized list while we were there. They will go through them all and pack up everything."

"Okay, good," she muttered. "It'll be one heck of a haul."

"It really is. They were pretty excited about one of the motorcycles and definitely a couple of the cars."

"Good to know," she muttered, with a shrug.

"You really don't care, do you?"

"I don't really care about any of it," she declared, "and I know that's foolish, … but it's just *stuff* to me. And right about now, I'm also worried about Thaddeus." She walked over to the hat rack in an alcove where she had left him perched and caught sight of him still sleeping.

Thaddeus opened an eye, yawned, stepped out onto her shoulder, and curled up against her. "Thaddeus is here," he murmured. "Thaddeus is here."

"I know, buddy. You just want to go home, don't you?"

He nuzzled up tightly against her neck, and she cuddled him for a few moments. She turned to spy on Mugs, as he jumped up onto the bed, joining Goliath, the Maine coon already fully stretched out there. She had to chuckle. "Scott would not like to see the animals on the bed. After all, he didn't want *us* on the beds." Then she sighed as she looked over at Mack. "We really do need to check each piece for hiding places."

He nodded. "Just point me in the right direction and tell me what to do. I will be the muscle."

And, with that, she got Mugs and Goliath off the bed and very quickly tore off the linens and checked under the mattress and even under the box springs.

Just as they were done, Scott walked in, talking animatedly on the phone. "Oh, there you are," he said to them, ending his phone call. He stopped to admire the bed. "This is such a beautiful piece." His hand brushed over the huge bedpost. "Ooh, they have finials atop," he cried out.

She gasped, pointing, and Mack just groaned. "Mathew always talked about them." She went to the newel post nearest her and stood on the mattress to twist off the top. "Yep," she exclaimed, as she reached in a hand and grinned. "This part is fun." And, with that, she handed a wad of cash to Mack.

He looked at it, just shook his head, and waited while she checked the other posts.

Scott was laughing. "This is incredibly rare—to get these pieces, I mean. And the movers are fast approaching the master. Also, how about the beds you're using, or not using actually? What will you do about that?" He hesitated, but she got the gist of it. "I mean, I know you'll still be here."

"*Right.*" She laughed. "We'll be fine with sleeping bags, and now it seems to be necessary."

"I'm all for it," Mack declared. "Those beds should go while the movers are here and are set up for the transport, rather than us dealing with it later. So, if we need sleeping bags, that's what we will do." He turned to Doreen. "Point me to the storage room, and I'll see if I can find three of them." She gave him directions on how to get there, and his phone rang as he took off. Meanwhile, she went over the rest of the furniture in the master bedroom, along with Scott.

As soon as they got through it all, he said, "Okay, I think the search for hidden places is all done here, as far as the master bedroom furniture is concerned."

"As far as the second floor is concerned too," she muttered. "Could anything else be here in the bed?" He frowned at her, and she shrugged. "I didn't want to torment Mack by asking when he was here."

"Understood," Scott replied, with a smile. "I do know that this bed usually has drawers along the sides. They are usually set back some, so that you can stand near the bed, like when making it or just getting in bed at night, and your feet won't touch anything."

He went along one side, checked, then back along the other side. "Just like this," he noted, and, sure enough, out popped some drawers.

"Thankfully these are empty," she muttered. Yet Doreen was amazed. "I slept in this room for a very long time, never knowing what was hidden in this bedroom set."

"Mathew seemed to be the kind of man who kept secrets."

"He was all about secrets," she confirmed, "and he was all about control."

"I'm sorry, Doreen," he murmured. "It sounds as if you didn't have an easy life here."

"A gilded cage is what I call it," she shared with a smile, as she looked at him.

Scott nodded. "Maybe, at one time, but now the cage is yours, and the door is wide open. It's pretty amazing what you've got going on here."

"All I need now," she pointed out, with a smile, "is to get this sorted and out of here as fast as I can. Since I want to sell the properties eventually, beginning with this one, I want it done as soon as possible, since quite a bit of upkeep is involved."

"I hadn't considered that angle," Scott replied, "but it makes perfect sense." As she watched, he walked around and checked out a few more things. "I still need to go through all his personal clothing as well." He looked at her. "Did he dress well?"

"Very."

"There's a huge market for that too, depending on the quality of the clothes."

"I know for a fact that he didn't think twice about spending forty thousand on a suit."

He nodded. "Let me take a look." He entered the walk-in closet, muttering to himself as he had a first look. When he rejoined her, he shared, "I'll need another expert for this."

"Go for it," she said. "Everything here needs to go … and fast."

"Got it." He smiled. "I suspect that we'll deal with a good share of this, the dress clothes at the very least. I do know someone who would probably want to sell it, if you're okay with that."

"If it's aboveboard and a reputable seller, then, by all

means, connect us up."

With that, he laughed and clarified, "We only deal with reputable."

"No offense intended, but Mathew did not."

"Point taken." And, with that, he headed into the hallway to make more calls.

When he came back, he told her, "My first contact is overseas, so I called somebody else, who is in Vancouver. He'll be here tonight."

"Oh wow," she noted.

He looked at her anxiously. "Unless I'm going too fast? I know this is a lot for you."

"No," she replied, "no such thing as too fast in this instance."

"That's what I thought, and, considering you've already got a police presence and an issue along that line, I'm sure the sooner, the better."

"Yes," she agreed. "The sooner, the better."

Chapter 10

ONLY AFTER DOREEN finally finished her inspection of the master bedroom, and Scott had gone to a nearby hotel for the night, did she really start to fade. She should have gotten the hint when Mack and Nick had taken turns coming in to see if she was ready to call it a day.

Mack shook his head. "I know we need to move on this, but I can't have you wearing yourself out."

"Too late," she muttered, as she sagged against him.

When Mugs started barking, she lifted one eyelid at him. He was at the window, and he was not a happy camper. Thaddeus squawked and flew over to look out the window with him. Mack was frowning now, as he looked outside. He turned to head to the front door. He called out for Nick to come with him.

She groaned, figuring that she needed to go with them, yet wanted nothing to do with whatever it was. Still, she decided to meet them halfway—or at least in the kitchen. When they made their way back to her again, she asked, "What's the problem?"

Mack lifted a note, showing it to her, while explaining how he found it taped to the front door. Nick nodded.

"*Give it to me*? But that could be about anything," she muttered. "I mean, look at this house. It's full of stuff. And you also don't know—"

Mack pointed at the note. "Turn it over. There's more."

Flipping over the note, she silently read the rest of the message. *I warned you. And you paid the price.* "Okay, but this …" She frowned. "This doesn't make any sense. *I warned you, and you paid the price?* Is our note writer speaking to our dead guy, Pete Singer? What good does that do, telling us this? What is happening here?"

Mack agreed. "We know when and where Mathew died, and we also know who killed him. But we don't know much about Pete Singer, the dead man in the greenhouse, despite my calls to Daniel's captain. While I don't expect an immediate return phone call, I do expect to hear from him within forty-eight hours, which is coming up soon. Plus, we have to consider that somebody potentially thought *Pete Singer* was Mathew."

Doreen shook her head, clearly confused. "So, what's the point of these threats to Mathew then? I mean, does somebody here not know that Mathew is dead already, since he was killed in Kelowna? Or, does somebody really think Pete Singer was Mathew? How could you be so mad at somebody, enough to kill them, and not know what they look like?"

Mack shrugged. "We could have somebody who's not quite all there."

She stared at him. "But you can't reason with someone like that," she muttered. Just then her phone rang, and it was Nan. "Hey, Nan."

Her grandmother asked, "Are you all right?"

"I'm fine. Sorry. I'm just exhausted. Don't worry about me."

"Oh, wow," she murmured. "Is that a good exhausted or bad?"

"It was good until we got a warning note taped to the front door."

Nan cried out, "Let me talk to Mack."

Doreen handed over her phone, almost too tired to care. Yet she could assume an onslaught from Nan followed.

Mack listened for a long while, then replied, "I promise. I'm looking after her. … Yes, I know. … I am very aware that you don't want anything to happen to her down here and that you are stuck in Kelowna. … I know. … I know. … Yes. … Yes. … No, you don't need to come down here."

Doreen rolled her eyes, listening in on the one-sided conversation. Nan was freaking out, and Doreen knew it.

By the time Mack was done with the call, he groaned, collapsed on the kitchen chair beside her, and said, "That was dirty pool." He and Nick shared a knowing glance.

She snickered. "Hey, she wanted to talk to you. I apparently didn't have the mental acuity to think about what she would do."

"Aha," he declared. "Seems you set me up."

She smiled. "You're so good at handling her."

"No, I'm really not," he muttered. He turned to her. "I need food, and I need it in a big way."

"Steakhouse?" she suggested.

Nick looked over at her. "Do you know a good one?"

"I don't really care which one—or even that it's steak," she said. "You guys can go. Just bring me back a to-go bag. I'll stay here with the animals."

Mack shook his head. "In that case, we'll just order in."

"Ordering in is plenty good enough for me," she muttered. "As long as I don't have to do anything more complicated than standing up."

"And that probably includes walking to the formal dining room to eat. Don't worry. We'll eat in the kitchen, so just sit tight right where you are," Mack added, giving her a smile.

He knew her so well.

Chapter 11

WHILE THE TRIO ate the roast chicken dinner they'd ordered in, Doreen said, "So that *Give it to me* note must be related to Pete Singer, the dead person in the greenhouse, because he definitely paid a price," she muttered. "So, we need to figure out why someone thinks he's Mathew. If Singer was the caretaker, gardener—even a thief for all we know—he paid a price that was most likely intended for Mathew."

"And that's all possible," Mack noted, "but we don't know that for sure." He shared a bite of chicken with Mugs. Then Goliath appeared, wanting some for himself. Mack accommodated him as well.

"No, we don't, yet it makes sense."

He smiled. "Everything in your world makes sense."

"No, none of this does," she stated, as she stared at him. "Look at this house with all the absolutely incredible treasures and huge sums of cash Mathew had stashed inside. Yet," she began, "it's entirely possible Mathew took something outright, even swindled or blackmailed people out of their money. So it's really not out of the realm of possibility that somebody wants something from him, thinks something is owed to them."

Nick shrugged. "Of course there is the reverse situation to consider too. With insanely rich people, they get sued all the time, usually in civil courts, by people hoping to get paid something because of the nuisance value alone, with no criminal action involved."

"Outside of cash, what could they want though? And who could it be?" Mack asked them.

"Your guess is as good as mine at this point, and I have no idea," Doreen replied.

"Still, we don't know enough. That's for sure," Mack pointed out. "So, we'll be a little bit handicapped for a while."

"We always are, it seems," she muttered. She munched her way through the big green salad that had come with the roast chicken and added, "Did anybody set up a list of things we still need to sort out?"

"I did," Nick confirmed, as he brought out a small notebook and put it on the table beside him. "I've contacted Mathew's probate lawyer about the safe deposit boxes. He says he didn't know anything about them, so I must contact the banks where Mathew has accounts. I do have a death certificate and everything else that's needed to prove Doreen is Mathew's sole heir. So we'll have to visit Mathew's local banks, change over the bank accounts into Doreen's name, then ask about any safe deposit boxes and see what's in there," he shared, lifting his gaze to look at her.

She nodded.

"Unless you already know what it is."

"No, I sure don't," she replied, but then she frowned. "Mathew did say it was worth more than money though." When both men stared at her, she shrugged. "I don't know what that means, and, for all I know, it's changed from the time that we had spoken about it. I do remember signing a bunch of papers. So, for all I know, they're in my name too. Thus you might want to bring that up with Mathew's probate attorney too."

"And that will be a whole different search, so do I have your permission to go on the hunt for it?" Nick asked her.

She nodded. "Of course."

He smiled. "Most people wouldn't be so agreeable."

"Presumably I'll be the one who has to look inside these boxes," she pointed out. "So it's not as if I won't see it with my own eyes. I highly suspect that the poor dead man, if he wasn't supposed to be here, could have been coming in to steal from the property and got caught. As you've seen, an awful lot is here to steal."

Mack interjected, "And, if that's the case, we also don't know what he may have *already* taken."

Doreen sighed. "That's the problem with Mathew. He always assumed everybody was out to steal from him, so he was very cautious in his dealings, always assuming the worst in people."

Mack nodded, looking over at his brother. "We also have to assume that—because of the way Mathew functioned—there is likely more than one safe deposit box."

"There should be financial records for the annual fees," Nick pointed out. "I'm not sure why his probate lawyer didn't see that."

Doreen snorted. "Again, that's Mathew, keeping secrets. For all I know, he's got that information in his office. We just haven't had a chance to get through that room yet."

Mack nodded. "Good point, so, if you don't mind, *I* will do that this evening." She looked over at him, and he nodded. "You're exhausted, and you need to get some rest," he explained. "We have to take care of so many things, what with these duffel bags of money still here, so we'll need to hide those and the cash bonds and the stock certificates, just in case there's trouble tonight."

"Trouble … tonight?" she repeated, her gaze turning owlish on him.

He nodded. "Remember the threatening note that just came to the door?"

"Right," she grumbled, with a sigh, "but trouble wouldn't be much fun."

"No, it wouldn't, but …" He looked over at his brother.

Nick nodded. "We have to presume that we'll have some visitors."

"Oh no, no, no, no, no," she wailed. "I am so tired, and so are the animals."

He laughed. "And we get that. As long as a lot of people are working here, we have less to worry about."

"I think a second team is taking over," she muttered. "Scott mentioned something about bringing in more people because there was just so much to do, and he wanted everything out within a week."

"A week?" Mack asked.

"I have to confess I had a similar reaction, and he just laughed. He initially thought four or five days would be enough, but to do that meant they must bring in another crew. So, I more or less just told him to do it. I mean, I don't know what I'm supposed to say, but we're down here already, and an awful lot of furniture needs to disappear."

"Not only has the bedroom furniture got to go," Mack noted, "but this whole first floor must be emptied too, plus whatever's left in the basement."

"I know. When it starts to leave fairly quickly, then it will look as if we're getting somewhere—at least on the second floor. However, when we consider the first floor and the basement too, then it just seems to be a massive amount still to go."

He smiled. "I am not worried about it. We'll stay here and get this done. Afterward it will seem like no time."

"I'm glad you have that level of confidence," she quipped, yawning. She grumbled, "I might just need a nap."

"You do that," he urged her. "Go pick out a place where you want to lie down. I did bring in the sleeping bags."

She groaned. "Oh *no.* … It's another sign of how tired and stressed I am. I'm so sorry."

Both men frowned at her. Mack asked, "What are you talking about?"

"The other quarters. … I'll use the term *servants' quarters*, but obviously the people who worked here weren't servants."

Mack and Nick stopped what they were doing and gave her puzzled looks.

She added, "A fully furnished apartment is over the main garage." The men were speechless, and she nodded. "I was too tired to remember. So I sent you to get all that camping equipment, but really we could just crash over there."

"We haven't even been in there," Mack stated, sitting back and staring at her.

"I know, and for that I apologize."

"Stop apologizing," he said. "What is it that you think will be there?"

She shrugged. "All I can tell you is that housing is there."

Mack and Nick looked at each other, and she yawned again.

"Okay," Mack replied. "Why don't you crash on the couch, and we'll take a look over the garage and figure out what we need to do from here."

"Good enough," she whispered, yawning yet again.

They got up, and she made her way to the couch, Mugs following her. As soon as she dropped onto the couch, they took off in the direction of the garage. A few minutes later she heard a meow, and Goliath, obviously having enough of all the strangers, hopped up on top of her.

Tears came to her eyes as she cuddled him. "We should have left you guys at home," she whispered. "I just couldn't imagine not having you here with me for this."

Goliath head-butted her, and instead of falling asleep, she spent the next twenty minutes cuddling him. When the men didn't return, she sat up slowly, picked up her phone, and texted Mack. But there was no answer.

Groaning, she made her way fully vertical and looked down at the animals. "Now we'll have a problem," she muttered. "Let's go find Mack."

With the animals in tow, and Thaddeus tucked into her neck grumbling softly, she headed to the servants' quarters. It was a phrase her husband had used all the years she had been with him. It was hardly appropriate, since the residents of those quarters weren't servants. However, from Mathew's point of view, they may as well have been.

As she got closer to the garage apartment, she heard raised voices. She froze. Somebody was yelling, and it wasn't Mack or Scott or Nick. She tiptoed closer, wondering who was there, and she saw a stranger waving a gun at the two brothers.

Mack took one look at her and shook his head slightly. She frowned, not sure what that meant, but it seemed as if she was not supposed to get involved. Yet how was she supposed to *not* get involved when somebody was literally waving a gun at them?

Finally the man with the gun slowed down his yelling and glared at Mack. "What are you doing here? This is my home."

Mack looked over at Nick, and then Doreen stepped up. "Actually it's my home." When the stranger turned to her in shock, she nodded. "I inherited it from Mathew."

His shoulders sagged. "He's dead?"

"Yes, he's dead," she stated, with a small smile. "You didn't know?"

He shook his head. "No, I didn't know. I was looking after the place for him. He told me how he was making a lot of changes and would be gone for a while. So I took a holiday, and, when I came back, I wasn't sure what was going on. Vehicles were everywhere, but I just stuck to my corner because he … didn't like questions."

She nodded. "That's very true." She pointed at the two men he still held the gun on. "Could you please drop the gun?" As he stared at the men, she added, "One is my fiancé, and the other is his brother. Nick happens to be my lawyer too. We came here to deal with the massive property and furniture issues because Mathew is gone and has been for some time."

He turned and eyed her suspiciously.

"I was his wife," she added.

"You aren't Robin."

"No, I'm not Robin, and Robin is also dead."

His eyebrows shot up. Then he asked hesitantly. "Did he kill her?"

"No," she replied, "although I understand that they

weren't doing that well."

"He used to yell at her a lot. A couple times he told her how he wished he'd never gotten rid of his wife." Then he frowned and asked, "Was that you?"

"Yes, that was me," she confirmed. "Yet it doesn't matter what he might have wanted back then. He did get rid of me, and I have this thing about people who try to get rid of me. I tend to stay gone."

He snorted at that and nodded. "Mathew was not a nice person."

"He most certainly was not," she agreed, with a nod. "Now, what were you supposed to do here?"

"I looked after the place when he was gone, and he was planning on doing a lot of traveling."

"When did you get back?" she asked, leaving the men to just stand there. The stranger still had his gun out, but she was trying to calm him down.

"I was gone until today," he shared. He sagged down onto the couch. "Now what will I do?" he cried out.

"Did he pay you?" Doreen asked.

"He paid me up until the end of this month because we set my services for one year, then would reassess," he explained, frowning at her. "He just told me to wait for instructions."

Doreen sighed. "At this point in time, I can tell you that he won't be giving you any more instructions."

"He had plans," he repeated, staring at her as if she should know about them.

"And do you know what those plans were?" she asked.

"No," he cried out, "I don't. I wish I did though because he told me how it would make him money."

"Everything Mathew did made him money," she murmured, "but not necessarily in a manner that other people would have appreciated." He frowned at that, and she nodded. "I'm sorry we surprised you. I sent these guys over here to see if the apartment was livable."

"It's very livable," he declared, "and it's mine."

"It *was* yours," she pointed out, "but, now that Mathew is gone, you don't have an employer, and all of this is being sold."

At that, tears began to well up in his eyes. "I have no place to go."

"How did you meet Mathew?" she asked, as she walked closer. "And what is your name?"

"Butch Weldon."

She kept an eye on the gun, and Mugs finally stepped forward, walked over to the man, then rubbed up against his leg. Without a thought, he put the gun on the kitchen table, as both Mack and Nick heaved a sigh of relief. Butch bent over and started cuddling Mugs. "He's a lovely dog," he noted finally.

"Yes, this is Mugs. He's mine," she noted.

"But there are pictures of him in the main house."

"Yes, Mugs was here toward the end of my marriage to Mathew too."

Butch nodded. "Mathew hated dogs."

"That pretty much sounds like Mathew," she muttered. "Mugs was looked after by the kitchen help and wasn't allowed to do much doglike stuff."

"I'm sure he's much happier now. Dogs are … dogs, and they just need to be loved."

"I won't argue with that," she said, with a smile. "I'm not sure what to do about you."

He looked over at her and shrugged. "Me neither. Do

you need a caretaker?"

"From what I understand, the property management company hired a caretaker," she shared, looking at him.

His face fell.

"So, the question is, if you're not that caretaker, where is the one who was hired?"

He shrugged.

"When were you hired for this job?"

"A year ago," he repeated, "yet I needed to go home and see my family. My ma isn't in very good shape."

"Okay," she muttered, frowning at that. "So you talked to Mathew about taking a break, going back home?"

"Yeah."

Mack looked over at her, one eyebrow raised, and she shrugged. "It just doesn't make any sense when Mathew's been dead for quite a while now."

"Are you thinking it wasn't Mathew I spoke to?" Butch asked in astonishment.

"Did you see him in person?" Doreen asked.

"No, not with the phone call, but I was here at the house earlier, when we first made this arrangement."

"How long ago?"

"Must have been a year ago because our original deal is up at the end of this month. The discussion was in his office, where he told me how he was making a bunch of changes. So, he would be gone for a while, but I could move in here to the apartment, and he would be in touch, but now you're saying he's dead?" He turned a suspicious gaze to each of them. "I don't even know who you are and whether I can believe you."

"No, of course not," she said. "Did you have anything to do with anybody else here?"

"No, I mean, I saw a few people around him back then. I guess he had a manservant, and I was going to contact him soon too."

"That won't do you any good either," Mack interjected, with half a smile. He reached into his pocket and pulled out his badge. "He's in prison for killing Mathew."

Butch looked at Mack's badge and sagged. "So, it's really true then. … Mathew is really dead."

"Yes, it's really true. I'm sorry."

"That's the first time I've ever been hired for a job where the boss is dead."

"You can stay here tonight," she offered, "and then we'll discuss things tomorrow. Did you have a conversation with anybody else?"

"Do you have a letter of employment?" Nick asked, cutting her off.

"Yeah, I do somewhere," he muttered, pulling out his phone. "I'm not really good on my phone though."

"Did you move in here?"

"No, not yet, I was going to spend the night, figure out what was going on here, and then go get my stuff," he muttered.

"And where else do you live?"

At that, he realized he was being interrogated, and he glared around at all three of them. "That's an awful lot of questions."

"You've got to look at it from our point of view," Mack said. "We don't know you, don't know anything about you, and yet you're here in her house, having been hired by a man who's been dead and gone for quite a while."

"I told him that I couldn't come right away, and he told me that was fine," Butch shared, "and he gave me the key to this apartment. He told me to keep my eye on the homes and the property."

When he held up the key, Doreen smiled. "I'll take that now, thank you."

He stared at the key, gave her a glare, but handed it over. "This isn't exactly how I thought things would go," he muttered.

"Of course not," she said.

"Why don't you keep the house?" he asked, almost pleading. "I can stay and look after it for you."

"Somebody might be needed for looking after the house for a time," she explained, "but my understanding from the other lawyer"—she turned to Nick—"was that somebody has already been hired."

"Ha," Butch snapped. "If he's hired, he should be here, making sure the police don't go where they don't belong."

Nick's lips twitched at that. "I do have a call into the other lawyer," he shared, "so we'll see what he says."

"And is there any chance that Mathew's probate attorney or even the property management company hired Butch?" Doreen asked Nick.

Nick shrugged. "I have no idea what's going on right now, but it's not working hours, and, if you want to talk to either, it'll probably cost you three hundred an hour if not double that." She stared at him. He nodded. "And, yes, the estate attorney will probably talk to me because it's related to existing business between us, but I'm not entirely sure."

Doreen frowned. "The other problem is this still won't be resolved tonight."

"That's true," Nick confirmed.

She turned to Butch. "Have you ever been through the main house?"

"Only when I was here with Mathew many months ago," he muttered.

"And how do you know Mathew?" Mack asked.

"We're old friends," Butch said, narrowing his gaze.

Doreen stiffened at that. Was Butch a criminal too, like Mathew?

Butch nodded at her reaction. "I know what you'll say, that he didn't have friends."

She laughed. "No, he didn't have many, that's for sure, but he did have a few."

"Yeah, and you're looking at him. I know that, to Mathew, I was down on my luck, but we did go way back. To be honest, I did beg for a place to stay and enough money for a few meals," he admitted.

She just nodded, not saying anything. She had more questions, but now wasn't the time. "We'll talk to you in the morning then." Then she yawned once more.

And, with that said, the group backtracked out of the garage apartment. Outside the door, she stopped and stared back at the apartment. Mugs sniffed the door, his head down but no tail wag. He was not at all sure about the new arrival. Then again … neither was she.

Mack came up behind her and asked, "What are you thinking?"

She winced. "I don't think he had a key to the main house, no matter what Daniel thinks. I think that's smoke and mirrors." She lowered her voice and said, "Yet I just … don't know if I believe Butch."

"Now you're making my heart sing," Mack stated, with a smile, "because I don't believe anything he told us. I figure, with Butch lying to us, with Butch telling us he knows Mathew from way back, without giving us specifics, I bet

Butch is a criminal."

"In that case, is there a reason," Nick asked, staring at the two of them, "that we're not kicking him out then?"

Mack fielded that question. "Because, one, it's nighttime. Two, we don't know what he's really after. And, three, we should give him enough rope to hang himself."

Chapter 12

DOREEN WENT TO bed in the same guest bedroom she'd been using, but tonight inside a sleeping bag instead of on a proper bed. Her four-legged animals didn't seem to care, and Thaddeus was using whatever high spot he chose as his new temporary roost. Before long she fell into an uneasy sleep, her animals wrapped around her. When she woke up in the middle of the night, she found Mack checking on her.

He brought along his sleeping bag and put it down beside her. Wrapping her up in his arms, he whispered, "Just rest. You're fine."

With a sigh, she closed her eyes and crashed again. When she woke in the morning, she was alone but smiled at Mack's empty sleeping bag still beside her. She expected her animals were with him too. So she got up, took a shower, and then got dressed. By the time she made it into the kitchen, still yawning, she found Nick and her animals. Scott was already here as well.

He grinned at her as if a kid in a candy shop.

She smiled back at him, shaking her head. "It's nice to know that you're doing well."

"Are you kidding me?" he practically squealed, rubbing his hands together. "This is a wonderful treasure trove."

She nodded. "You can thank Mathew for that. None of this had anything to do with me."

"Ah, but it's because of you that I'm here," he noted, still beaming. "So I need to thank *you*."

"Consider me thanked," she replied, now laughing. She motioned at the coffeepot. "I sure hope some is left for me."

"If not," Nick interjected, "it's pretty easy to put another pot on."

"I know," she scoffed, "but I have to admit I'm feeling pretty groggy."

"That's understandable. Did you get some sleep at least?"

"I did, fitful at first, but better after Mack joined me," she muttered. "Where is he?"

Nick shrugged. "I think he went looking for our supposed caretaker."

She frowned and suggested, "Maybe we should go look too."

Scott raised one eyebrow and asked, "Is there a reason?"

Mugs barked from the doorway, heading toward the garage apartment, and she nodded.

"Yeah, there absolutely is a reason." She groaned, snatched up her coffee cup, carrying it with her, and followed Mugs to where she assumed Mack was. She knocked on the door to the garage apartment but no answer came. So, she opened it and stepped inside, seeing no one. She frowned, made her way to the bedroom, then gasped.

Nick stepped up beside her and groaned. "Are you kidding me?" he muttered.

Butch Weldon was on the bed, staring up at the ceiling,

apparently dead. Doreen wondered if that was his real name. She also wondered what his real job was here. And how he met Mathew. Butch had never answered that question last night. She figured they would discuss it today. Not now though. She sighed.

Mugs started sniffing around, as if looking for clues.

She groaned. "Buddy, I don't know what's going on here, but we need to find Mack."

Mack spoke from the doorway and announced, "I'm right here, and I've already called the cops. I went looking to see how somebody got in or out."

She turned to him. "It wasn't me."

"I know," he said, then chuckled. "However, I'm assuming from *this*"—he motioned toward the dead man in the bed—"that somebody came in and took care of *loose ends.*"

She grimaced. "I didn't look, but do you want to tell me how he was killed?"

"Gunshot," he replied, "small caliber, straight to the heart."

"While he was sleeping?"

"I would suspect so."

"So, he had a partner," she whispered, "obviously disgruntled."

Mack corrected her, "And again we don't know that there is a partner."

She nodded while staring around at the room. "Mathew's legacy still lives on, doesn't it?"

"Apparently," Mack muttered, "and Daniel is coming back."

She nodded. "He'll love this. He'll blame me for this death too."

"Yet we didn't do anything, and we will stand firm on

that. Plus, GSR tests would prove us out."

"Still," she noted, "that doesn't mean certain people won't see how they can mold the evidence to fit."

At her side, Nick just grinned at his brother. "Interesting that you two ever got together at all."

"Right," he muttered. "It's almost as if… she doesn't trust me."

"I trust you just fine," she declared, turning to him. "I'm just a whole lot less trusting of everybody else in law enforcement. Yet I believe you. I believe the captain, I even believe Darren and Chester and Arnold," she stated, "but I also know that it's not quite so cut-and-dried with other people."

"Nope, that's true," Mack conceded. "And this has become one of the craziest cases ever. I did leave a hair in place on the front door to this garage apartment, so, if the connection was severed, we would know."

She nodded. "And, of course, it was."

"Yes," he stated, "it was."

"So, Butch left the apartment in the middle of the night? To do what? Or Butch didn't lock the inside of the door, just allowing his killer to waltz inside and end his life?" she asked, staring at Mack steadily. "Or Butch *did* lock the door, but the killer had a key to the apartment. So Butch shared his key? Or some other former employee of Mathew still had a key to this apartment? We need that list of Mathew's former employees. How come we don't have that yet?"

Mack looked at her and sighed. "I keep forgetting how quickly that mind of yours works."

"It's the only thing that makes sense."

Nick piped up, "Obviously Daniel isn't cooperating, so I'll remind the probate attorney, who should have that info."

She snorted. "And Daniel will now pin this second murder on us. He'll think it's one of us because, in his mind, who else could it be? From his perspective, who else would have had access? Plus, he doesn't have to look any further for suspects."

"It could be any number of people," Nick pointed out. "And considering the amount of, … I'll call it *treasure*," he pointed out, for want of a better word, "a lot of people could be enticed, a lot of bad people mostly. Maybe somebody looking for something of theirs, expecting to get payback for something, or just someone checking out an unoccupied house."

Mack shook his head. "It's not that hard to get inside this garage apartment. That is a very simple door lock system," he noted, "which surprises me, with your ex being as paranoid as he was."

"True," Doreen conceded, "yet each exterior door has its own key. Plus, the house was better secured than this apartment. However, that's a good point too," she noted, frowning. "I suspect somebody must have a duplicate key to that garage apartment, and it isn't that hard to get keys made, is it?"

"No, it sure isn't. Particularly if you live on the edge of the law, there's always somebody who would make keys."

"Right," she replied, "so it's all a little dodgy, but we just need to find out who might have a key. Again we need that former employee list because the key to the garage apartment doesn't get anyone inside this mansion."

At that, Nick stared at her and clarified, "That won't be just … *finding* somebody. It could be any employee, temp or full-time. You even mentioned, Doreen, how Mathew's bodyguards and whatnot used the garage apartment as well.

So we need a list of security people, armed guards, who probably won't be on the standard employee list. This would entail a legal agreement to hire these people from a bonded company that specializes in that." He turned to Doreen. "You really don't think Robin gave out keys to the house to anybody, right?

Doreen sighed. "I really don't think so. She obviously had no friends. She ran with the likes of Mathew, so surely she was wise not to share the keys to this house with anyone. She surely didn't have any family either. After all, she left her estate to *me*. To me of all people."

Nick gave her a one-arm shrug. "Probably restitution or guilt or both. However, I agree with you. Doesn't sound as if Robin would be handing out keys like candy."

"Right. Many people could have had keys to this place, but Mathew was diligent about changing locks with each employee dismissal. So, since Mugs hasn't barked once during the nighttime, I maintain that nobody has been inside, at least since we got here. … I presume now," she added, turning to Mack, "that we're not buying Butch's story at all."

"No, I would think not," he agreed, with a nod. "In fact, he may have been the one to leave us that strange note taped to the front door. Did he think we would just hand something over? Regardless I didn't think Butch was hired as a caretaker either. So where's the real caretaker?"

"That's another really good question," Doreen declared, as she turned to Nick. "You really need to visit Mathew's probate attorney—or the property management company itself—to get more info, more details about Butch, if he was really hired by Mathew to begin with or by Mathew's agents, including asking again for Mathew's roster of former employees. If you have to stand over the estate attorney, watching him printing out a copy, then do that. Don't come home empty-handed."

"I was thinking about all that too," Nick shared. "I'll make an appointment to see the probate attorney this morning, then I can go from there. Seems it's needed because we have a lot of missing details, including the contact information for this caretaker."

She turned to him and asked, "Is there any chance Mathew's probate lawyer is involved in all this?"

Nick winced. "I know that your opinion of lawyers is right up there with cops, but—"

"No, probably worse," she interrupted, cutting him off. As he stared at her, she snorted. "I'm kidding."

"No, you're not," he acknowledged. "However, not all lawyers are like Robin."

"No, of course not," she declared in a deadpan tone. "They're worse."

He sighed. "Okay, fine. I can see you're having a grand old time with this."

She snorted. "It's not so much that I'm having fun with it, but I think that local estate lawyer has multiple things to discuss with you. Things definitely feel dodgy, and I'm beginning to have my doubts about him." She asked, "Could he have something to do with this? I mean, think about it."

"Why would you think that?"

"Would he have had any idea of all the treasure here for the taking?" she asked.

Nick replied, "Sure. The probate attorney prepares an inventory of the assets to be distributed. Now it's not detailed. Instead of noting *ten bedroom sets on the second floor*, it will just list *household furniture*. It may even specify *antique*. It's not a robber's list of every expensive item within the house or the garage."

Doreen frowned. "I think that's the biggest issue for me. With so much of this just literally being cash, anybody could have come in here and just taken it all."

"Right there," Nick noted, "is the crux of the matter. A generic entry of *cash* could include the green stuff as well as the bonds that represent cash. Still, I wouldn't think that would be clarified on the inventory that is a matter of record with the court."

"Which means," Mack shared, "someone couldn't really tell from the court's inventory. They would have to know about it firsthand or from someone else who had seen it themselves."

Doreen nodded. "Exactly, and that is possible, given how much is here. I mean, I know that his right-hand man is in jail, but could Mathew have done all this stashing of getaway cash over time without anybody else knowing?"

"It's possible, given how paranoid he was," Nick offered. "There again, most people don't notice when the cleaning ladies are around or when the gardener is outside the window." The two brothers shared a look. "Or the caretaker." Nick shrugged. "I need to talk to the estate attorney, don't I?"

"Yeah," she agreed. "Do I need to come with you?"

"Nope, you sure don't," he stated, with a stern look. "Better in this case that it's lawyer to lawyer."

"Good enough," she conceded. "I really didn't want to have anything to do with him anyway."

Nick burst out laughing at that and nodded. "I can see that's most likely the case. … Let me just add in, Mathew's probate attorney was his estate planner for purposes of the will and related documents. However, the same guy was his personal attorney for some business-related matters too. He was the guy Mathew shared things with that he wouldn't tell his usual business attorney."

Doreen sighed. "So what's new?" she scoffed. "That's just Mathew being Mathew. *Secretive.*"

Nick nodded. "So I get tidbits of insight into Mathew from the probate guy. Just saying that I trust him. He's got info we can't get from just anybody."

Doreen nodded. "I get it."

Nick smiled. "That's all I'm saying. Besides, you've got enough going on here to keep you busy."

"More than busy," she grumbled, as she glanced around. "It's definitely a little on the hairy side right now. Particularly with this additional death."

"Agreed," Nick replied.

They all returned to the kitchen, taking a break before another round of police and the coroner and forensics came to Mathew's house.

The front doorbell rang, sending Mugs into a barking fit again. Mugs would really struggle with that each time. In comparison Thaddeus and Goliath stayed close to Doreen but out of the way.

Doreen found Daniel at the front door, a sneer on his face.

"Another dead body?" he snapped. "You know you will be my usual suspect, right?"

"I didn't kill anybody, Daniel. Just do your job."

"I am doing my job, and you are the most likely suspect," he snapped.

"You haven't even taken a look at the crime scene, so how can you say that?" Doreen asked, frowning.

"The usual motive for murder is money." Daniel stared

at Doreen.

"Doreen has no greed in her," Mack stated.

Daniel snorted. "I hear you say that, but a lot of money is involved here."

Doreen laughed. "I keep telling you, Daniel, that I didn't kill anybody, that Mathew left me in his will. So Mathew left me this money. So killing Pete Singer, and now Butch Weldon, didn't land Mathew's estate in my name. Seems *you* are more taken by Mathew's money than I ever was. Regardless, why are you discussing Mathew's murder, which has already been solved, done, and dusted?" she asked, staring at him. "That has nothing to do with what happened here."

"And maybe you did have something to do with that, and maybe the detectives up there closed it very quickly because you were a friend of the police."

Mack stiffened at that and turned around, looking far less patient and slightly ferocious.

Daniel held up his hand. "Of course I have to look at everything."

That did not appease Mack. "As will we," Mack declared.

Smiling, Doreen looked over at Daniel and asked, "Are you done?"

"Why? Will you kick me out?"

"As soon as you're done, sure," she declared. "I have seen enough police procedures to understand when someone … oversteps the line."

"I have every right to be here. We now have two dead men on your property. For the first one, you supposedly weren't here, but, for the second, you were sleeping right next door."

Doreen studied him for a long minute, noting how uneasy Daniel was. "First, you said you were heading up this investigation. We've been here for two days now. Yet you haven't found who murdered Pete Singer? You haven't narrowed down any suspects, other than us, notably me? Seems slow response times are to be expected in this city." Daniel spat out a retort, which she ignored. "Second, you told us you have cleared us all. Yet you continue to just focus on us as suspects. Why is that, Daniel?"

"*Detective* Sherwood," he snapped.

"Three, *Daniel*, Mack's captain confirms he nor anyone else in the department was contacted by anyone at all to confirm Mack's alibi for Pete's death. Same with the Merrit restaurant where we had brunch. Same with the gas station where both Mack and Nick filled up their vehicles. Same with Rosemoor, where Nan lives, confirming my daily or more visits there. Care to explain to us, *Daniel*?"

"I don't have to explain myself to you," he spat.

"But you will to your captain. We'll give him a call."

When he huffed but didn't reply otherwise, she added, with a knowing smile, "I note that you didn't check any of us—our hands or our clothing—for gunshot residue when investigating Pete Singer's death. Didn't mention it now when investigating Butch Weldon's death. So is this just police harassment?"

Mack silently moved to stand behind Doreen. Nick soon took his position with them as well.

"My final point," she added, "is that the servants' quarters might as well have been a house away, and you know very well that it is a separate structure from the main house." Daniel blinked at that, and she nodded. "You can see for yourself how far that apartment is from where we were sleeping, so to suggest otherwise is just you being testy and trying to get a rise out of me. What bothers me most, yet apparently has gone unnoticed or doesn't bother you in the least, is the fact that whoever killed him may have had a key to the garage apartment."

He stared at her and then asked, "How do you figure?"

"Short of Butch not locking his door at night, the *logical* question becomes, how did the killer get inside the garage apartment? There is no other way to get up there but through that one door. That door has its own key. It is not a key that works elsewhere on this property."

"Any idea who might have a key to the apartment?" Daniel asked.

"I don't know anything about this house or that garage apartment anymore. The sooner I am free and clear of this place, the better. Yet, in the meantime, you should be checking Mathew's former employees. Why haven't you shared that info with us yet, Daniel? Nick has asked you twice."

"You are not a part of this investigation," he snapped.

"No worries," she quipped, with a smirk. "We'll get it directly from Mathew's probate attorney."

"You can't just call up a lawyer and demand things," Daniel snapped.

"I can, as Mathew's executor of his estate and his sole heir." She beamed at Daniel, enjoying his discomfort. "Plus Nick is my probate attorney, so he too can ask this of Mathew's probate attorney."

"Sure, waste his time," Daniel muttered, glaring daggers at her. "But, as you said, you have lots of money."

"I have never said that. This is *Mathew's* money. *You* keep saying that I have *lots of money*, enamored as you are by just money," she clarified. "As for my payday from Mathew's estate, that hasn't happened yet. So I can't spend money I don't even have. However, the probate attorney will charge the estate for his time and costs involved as this would be deemed a necessary expense, since we can't get any cooperation out of you."

Daniel didn't say anything at all, just studied her closely. "The dog didn't wake you up in the night, *huh*?"

"No, Mugs didn't, and I would expect that he would wake me up if needed. However, everyone is exhausted right now, including the animals," she explained. "And whether you choose to believe it or not, these animals generally are very good watch animals, but everybody is entitled to a holiday, which is what we thought this would be, by the way. Not necessarily a fun one, more of a working holiday, but it's turned out to be incredibly stressful instead."

"It sounds to me as if you're doing very well out of it."

"Wow. You just cannot get your focus off Mathew's money. Jealous much?"

He seemed startled and asked, "Aren't all these experts and specialists removing a lot of the property from the house?"

"Sure," she agreed, with a nod. "There's no money until something is sold, and there is no confirmed sales price until the buyers are involved," she explained, with a shrug. "Still, it all had to go. So what would you have me do, take it to the local thrift store? Have a garage sale?"

When he just stared at her, she went on. "I get that, for you, all you see is some fortune here. And maybe there is a fortune here, though hopefully you realize it will likely take years to sell all this. I also get that you don't care one bit about what my life was like as soon as Mathew ditched me for Robin, or what it's like emotionally for me to come back here and deal with it all. Could I have assigned it to someone else? Maybe so, but I thought it would be best to oversee things myself. However, considering the current situation, it's definitely a decision I'm regretting."

"Maybe," Daniel noted, "but maybe you're only regretting it because you got caught."

"Caught at what? I haven't been caught doing anything wrong," she pointed out, still giving him that knowing smile, "because *I* didn't do anything wrong."

Just then Scott cleared his throat at the door. She looked over at him. "If you're done here," Scott said, "I could use your help."

She looked back at Daniel. "Are you done?"

He stood up, headed to the front door, and replied, "For the moment." Then he turned and, with a snarky smile, said, "Don't leave town."

She raised her eyebrows at that. "You've just been dying to use that line from the movies, haven't you?" She laughed. "As you well know, our home isn't here, and I can assure you that, when I'm done with my business here, I'm going home."

"I must warn you that, if you choose to leave without permission, we'll just haul you right back. And, at this point in time, I'm looking forward to it."

"Stop comparing yourself to Mathew and do your job properly, Daniel," Doreen replied. "Where is your captain today? I think I'll give him a call. I'm sure his permission to leave town overrides yours."

With that, Daniel turned toward the front door and said, "I'll let myself out."

As soon as he was gone, she turned to Mack, who stared

at the door in consternation. Doreen raised her hands to Mack. "I'm sure you didn't appreciate my comments to Daniel. But can he really stop us from going?"

"It's an interesting tactic and also telling that he doesn't consider you off the hook."

"I'm not off the hook?" she asked. "Even if I don't own a gun?"

"No, but you also know Mathew had a weapon here, other than the one we've already found."

"The one that hasn't been shot in forever?" she asked. "If he did have more, I don't know where they would be. Yet surely he has some, as paranoid as he was." She sighed and turned to Scott. "Sorry, Scott. It's been a day already."

"He can't really think you had anything to do with it, can he?" he asked her, frowning at Mack and Nick.

Mack shrugged. "I'm not sure what he thinks. At this point, all I can say is he's being very suspicious, as cops tend to be. However, it is interesting that only Daniel is here for these suspicious discussions with Doreen. He never arrives with a partner. So I may give his captain another call to see if I can update him on this and the other things Daniel has done."

Nick snorted at that. "Agreed."

Scott shook his head. "I hear you there."

"Wait," Doreen suggested. "Before you make that call, and after Daniel leaves, can we search the garage apartment and see if we can find Butch's gun or other evidence? It would be great to show that Daniel's not doing the basics. Then you can call Oren." She turned to Scott. "So, we have a little bit of time. Did you need us?"

Scott nodded. "Let's go check out the basement, and, if time allows, the kitchen. The artwork is gone, but the storage area is awaiting your approval. We have one stack for donations. Then a few things we will take to auction."

With a nod, the four of them went to the basement. It didn't take long for Doreen to approve Scott's plan for the storage area. He even offered to call the two women's shelters to arrange for them to pick up what they wanted. Then all four returned to the main floor.

"I need to show you something else in progress." Nick motioned to the kitchen. "I took it upon myself to bring in someone to pull out all the expired food and a Dumpster will be delivered to the back of the house and will cart off the first load immediately, per Amos's instructions, so none of the neighbors are *inconvenienced.*" He took them to the second pantry, where a couple men still worked. "They will cull out all of the expired foods here as well as sort the freezers for you. If you have anything you know needs to go to the dump, it will return tomorrow for a second load. They are boxing anything sealed that can go to the food bank after we pack anything we want."

Doreen smiled in delight. "Oh thank you! That's a great answer."

Leaving the workers to get on with their jobs, she led the men back to the front room. A quick glance out the front window confirmed that Daniel's unmarked cruiser was gone. Doreen grinned and turned to the men, specifically Scott. "We won't be long. Where should I meet you?"

Scott smiled, apparently enjoying Daniel getting in further trouble. "Take your time. I'll be in the private art gallery."

With that, the trio traipsed up to the garage apartment, all donning plastic gloves, even those blue booties that are supposed to be sterile for police purposes. As Mack handed those out, she raised her eyebrows. "Even on vacation you bring your forensic gear?" she asked.

Mack simply shrugged and smiled.

"So, do we each start at a separate wall and work toward the last one?" Doreen suggested.

"Sound good," Nick replied, looking to Mack to confirm.

Mack nodded. "Let's do this."

In less than ten minutes, Mack found Butch's gun, hidden away in the toilet tank in a waterproof bag. He yelled out, "Found it."

Doreen reached him first and had to laugh. Mack joined her, having a good belly laugh. Nick came in frowning. "What's so funny?" Then he saw the treasure dripping wet still being held over the toilet tank.

Nick muttered, "Must be a criminal thing."

Doreen agreed. "So now you really do have something more to tell Captain Hawkins," she told Mack, who had already pulled out his phone. The three of them walked from the latest crime scene, ending up at the kitchen in the main house.

"Before I forget," he told Doreen, "Captain Hawkins called me earlier and confirmed that the street cams had been disabled that would have spotted our trespassers on the property before our arrival."

Doreen smirked. "Like somebody with knowledge of them, say a bad cop, who may have done that on purpose?" Doreen turned to Nick. "What do you wanna bet that Butch's gun has been recently fired?"

Nick shook his head. "But he never fired at us."

"True," Doreen stated, "but maybe Butch was the one to kill Pete and to bury him in the onion patch. Wanna bet that

Pete is a criminal too, maybe recently released from prison?"

"Oh wow," Nick muttered. "It's scary how your mind works."

"I'm sure Mack will ask for the results of any tests on the gun, the ownership, et cetera. And we should have those answers soon, now that Oren is working directly with us, even if Daniel has no clue about all that's going on in the background. Sorry to miss hearing the fireworks from Mack's phone call, but Scott needs me."

The front doorbell rang again. Nick offered to see who was there, and Doreen hung around to find out as well.

Nick returned quickly. "A parcel is here. I signed for it."

She frowned at it and shook her head. "I'm not expecting a delivery." She pointed at the label. "That's got Mathew's name on it."

Mack finished his phone call with Oren and rejoined them. "You can open it," Mack told her. "It is yours after all."

"How can it be mine?" she muttered.

"It's yours in the sense that he's no longer here. So, it's something to be dealt with. His estate entails other things, such as his income tax filings, outstanding debts, and related things."

"Which thankfully," Nick noted, "his probate attorney is handling all that, even by setting up the property management company to oversee this property."

"Good enough," Doreen muttered, with a sigh of relief.

Mack looked over at his brother. "Do we trust those people?"

Nick raised his eyebrows, contemplating his question. "I had to think about it because, considering the *business* Mathew was in, I think he attracted all the wrong people."

"He did, indeed," she murmured. "In a way, I feel sorry for him. Although he seemed to be so very successful, he was not well loved, and he wasn't respected as much as he was feared."

"But he fostered that fear himself," Mack clarified. "Plus, he did it because that's the type of person he was."

"Maybe, but he could have lived a better life."

"Absolutely, but it would have meant being a better person."

"Yeah, that wasn't his thing." She looked down at the parcel and muttered, "Fine. I'll open it." She got a kitchen knife and popped the strings on it. She opened the package and found a smaller box.

When she frowned at it, Mack asked, "What's the matter?"

"You open it," she stated suddenly. "I don't like anything about it."

He eyed it suspiciously, and even Scott, who'd just arrived, stepped back. Nick looked over at Mack and asked him, "We aren't expecting this to be a bomb or anything, right?"

"I would hope not," Mack said, studying it oddly.

Just then Mugs came over, sniffed it, and started to bark, a really ugly bark.

Thaddeus squawked and hid in her hair. There was no sign of Goliath.

"That's an interesting reaction," Nick noted.

Scott took several more steps backward.

Mack shook his head. "I'm not saying it's a bomb, but obviously Mugs doesn't like it."

Doreen interjected, "My mind immediately thinks of scary movies, where somebody's ear might be in there or something."

Nick stared at her in horror. "Why on earth would you say that?" he cried out, staring down at the box, then backing up to join Scott.

"I'm just saying out loud what everybody here is thinking," she stated. "You guys seem to be reacting in just that way."

Nick pointed out, "Hey, your dog is setting off the alarm."

Mack agreed with him. "Mugs's reaction concerns me the most."

"So, what do we do?" she asked.

Just then the doorbell rang again. Nick announced, "I'll get it." And, with that, he soon returned with Detective Daniel Sherwood.

Doreen frowned at him. "Why are you back so soon?" she asked.

Daniel ignored her question and asked her one, "What is going on here? Nick mentioned a delivery."

She pointed to the package. "Nobody wants to open this."

"Why not?"

"I'm not sure, but Mugs is really against it. And we have really good evidence that he's always been great with his nose."

"Oh for heaven's sake," Daniel snapped. "I'll do it." As he did, everybody stepped back.

Doreen looked inside the little box, now opened, seeing only tissue paper, and muttered, "At least it's not a bomb."

"Not one you can see," Nick noted.

The detective snorted and asked her, "Did you really think it was?"

"I don't really want to open up surprise packages addressed to my dead husband and delivered to my dead husband's home, where we find a dead body buried in the onion patch as soon as we arrive here and most recently one in the garage apartment," she murmured, glancing over at Mack.

Mugs barked several times. She looked down at him and said, "You were right, honey."

"What do you mean, he was right?" Daniel asked. "It wasn't a bomb."

"We didn't *say* it was a bomb," she clarified, looking at him. "We just didn't like the way Mugs reacted to this package."

Daniel shrugged. "He's hardly a trained police dog, so I wouldn't worry about it."

A hint of something akin to disgust filled his tone, enough so that she didn't like anything about it. "Since when did you become so critical, Daniel?"

"When I became a cop and learned that the world was not a nice place."

She had to consider that, conceding he really did have a point. "I get that, but you didn't use to hate dogs."

"I don't hate dogs," he argued, staring at her. "Yet I really don't want a dog making decisions for us."

She laughed. "What decision?" she asked, scoffing at him. "We were going to open this package anyway, but we did have to deal with some apprehensions beforehand."

Daniel shrugged. "I just want to make sure that we aren't dealing with something more here."

"I think we're dealing with plenty," she pointed out.

Doreen retrieved the kitchen knife and dragged away the tissue paper on top. For Daniel's benefit, she explained, "Since I've already touched both the outer box and the inner box, I'm going to shake out what's left." One handwritten note fell out. Another seemed stuck in the bottom of the little box. She gasped and pointed to the first message.

I told you that you would pay, Daniel.

She looked over at the detective in shock and then at Mack.

Mack frowned and asked, "Daniel, does this mean anything to you? Who would send a message to you here? And why was this delivery addressed to Mathew? He's been dead for months. Wouldn't the sender know that already?"

Doreen glanced at the three men nearby, with nobody responding, then took a deep breath and nodded. "Daniel? What's going on here?"

"I don't know," he snapped. "I'm not the only person named *Daniel* in this world."

"Funny how someone named Daniel has been around for days though?" Doreen noted, studying him.

"Somebody's attempt at bad humor."

As she shook her head, she pulled out the second handwritten note, accompanied by a picture. She read the note out loud. "*In the wrong place at the wrong time, Daniel. Not our problem, It's for you to find.*" Bewildered, she noted, "It's a rhyme, a note addressed to you again. Plus, this photo is of our dead man from the onion patch," she muttered, handing it to Mack.

Mack continued to stare at Daniel.

Doreen added, "I don't know what's going on, and it would be really nice if you could explain this to us, Daniel," she declared.

Daniel swallowed, then sneered at her. "Did you send this package here, Doreen? Trying to divert attention away from you? Because you're sitting very pretty on a very large sum of money now, aren't you?"

She snorted, glaring at him. "Wow. Daniel, do you realize you were called out here, twice now, to investigate the murders on this property?"

"I am well aware of that," Daniel snapped.

"But all of Mathew's money has your focus," Doreen pointed out. "How is that doing your job here? You just seem jealous."

"You are a suspect, Doreen," Daniel stated gleefully. "You came into a lot of money here."

She nodded. "Yes, I did become the sole heir of Mathew's estate. However, I didn't kill Mathew for it, which is the only way that works. I surely didn't kill anybody else. So tell me, Daniel. How does me killing the guy in the onion patch end up with me inheriting Mathew's estate? Is Pete Singer related to Mathew in any way? As you well know, I didn't leave Mathew, but I should have. *He's* the one who kicked me out. Why didn't he update his will way back then? It's his fault that he failed to change his will, not some supersecret plan I had going on. I mean, really, Daniel? Look at the facts. I don't know why you are so fixated on Mathew's money. Regardless, I really couldn't care less about *Mathew's stuff*. Mainly because it was all about him. Also," she added, shooting daggers at Daniel with her gaze, "I was already set up to receive a very large amount anyway from my grandmother, who loves me very much. Mathew never loved me. He made that very clear throughout our entire marriage."

"Yes, but once he divorced you"—then Daniel frowned—"I guess you still would have gotten a large chunk due to being married for all those years."

"Well, I *should* have gotten a very large chunk," she

agreed. "Even though he tried at every stage to not give me my due as we discussed protracted divorce proceedings. Regardless that's still not the point."

"Are you sure?" he asked, eyeing her quizzically. "Because I'm not so sure about that."

Doreen snapped, "That's because you're looking for somebody to be in the wrong, and no matter how much you want it to be me, it's not."

He shrugged. "That's what you say."

"And it's the truth," she declared. "Look. I don't expect you to be some long-lost friend and automatically believe me. Just do your job, figure it out, and then you'll know the truth too," she stated. "I have never been mean to anybody. That was all Mathew."

"Until you found yourself homeless and on the streets."

"Not even then. Thankfully my grandmother stepped in and saved me," she countered, scoffing. "Without my grandmother, … things could have been very different, but she gave me a home, and I found a purpose in everything else I did after that," Doreen told Daniel. "But I can see that, for you, it's apparently all about money."

"For most people it's all about money."

"Not Doreen," Mack declared.

Doreen shook her head. "Don't waste your breath, Mack. And, Daniel, it doesn't matter if you believe me or not, but I did expect you to do your job." And with that, she picked up her phone and began taking photos of the contents of the delivery box.

He stood behind her. "You do know we need the contents of that box?"

"You didn't ask for it yet, and you aren't leaving yet either, and I doubt Mack would allow you to take this evidence anyway, not with your name clearly on both messages," she snapped, as she took pictures of it all.

"Just *Daniel* is on those notes. Doesn't mean they are for me. Now what are you doing?" he asked in exasperation.

"You're making me doubt that you'll do your job properly, and that leaves me in the position where I need to make sure that someone is looking after *my* rights. So I will document any evidence before I turn it over … to your captain."

"What are you talking about?" Daniel cried out. "I'm right here, aren't I? I'm the lead detective."

"Yes, you're here," she confirmed, "in name only, as I'm not sure you can be objective. Now, with your name on these two notes, I really doubt you can be by the book. But hear me when I say that I am not about to have anybody bulldoze me into a murder charge or two, when I had nothing to do with either death here."

"He knows you didn't have anything to do with it," Mack interjected. "I presume he knows that these notes put him in a bad light right about now." He turned to face Daniel. By this time, Nick and Scott stood with Mack, making a line of defense between Daniel and Doreen. Also adding in some barrier before he grabbed the evidence and destroyed it all. "Sorry, Daniel, but you know I must report this to your captain."

Daniel glared at him.

Doreen asked, "Don't you work with a partner? I only ever speak with you. Don't you work in pairs, have a backup?"

He shook his head at her. "I don't need backup."

Doreen interjected, "Why don't you try to redeem your reputation by sharing some details with us? As in, how long has Pete Singer been dead?" she asked.

He sighed and replied, "I haven't got the autopsy report yet, so I don't know. These things take time."

"It *all* takes time," she stated, looking at him, "but that's really got nothing to do with it. She should have been able to give you an estimated time of death fairly quickly."

"She?" Daniel repeated.

Doreen shrugged. "The coroner we work with in Kelowna is female."

"That's nice, but we have a male, and he's swamped."

"He still should have been able to give you a rough estimate for a time of death."

"And you're talking about the movies, not real life," Daniel said in exasperation. "It can take a lot longer. This guy was buried, and we don't know for how long."

"It doesn't take that long for a seasoned coroner," she declared.

"And how would you know?" Daniel asked, turning to her.

She stared at him and asked, "Seriously?"

When he didn't respond, she went on.

"Pete's exposed nose was fairly intact. No degradation. No bugs or animals eating it. So the rest of him was buried, but I doubt he was buried for longer than … a couple days at the most." Daniel stared at her, flummoxed, and she continued. "No, of course I can't prove that, and I don't have any insider knowledge. Yet it doesn't take that much to figure out the body is in decent shape, as in *fresh*. Not only that," she added, "I detected almost no dead-body-decaying smell in that room. There was a little but not like full decomp can be."

"Just what do you know about decomp?" Daniel snapped.

Nick laughed. "She knows a fair bit."

Mack nodded. "She's become quite a successful amateur sleuth."

"Good God," Daniel muttered. "What kind of a hick town is it if your department lets somebody like her get involved in your cases?"

Mack stiffened and Doreen growled, her voice low as she spoke. "Somebody like me? By all means, please elaborate."

Mugs strode up to Daniel, walked around him, and lifted his leg. It took Doreen a moment to register what he was doing. Then she called out, "Mugs, no!"

But it was too late. Mugs managed to soil Daniel's pant leg. Daniel lashed out to kick at Mugs, but he was already out of the way and safely behind Nick.

"Oh my gosh, I'm so sorry," she cried out. "He doesn't normally do that."

"He just did it," Daniel snapped, shaking his leg and sending droplets flying all over. "Good God, what an absolute disaster."

Mack nudged her off to the side and behind him. He already had his phone in hand. He stared at Daniel and called his captain. "Captain Hawkins, Corporal Mack Moreau of the Kelowna RCMP. We have some evidence here that names a Daniel and we think you should be involved in retaining said evidence. … Yes, sir." He put his phone on Speaker, so everyone could hear.

"Detective Daniel Sherwood," Captain Hawkins announced, "you are no longer in charge of any investigation regarding deaths on the property in question. Stand down. I will be there shortly." Then the call ended abruptly.

Daniel seemed nervous to Doreen, ready to take flight. Mack saw it too. "People who run look guilty, Daniel."

Daniel just glared harder at them but remained in place.

"Wise decision," Mack muttered.

Just then came a knock on the door, with Mugs barking madly at the noise.

She looked over at Mack and asked, "Are you ready for this?"

"Heck no," he muttered, "but I don't see that we have any choice."

And, with that, their day officially began, first with Detective Davis arriving to oversee Daniel, as everyone awaited the captain's appearance. Soon afterward came Scott and his crew. As the Christie's crew worked, finally Captain Hawkins arrived, with a glare for Daniel, but spoke to Mack, Nick, and Doreen. Gathering this latest evidence, including Butch's gun, Captain Hawkins ordered Detective Davis to escort Detective Sherwood to the department for interrogation. Little did Daniel know that Doreen and Mack had been feeding info to Captain Hawkins long before this delivery arrived. Daniel would find out soon enough.

With them now gone, Doreen had been called to the second floor. Scott and his team of experts weren't interested in the knick-knacks or bedding or decor or things of that sort on the second floor, so she sorted through all that was left in each of the guest bedrooms. Eventually she found her way to the master bedroom. She identified things to donate to the local women's shelter, others to antique or specialty shops. She planned to call somebody to pick it up later. Soon, the second floor would be entirely empty. She looked forward to that accomplishment.

At one point, Mack called her downstairs, saying, "The police need to talk to you."

"Of course they do." She walked into the kitchen to find

Mack and Nick and another officer sitting here, having coffee. She greeted them, asking if anybody needed fresh coffee, but nobody did. So she walked over to the coffeepot and poured herself a cup, then sat with them at the kitchen table.

"I'm Detective Clark. I'll be taking over the lead in the investigations of the deaths of Pete Singer and Butch Weldon. So, I need to go over some questions with you."

She nodded.

Then he lunged into his questions about the stranger they had met last night. "Why would you have left him in the apartment?" he asked.

"I wouldn't just kick him out, not knowing whether his story was true or not. We didn't have any way to prove or disprove his story at that moment, and I wouldn't leave the man on the streets when we have a space for him in the garage apartment."

"And yet he could have murdered you in your sleep."

"The chance of his murdering us all in our sleep wasn't that great. He couldn't gain entry to the main house from the garage apartment, not without breaking inside. Plus, I had Mack, an experienced detective, and Nick, my attorney, not to mention the animals. Mugs never barked."

"Speaking of which," Clark noted, seeing Mugs at Doreen's feet, staring directly at Clark, "your dog doesn't seem to like me."

"Mugs is very protective of me. So, at the rate you are interrogating me, he'll like you less and less," she explained, with a shrug. Hearing Mack clear his throat, she looked over at him. "I'm just calling it like it is." She frowned at him and rolled her eyes, then turned back to Detective Clark. "Please continue."

He asked more questions, some that Daniel had already asked, but she answered them to bring Clark up to speed faster. “Did you find the gun?” Doreen asked him.

“I cannot discuss this case or the other one with you.”

Undeterred, Doreen proceeded with her own questions. “So you didn’t find the gun that shot and killed Pete? And you didn’t run ballistics on Butch’s own gun either?”

Detective Clark frowned, seemed upset. “Please answer my questions here. So the man in the garage apartment never came inside this house, whether you saw him or not?”

Doreen shrugged. “If we can believe what Butch told us last night, he was inside the house many months ago, speaking with and working with my late husband. So Butch has never been inside this house since we arrived here, about a week ago. Mugs would have barked had Butch been inside here with us. Yet Butch told us that he had just arrived last night.”

“So you didn’t know Butch Weldon?”

She shook her head. “Not before meeting him last night.”

“And the earlier dead man on this property, Pete Singer, did you know him?”

“Nope. Never knew him.”

When Detective Clark ran out of questions, he finally left.

Doreen was relieved. She had a ton of stuff to still deal with here. And on that note, she walked back to the master bedroom, relieved to find Scott still there.

She gave him an apologetic look and shared the latest on speaking to the new lead detective on these murder cases.

“Your life is never dull, is it?” Scott asked in wonder.

“We’ll know more later. So what’s up here?”

He pointed. "Taking apart the master bedroom suite, we found a few secret drawers here, when the back on this dresser … falls away."

She followed him to the rear of the dresser. She wasn't a fan of this bedroom furniture to begin with. Yet she ignored it for all those years she had lived here. It was very ornate, very stifling as far as she was concerned, but Mathew selected it for whatever reason, and it had survived the years well. Yet, if secret drawers were everywhere, Mathew would definitely have loved this furniture and may have chosen it for just that perk.

Scott pointed out the hidden drawer and shared, "I didn't look at the contents, leaving that to you."

She nodded, bent down, pulled it open, then stopped and stared. She pulled out her phone and called Mack. "Hey, you need to come up here too."

"Do I need to?" he repeated in a wary voice.

"Yeah, I'm sorry, but I wouldn't know what to do with this."

Chapter 13

DOREEN STARED DOWN at the contents in the secret drawer in the back of one of the master suite's dressers. As she and Scott waited until Mack showed up, Mugs wandered around, sniffing, his nose heavy to the ground. She watched him and noted how he was more interested in that than the contents of the drawer. When Mack showed up, she pointed at the drawer.

He walked over, pulled it open, and sighed. "Of course."

"What is it?" Scott asked, standing at the front of the dresser.

"A weapon."

Scott stared at her in surprise, and she nodded. "It's a gun, the second one we've found so far. I'll add this one to the first one in Mathew's home office desk for now."

"Oh dear," Scott muttered.

Doreen asked Scott, "Did you say more secret drawers are in this dresser?"

"Yes, I will open that next."

Mack always carried plastic gloves and donned one and quickly picked up the weapon and sniffed it. "Hasn't been fired recently either." Then he took it away.

"I'm really glad he's here to handle that stuff," she muttered.

Scott noted, "I had no idea that your ex-husband was so into weapons."

"With the dodgy lifestyle he had, and so much money stashed in this place, I guess it makes sense."

"It does, indeed. The problem with amassing such valuable stuff is that you then have to protect it," Scott explained. "That tends to drive a lot of people mad because the last thing they want to do is lose everything they've invested in."

"And yet it seems counterproductive to worry so about it because then these things you've coveted and worked so hard to get become the very things that drag you down and that rob you of joy. I know firsthand that Mathew got so paranoid that he couldn't enjoy these things at all."

Mack returned and rejoined them. "I imagine Mathew's actions were counterproductive," Mack acknowledged.

Scott agreed. "In my line of work, I find collecting anything to extremes can be a cold and calculating hobby in very slow and insidious ways. We've dealt with a lot of collectors, and sometimes they're really well adjusted, but other times it just becomes an obsession."

"I don't know if Mathew was to the obsession level but probably not far off," she admitted. "Maybe he got something worthwhile from amassing these things, but I never got to see much of them," she noted. "What did he do with them? Just stare at them all day? And now he's left me with this mess here."

Scott pointed out another hidden drawer. "You need to look at this one too."

She took a hesitant step forward, slowly pulled it open,

and then smiled. "This one's empty."

"Good for that," he muttered with relief.

"Any others?"

"No, I think that's it," Scott said. "Wasn't that gun enough?"

"Absolutely." She looked around the master and asked, "How are we doing?"

"I have someone here to help—"

Just then a person stepped out of the huge master closet, somebody Doreen had never seen before. He walked over, smiled at her, and announced, "I'm Jewels."

He was extremely well dressed, exhibiting fashion-diva vibes, not a hair out of place. If she had any energy left, she would be jealous, but she was just too overwhelmed by the rest of it. She smiled at him. "Hey." Scott's introduction shared how Jewels was here about the clothing.

Jewels began, "I found suits that have never been worn, still hanging in their bags."

"That would be Mathew. If he liked something, he purchased multiples, so he never ran out of something, keeping them in perfect, pristine condition until he might need to use them."

"Interesting system," Jewels noted. "And do you want to keep anything in these closets?"

She shook her head. "No."

"What about the women's clothing?"

"Absolutely not," she stated. "My husband kicked me out a long time ago, so none of that stuff is mine."

"Some of it is beautiful though."

"Maybe," she conceded, her mind thinking that maybe she should try to sell it on consignment. Yet she instantly realized she would just be dealing with all that so much longer. So there was a point. Time to let it all go. She smiled at him and replied, "If you guys can sell, use, or whatever regarding anything in there, please do."

He nodded. "I'll give you a full listing. I'm working on it as I go." Still muttering to himself, he headed back into the massive closet.

She looked over at Scott. "Mathew's closet needed a special clothing expert? Really?"

He nodded. "You have no idea."

"Apparently not," she muttered.

Scott shrugged. "Clothing of this level can just be cleaned—or dry-cleaned as needed—and an awful lot of buyers are out there for these slightly used items."

"That's good," she stated, "because I don't know anybody. I guess that's not totally true. I did sell an awful lot of my grandmother's clothes way back when."

"She probably had quite the clothing collection in her day," Scott noted, with a laugh. "I do remember meeting her, and she still phones me on a regular basis."

Doreen frowned at her phone, not hearing from Nan today. "Speaking of which, if we're done here, I'll give her a quick call."

"We're absolutely done," Scott declared, beaming. "The remaining furniture in any other guest bedroom should be all gone today—except for small decor pieces, which we are not interested in. They want to get onto this master tomorrow."

"Perfect. … A lot of stuff is still here, isn't there?"

"Yes, but hopefully we will get through it in one more day." He added, "We haven't discussed the living room furniture."

"Take everything you think you can sell," she said. "Anything else can be donated to the local women's shelter."

"Are you sure?"

"Absolutely sure."

He added a bit reluctantly, "I did take a little sneak peek in the main kitchen area. Do you want me to bring in any experts?"

She frowned at him and asked, "What stuff in the kitchen?"

"Mathew had china, very expensive china."

"Oh, that's right. We never used it, which I never understood."

"Of course not," Scott exclaimed in astonishment. "Some of those pieces are not for using."

She winced. "Every piece in my house in Kelowna is a piece to use," she muttered. "I won't have it any other way."

He smiled. "I gather then that I can take a good look and whatever we think we can sell …"

"Absolutely," she murmured, cutting him off, "the more you take, the better. Everything that you don't take, I still have to deal with. I'm trying to avoid that, if possible."

AND THAT PATTERN continued for the next day and the day after. Thankfully Scott reported all jewelry and loose stones had been removed from the house and was already in the air. Detective Clark was around part of the time, asking questions, and she did her best to answer them. Butch's body had been removed from the apartment, and the bedding he had been on was removed by forensics. The remaining contents of the room would go to charity when the cops were done with the crime scene.

Not much was there in the garage apartment, and it certainly wasn't of the same quality as the contents of the main house. She and Mack did another search of the apartment, looking for anything related to Butch that the forensics team may have missed.

"By the way," he whispered, in case anybody was nearby, "Captain Hawkins confirmed Butch's gun was the one used to kill Pete. Seems they were jailbirds together too."

"Makes sense," she muttered, "since Mathew was working with them. Does Detective Clark know that the gun ties Butch to Pete?"

"Yes, as Captain Hawkins informed him of that."

"Is he checking with the prison for more info on our two dead guys and gonna share it with you?"

Mack grinned. "A professional courtesy has been extended to share info with me, so yes."

Doreen muttered. "Good. Should we have Nan and crew see if they can find out anything else on these two?"

Mack had to grimace. "As much as I don't want to encourage them, I sent Nan a photo of Butch. I presumed they were working without my authorization already, so I caved."

Doreen chuckled. "Sounds good."

"Now," Mack said, pointing around at the furnishings still in the garage apartment, "what is your plan for these contents?"

She told him how a local women's shelter came looking for some furnishings earlier, and she expected them later today. "They will come through first, taking what they want. Then I found another local charity, already spoke to them on the phone. They talked about some garage sale or consignment or something, but I don't care. As long as they make a few bucks or can use it to help somebody out, I am happy for them to take whatever's left. I'll call them to come as soon as the first charity is gone from here."

Chapter 14

DOREEN SAT DOWN for a cup of tea the next day, and Nan video-called her. Doreen stared at her beloved grandmother's face and sighed. "I wish I was home."

"I wish you were too," she said, with a kind smile. "We are missing out on all the excitement."

"I guess in a way you are, but it's not all that much fun, considering we now have had two deaths on the property."

"That's one of the reasons I wanted to call this morning," Nan began. "We do have some information on him."

She asked, "On whom?"

"On the dead man. The second one. Butch Weldon."

Doreen stared at her. "Wow. That's fast. Mack only gave you the photo yesterday."

She laughed. "Yes. I was so pleased when Mack sent us a photo. I guess he doesn't totally trust the local authorities either. He did tell me that we weren't to go through proper channels, so we contacted Chester. He ran it through the database, and Butch has a record," she declared proudly.

"Oh my," Doreen muttered, and then she laughed. "It was a really smart idea to contact Chester. I'm surprised you didn't contact Darren."

"We wanted to but didn't because we don't want to get him in trouble. Chester didn't seem to think that he would get in trouble for anything, so it wasn't an issue."

"It might well have gotten him into trouble, but, as it is, thank you. So, Butch has a record then. What can you tell me about him?"

"I just sent you the file. Chester gave us a full rundown," she stated. "Since Mack wanted us to be acting on our own accord, I did tell Chester that I was acting on your behalf and that you had such terrible reception in that monster house of yours down there that we needed his help."

"Oh my." She started to laugh. "I can almost see him wanting to believe that enough to help out."

"He absolutely did help out," Nan confirmed, chuckling. "But Mack can't get mad at him. Remind him how he gave me the photo. No matter, you may have to fix it."

She opened the file and began reading it. "So, Butch was only let out of jail a few months ago," Doreen noted. "Yeah, he told me how his ma wasn't doing too well. So he lied about that for sure."

Nan continued. "And we asked for a list of his cellmates. Now this part," she said, raising a hand in excitement, "we're really proud of."

"Can't wait to hear it, Nan."

"Maisie phoned the prison, and eventually she spoke to Butch's last cellmate, before Butch was sprung."

"Oh my," Doreen stared at Nan in shock. "And what did Maisie find out?" Doreen asked.

"Butch was coming back to get something owed to him. And he apparently told his last cellmate he would get it, … no matter what."

"He did get something," she muttered, "but not what he expected."

"Right, since he's dead now," Nan agreed. "However, Butch had a former cellmate buddy, and that guy was also released not very long after Butch got out. This guy, Sam, had been friends with him in prison."

"And how did you find out about him?"

"We talked to the security guard and to the prison administration, asking if anybody there had been friendly with Butch. The admin office didn't know about friends, but the guard mentioned how Butch had shared a cell with Sam at some point, and they'd seemed friendly enough."

"Amazing," Doreen muttered, "and you realize that guard probably wasn't allowed to talk to you."

"The thing was, Maisie played ditzy, supposedly not understanding half the questions the intake guy asked, so he probably just got frustrated and put her through to that guard, who was easily duped by her as well. You know how she gets, like she's getting ready for a part in some play."

"Now that sounds exactly like Maisie," Doreen noted, shaking her head.

"Anyway, you are probably looking for this other guy, Sam, who said he would join Butch. They were both sure a lot of money was in that big house."

"But where did they hear that? Butch said he had met with Mathew inside the house many months ago. But still? It's not that Mathew would have given Butch a tour of all the hidey-holes with his *running money.* So, yes, there is definitely a lot of money in the big house," Doreen confirmed, "and we still haven't gotten to a bank to put it away safely."

"You need to do that soon," Nan urged in a loud tone. "You do not want to be sleeping where all that money is."

Doreen ended the call the phone, turned to Mack,

standing right behind her. She smiled at him. "How much of that did you hear?"

"Most of it, not all though," he said, through gritted teeth.

"Will Chester get in trouble?"

He shook his head. "No, I sent the photo because of Daniel freezing me out of his investigation, which made me question whether I could fully trust Detective Clark—even Captain Hawkins," he admitted. "It's been incredibly frustrating not being in on the local investigation."

Doreen smiled. "Now you know how I feel."

He rolled his eyes at that. "And your new friend Clark hasn't been willing to share much of anything."

"No, of course not," she confirmed, "especially when you and I are looking to be really good suspects even to the latest detective on these cases."

"Which is complete and total bull-crap."

"Of course it is," she declared. "You and I both know that, but he's trying to close a case. I hope he's at least better at investigating than Daniel was. I don't think the facts were really on Daniel's mind too much."

He smiled at her. "I want to trust and believe in law enforcement, as least in Captain Hawkins, as Daniel clearly had his own agenda."

"Finally you owned up to it. You didn't trust Daniel either. However, mostly because of you, I will trust that Captain Hawkins is honest and open-minded."

Mack looked over at her, a big grin on his face. "I'm really glad to hear that. So, what all did Nan say exactly?"

"You may have heard the bulk of it," she began, "but, as far as she's concerned, our supposed caretaker, Butch, had a partner, Sam, both cellmates for a while. So that partner is likely nearby with a key to the garage apartment, for all that does for them. It doesn't get them into this main house. Regardless, Butch had a key, so maybe he copied one to give to Sam. And, if Sam heard about the bags of money inside the main house," she theorized, "then I'm sure he's still eager to look for them."

"But," Mack pointed out, "they can't get in the house. Not without a key to one of these doors. Not with all of us here. Not with the cops here almost every day too."

"Right," she agreed, "unless somebody got inside, dressed as a mover, an EMT, a ... *cop*." She shared a glance with Mack, who seemed to agree with her.

"This place is big enough that I'm not sure anybody ever has to leave the house for fear of being found," Mack added. "In that same vein, somebody could be hiding in this mansion. It's big enough, for sure. So somebody could *be* in the house now."

"I don't think so because Mugs never barked, unless at Daniel," she noted. "It happened before though."

"What happened before?" Mack asked her.

"Someone hiding in this mansion. Mathew hired somebody, didn't like their performance, fired them, but they were still in the house days later, and my husband didn't know because they'd been hiding."

Mack frowned. "Odd, but it could happen. Our dead guy, Pete Singer, was found in the greenhouse, which is directly connected to the main house. Maybe he's related to Sam or Butch or just another jailbird set free. Maybe he was scouting out the place, until the other two were both out of prison. Still, we now know Butch killed Pete. So who killed Butch?"

"Sam, maybe. That would make a lot of sense to me, not

having to share the loot," she suggested. "Will you bring it up with Detective Clark or with Captain Hawkins?"

Mack sighed. "We'll make sure the Vancouver police solve these murders correctly on their end. Otherwise we will always seem to be a part of this."

Doreen noted, "But we are a part of it, in a way, just not the murdering part. I wasn't expecting to have to defend myself. Every time Daniel was here, he got more aggressive with me than the last time."

"And," Mack added, "he never offered the professional courtesies that I got from other departments. At least Detective Clark isn't like that."

"I noticed," she muttered.

"Let me talk to my captain and see if we can coordinate our departments and get Pete's fingerprints run against any recently released inmates."

"Other than the killer, there may still be a third person, an informant or silent partner or whatever," she pointed out. "One who told Sam and Butch about what's in Mathew's house."

"And that could have been another disgruntled employee, another criminal, a friend or a cousin to said ex-employee or criminal, or just somebody with some connection to this house, like repairmen or cleaners or painters or whatnot."

"Goodness, that's a pretty large pool."

"So, for a start, we'll need employment records of those hired by Mathew and then get it cross-referenced with our dead criminals and any cellmates and such," he suggested, thinking out loud.

She beamed at him. "Now that's the Mack I'm used to."

He snorted. "This Mack has been a little overwhelmed by the size of the job here just to gut this house for sale, much less the size of this house and the cash money we found, … with more money popping up every time I turn around."

"Which also goes along with the criminal activity scene that Mathew was involved in because, for almost anybody, if they knew cash bonds were here, literally anyone could have grabbed those."

"Which is also why I'm surprised that previous employees didn't."

"Maybe they did," she pointed out. "We know what we've found but not what we haven't, if you get my drift."

"Yeah, good point. Is it just me or is the *simply getting rid of the house* job here getting bigger and more complicated by the day?"

She nodded. "It is and it isn't. I get it that we're up against something we couldn't have anticipated with these two murders and one bad cop, but we are up for the job," she declared, smiling at him encouragingly.

He laughed. "We are?"

"Sure," she declared, grinning. "The whole team is here, the front-line team anyway, plus Nan and the crew back home are all doing a heck of a job."

With that, her phone rang again. It was Nan.

"Maisie is here," she began. "She wants to tell you all about it herself."

Doreen smiled at Mack, and it wasn't very long before she was telling Maisie what a great job she'd done.

"It was fun. I mean, oh my," Maisie exclaimed, excited, "to think I talked to a criminal."

"I'm surprised that the security guard or whoever you were on the phone with let you talk to anyone."

"The prisoners are allowed phone calls, but I had to find

out the name of Butch's last cellmate first before they would connect me. I told the guy on the phone that I was a pen pal to many inmates in several prisons and how I might have the name mixed up with another guy in another place, as I kept guessing his name. Finally the guard got exasperated and told me *Jake* was the last one to bunk with Butch. Then a few minutes later he came on the line."

"And this Jake was interested in talking to you?" Mack asked.

"He was but not right away. So I told him that I was a lawyer, an activist, looking at people who were wrongfully imprisoned."

"Ah, now makes more sense," Mack said.

Doreen nodded. "I was wondering why the prisoners would talk to you."

"It was your grandmother's idea," Maisie admitted reluctantly, as if forced to give Nan the credit.

"Of course it was," Doreen murmured. "Did Jake say anything else, maybe indicating other people could be involved in this?"

"Just somebody named … Sam. Maybe it was Sam. I told you his name earlier. Sam heard something about the property. Sam and Butch figured they hadn't been paid properly after doing some jobs for this person in this big fat house, so they were owed some money. So, they would come get it."

"Did Jake hear about where it was?"

"I don't think so, but Sam was pretty sure it was there, and apparently he was jealous, thinking Butch would get a huge haul now that he got free, while Sam was still locked up and was missing out on the fun."

"Sometimes that's what happens when you go to jail,"

Doreen noted.

Maisie laughed. "I might have pointed out something along that line to him myself. I must admit that Jake wasn't very happy with me by the time I ended the call. Yet he was hoping we would find his friends. I didn't tell him if they were alive or dead because he might have stopped talking to me," she explained in that birdlike voice of hers.

"True, and you did great. What I'm trying to figure out is how they knew about the house in the first place?"

"Jake didn't name names, but Sam and Butch both talked about having done a job for some big fat whale."

"Yeah, that could be Mathew," she muttered.

Maisie didn't have anything else to add. When the phone changed hands, and Nan came back on, she added, speaking to Maisie, "Now, Maisie, you've done well. I told you that already."

More conversation went on in the background, and then Nan groaned and told Doreen, "Now you have to talk to Richie. He wants to do something to help too."

"He might want to," Doreen noted, "but I'm not sure what he can do now."

Nan pointed out, "I'm the one who contacted Chester. Maisie contacted the prison, and now Richie needs a job."

Doreen sighed and asked, "So, does he have any connections down here in the lower mainland?"

"No, I do. I told you that."

"Right, and did you ever come up with … whatever memory you had regarding Daniel?"

"Only that he's associated with Mathew. And you know how I feel about Mathew's friends."

"Which is hardly fair as technically you could say Daniel was my friend too," Doreen said gently. "I know it's easy to hate Mathew and everyone in his world, but it's not always that way."

"And sometimes it is," Nan muttered. "Anyway, I'm sticking to my intuition. I don't like Daniel. I didn't like Mathew either, and see how that turned out?"

"And you didn't find anything more in your research, maybe about Daniel's family?"

"No, well, maybe you should ask … Let me talk to Richie."

Then Richie came on the phone, and Doreen began, "Richie, I know that you don't want to bother your grandson …"

"Oh, I'm happy to bother him," he stated. "Give me a reason. I'm very happy to."

She looked over at Mack, who just shrugged as if to say, *Whatever*. "I'm wondering, since we seem to have gotten ourselves into a bit of a bind down here …"

"Oh, have you ever," he declared joyfully.

Doreen winced at such unmitigated helpfulness. She continued. "Could you have Darren discreetly run the details on Detective Daniel Sherwood and see if anything of interest is in his record? I don't know what Darren may find, and maybe nothing, but we need more than info on Daniel himself. We need info on Daniel's family, if possible, without anybody getting caught or in trouble."

"Oh, you really don't like him, do you?" Richie asked her.

"What bothers me is this second man who was killed on the property. Somebody had a key for the garage apartment. I'm wondering if Daniel does, but we've certainly let him inside, and he's been here a lot and could have easily gotten a mole inside."

Shocked delight filled Richie's tone. "I'm on it. Don't you worry. I'm on it."

And, once again, the phone was handed over to Nan.

"I feel as if I'm the director here," Nan muttered. "And honestly, sometimes it's just the crazy house that Rosemoor is."

Doreen burst into laughter. "Yet, I must say, you're doing an absolutely wonderful job."

Nan perked up and declared, "I am, aren't I? You know, you could hire me full-time to do this for you."

"The last thing you want," Doreen replied, feeling a shudder come over her, "is to have any full-time work. You wouldn't have time to do anything else."

"You're right about that," she muttered. "That sounds absolutely awful."

Doreen chuckled. "Therefore, we'll just keep it in the friendly spirit it is."

"That's good," she muttered. "But you need to stop getting into trouble, child. It was supposed to be a holiday for you."

"Who knew coming down here would get me into trouble?" she muttered. "We've just been trying to take care of removing all the contents of the house, but, of course, Mathew had things hidden everywhere, and, as soon as there's treasure, people are all over it."

Nan chuckled. "They absolutely are," she agreed, "so make sure you get the safe deposit boxes sorted too."

"I think Nick has already gone to deal with Mathew's probate lawyer to get as much banking information as he can."

"Good. He should at least be able to open some doors."

"He should open enough that I can go take a look,"

Doreen stated.

"Did you ever go to the bank with Mathew when you two were married?"

"Sure, lots of times. But it's not as if I was let in on any details. Remember that I was led around more than anything."

"*Tsk-tsk*," Nan muttered. "You could have learned so much about his business."

"Sure, and what would it have done, except get me killed too?"

After a shocked moment of silence, Nan replied, "Good point."

Chapter 15

DOREEN WENT TO bed that night, tired and worn out. All of this was mentally draining, and adding in the second death on the property had elevated her stress level to the point that she was antsy to get everything completed and just get back home. She was tempted to tell Scott to take everything, from all the houses Mathew owned in Vancouver. Scott should just coordinate with Mathew's probate attorney here in town, even the property management company—once both had been properly vetted, once she felt certain that neither were involved in killing these people nor wanting to get "what was owed them" from Mathew. Somehow, amid all these thoughts racing around her brain, she eventually slept.

The next morning and later into that day, an unbelievable amount of the large furniture was removed from the house, plus Mathew's clothing, even some remaining artwork. That was good. As long as it was leaving, and she was getting an itemized list of it, she was happy.

She knew Mack was happy to see it all leaving as well. The more that went, the better, as far as he was concerned, and he was right. As she glanced around the house that was still so full, she didn't even remember seeing most of it before, although she knew a lot of it had been here even when she had lived here. It just seemed to be even more than she had remembered. With such a large house, it was still amazing how much could fill it.

Yet it still remained to be a very daunting job. The animals all appeared to agree as Mugs and Goliath were wrapped around each other, both snoring heavily. Thaddeus snoozed on a temporary roost Mack had set up for him in Doreen's designated bedroom.

She walked into the kitchen to find Mack making breakfast. She perked up and asked, "Home-cooked food? Really?"

"I wanted pancakes," he said, smiling at her.

"I'm more than happy with pancakes," she stated, as she crashed down on a stool.

"Bad night?"

"Yeah, I kept hearing people walking through the house all night." When he stopped and turned to her, she shrugged. "Mugs never got upset about it, so I figured everything was just fine."

"How many people would Mugs have recognized from before?"

She frowned at him, considering that. "I don't know. I assumed it was just my … nightmares."

"Did you get up?"

"No, I didn't, … but now I'm questioning that. I do keep revisiting my worst-case scenario that somebody is hiding somewhere in this mausoleum, and we don't know it yet."

He stared at her and nodded. "Something I have considered too."

"With two dead bodies, scary stuff is going on," she muttered.

Goliath sauntered into the kitchen and stopped, shot his back leg up to the sky, and proceeded to clean himself.

She looked at him and sighed. "You know, as manners go, you really don't have any, Goliath," she muttered.

He completely ignored her and kept cleaning. Mugs came by, waited for a moment, then barked right in Goliath's ear. The big cat shot up in the air, landed on all four feet, and turned on Mugs. Just like that, the chase was on. They ran through the kitchen and the rest of the house. She burst out laughing at their antics, thankful for anything humorous going on.

Nick, who had just entered the kitchen, looked at the animals in horror. "What was that all about?" he asked.

"They're just blowing off steam," she explained, still chuckling. "Everybody's pretty fed up with being here."

"Yeah, me too," he admitted.

"You never did get a chance to tell us what happened with Mathew's probate attorney, since you got in so late last night."

"Yeah. I hadn't expected to be nearly that late, but he got held up, and the interruptions just went on and on and on."

"So, where are we at?" she asked, as he poured coffee, sniffed the pancakes, then snagged one off the plate before Mack had time to smack him. She snorted. "How come you get away with that?"

He grinned. "Years of experience as his brother."

"I didn't have any brothers … or sisters," she muttered.

Mack pulled out a plate, dumped four pancakes on it, and brought it over to her.

She chuckled. "You are the nicest man."

"Yeah, I am," he declared, "and keep remembering that."

She smiled and waited for Nick to come sit down. He frowned at the pancakes on her plate. "I don't have to steal pancakes. Mack shares," she stated, with a smile.

He snorted at that and shook his head. "You two are something else."

"Of course we are," she muttered. "So, enough dithering around. What did you find out?"

"Three banks," Nick replied, snagging a pancake off her special plateful, "each with at least one safe deposit box."

"Okay," Doreen said, "I vaguely remember two. I don't recall hearing about a third." When he just stared at her, she shrugged. "As I explained to Nan earlier, it's not as if I had anything to do with Mathew's money. I would have gone to a safe deposit box in some bank with him, but I might have been told to stay outside of the private viewing area, or I might have been told to sign something," she shared. "At that point in my life, I did not have the wherewithal to do anything but follow orders."

Nick nodded.

Doreen continued. "I know that may be shocking, considering the way you see me now, but the transformation didn't happen overnight."

"Right," Nick acknowledged. "And that is something I do need to remember. You were groomed into that life for a very long time."

"I don't even know when I became that version of me. I just know that there was always that fear about ..." She took a deep breath and added, "It wasn't even fear at that point. It was automated responses. Everything was just done because I was told to do it. When you feel you can't get out, you don't fight anymore," she muttered. "Believe me when I say that, looking at that life now, from this point of view, I'm thinking I was an absolute idiot."

"No, you weren't, and look where you're standing now," Nick pointed out. "And the one person who was the actual idiot is dead and gone."

She smiled at him. "I'm not sure Mathew was an idiot. He just believed he would be labeled a loser if he didn't own everything there was to own, and he just couldn't handle that."

"It's not an issue now," Mack stated, as he placed a plate of pancakes in the center of the table. "You can do anything you want now, Doreen."

"And that's a good thing," she declared with a smile, as she poured maple syrup all over her pancakes.

Mack now sat down with them, and she looked over at Nick. "So, what are we doing today?"

"We'll go to the banks today," he suggested, looking over at Mack.

Mack nodded, staring at them. "Good. I want to do that, preferably soon. … A lot of money is here."

"I know," she muttered. "Can we just take it in the duffel bags?"

Nick interjected, "That's one of the issues I had to resolve yesterday, but we are cleared with an appointment today. We'll bring the duffel bags and deposit that cash into a new account in your name only," he explained, "so you can access it from wherever because that's important. Plus, we need to get Mathew's remaining money in the existing bank accounts transferred over to you as well."

"*Right*," she grumbled. "So lots of paperwork."

"Exactly," Nick agreed, with a smile, "but this is paperwork that most people would be happy to do."

She shrugged.

Nick looked over at Mack, who was grinning broadly at Doreen. Nick shook his head and admitted, "I've never met anybody quite like you."

"Yeah, but that's because you're seeing it as *my* money, and I still see it as Mathew's money."

"It's not Mathew's money anymore," he argued.

She sighed, tired of that argument. "Now the question is, how do we get the duffel bags out of here without anybody knowing?"

Nick stared at her, then over at Mack. "Do you think anybody knows?" he asked his brother.

"Not at the moment. However, if anybody's sticking around this place, they'll be watching this house like a hawk. That would be my take," Mack suggested, looking at her. "We gotta take care of the cash in the duffel bags and those bonds," he pointed out, "because those are as good as cash."

"Plus," Nick mentioned, "those original stock certificates, which are proof of ownership."

"Right, I agree," Doreen confirmed. "So somebody heard that this place was a treasure trove, and the question is, how will we figure out who that is and where they are? What if they are in the house now?"

"Do you really think somebody was in the house overnight, just because of some nightmares?" Mack asked her.

She nodded. "I just couldn't stop thinking about," she muttered. "This place is massive. They could be hidden anywhere. Plus, I'm done here. I'm tired of sleeping on the floor."

"And yet you have a new air mattress," he pointed out.

She shrugged. "Apparently I'm getting spoiled in my old age."

He laughed. "Does that mean no camping?"

She shrugged. "I don't know what that even means," she admitted. "If it means sleeping on an uncomfortable air mattress, then maybe no camping."

"Have you never been camping?" he asked her.

She frowned at him. "When would I have gone camping?"

He winced and nodded. "Good point. We'll have to fix that."

"If you say so," she muttered, rolling her eyes. "Can't say I'm any too eager if that means sleepless nights."

"You'll love camping," he told her, with a smile, "and, if nothing else, we can always rent a cabin."

"Oh, a cabin sounds good," she said brightly.

He rolled his eyes and asked, "Will you finally tell me that you don't like something?"

"There's lots I don't like," she declared, "and sleeping in a sleeping bag or on an air mattress is one of them."

He laughed. "I'll keep that in mind."

"Good enough," she said.

They quickly finished up breakfast, let the moving crew all back into the house again, and then Nick announced, "Let's go. We need to get to the bank so we'll be there when they open. We have to make it to our meeting on time."

They loaded up the duffel bags, the bonds, even the stock certificates and various other critical paperwork they had collected.

Nick noted, "Luckily Mathew had a working scanner in his home office. I already scanned these documents, before we put them in the safe deposit boxes."

Doreen frowned at the animals. "I don't want to leave them behind."

Mack turned to Nick and said, "I don't know that the

banks are prepared for her."

Nick gave a one-arm shrug. "They do allow a certain leeway for eccentric people with money," he offered, with a sideways glance at her.

She glared at him. "A lot of strangers are here, and that upsets the animals. Thaddeus hasn't been doing well, and I don't know why. I just don't want to leave them alone with strangers lurking around the house."

"Do you want me to stay behind?" Nick asked.

"No," she replied instantly. "You need to come too."

They just waited for her to digest this problem and to work out a solution.

She nodded and announced, "We'll take them with us. That's all there is to it. If the banks want to see eccentric, they will see eccentric." Mack winced, and she glared at him. "Don't tell me that you think I should leave them behind."

"It's not that I think you should leave them behind," he began, "and I understand why you don't want to. Yet, in some circumstances, they just can't be—"

"But what if something happens to them here? This isn't their home," Doreen interrupted, glaring at him. "And we could be gone for hours. Think about it. How will they feel being here for hours without any of us with them? What with all the men going back and forth and the doors opening," she argued, "we'll lose Goliath—even Mugs and Thaddeus—and I certainly don't want to lock them up in one of the rooms. What if someone opens the door to that room and lets them all out?"

Now, with Mack and Nick on board, she packed up the animals, along with their other treasures. When they arrived at the first bank, the manager was waiting for them.

Mack looked over at his brother. "What kind of reaction

do you think we'll get when they see the animals?"

"Honest to God, with the amount of money she's bringing in, he should be singing her praises, bending over backward, and possibly hugging and kissing those animals," he muttered.

Mack sighed. "We'll see if they give us a problem."

"I doubt it," Nick said, "but you never know."

As they got out, with the four-legged animals on leashes, the banker looked at Doreen, surprised, but then smiled. "I don't think I've ever seen a cat on a leash before."

"This one's been especially trained," she replied. "And, of course, when you have therapy animals, it's pretty necessary." She figured that angle would seal the deal, keeping her animals with her.

"Of course, of course," he agreed. "Come on in."

They went inside, headed to his office, where he offered them tea. She accepted and settled back with her animals on their best behavior.

The manager began, "I understand we have quite a few issues to deal with."

"I don't know about *issues*," she clarified, "depending on the banking process, but I have a rather large deposit."

The bank manager almost salivated at the term. "When you say *large*?"

"Yes," she repeated, "*large*." Then she pointed to the two duffel bags.

His eyebrows shot up, and he seemed to be at a loss for words.

"So," she added, "this is my lawyer, and he set up this appointment. This is my fiancé, who happens to also be a Kelowna police detective. I inherited my estranged husband's property, and he had this money in a home safe."

"Oh my." The banker eyed them all nervously. "So, this is all legal and aboveboard?"

"Yes," she stated. Both Mack and Nick nodded. Nick produced documentation to ease his mind: Mathew's death certificate and the probate document appointing Doreen as both executrix and sole heir.

The manager read both documents, smiling again. "In that case," he replied, rubbing his hands together, "do we know how much it is?"

"I haven't counted it," she replied, shrugging.

"Then we will get it counted immediately."

"I want that process witnessed by us," she murmured.

Mack nodded. "That's a good idea. Would you mind?"

"Not at all." He picked up the two duffel bags and went to the room next door, right beside the manager's office.

The two offices shared one inner wall that was completely glass, so Doreen and Mack and Nick could see without getting up from their seats. A woman entered the second office with a cash-counting machine. She plugged it in and immediately inserted the money, batch by batch. Doreen watched for a minute and then shrugged and sat back. However, the bank manager stared in fascination, his gaze switching back and forth again.

"I guess it's rather a large amount, and you don't see that on a regular basis," she noted rather delicately.

He flushed. "No, we don't generally see hoards coming in from paranoid …" He stopped and winced, looking a little flushed in the face, almost stammering, "From … customers."

"For the record, I wasn't the paranoid one," she stated.

He smiled gratefully at her for letting him off the hook. "So, we just need to wait for that process," he noted. "I gather you were also inquiring about some other accounts. Which accounts do you wish to go through?"

At that Nick handed over some paperwork and explained, "We need to transfer all her late husband's accounts into her name only, and we also need access to any safe deposit boxes here in his name."

"Oh my," he muttered, "let me get somebody else to help."

And, with that, it all began, and it took hours. She couldn't believe that it literally took hours before the money was counted, the accounts were changed, and they were finally being led to the safe deposit boxes.

She asked Mack in an undertone, "What about the paperwork for the stocks and bonds and riders and all?"

"We'll put that in a safe deposit box as well."

"Good, because the bank manager doesn't need to know anything about that, does he?"

"No, I think we've overwhelmed him enough for one day."

She laughed. "I think this may be a once-in-a-lifetime occurrence for him."

"Probably a good thing at that," he whispered, smiling at her. "Are you sure you want to do this?"

"Do what?" she asked, with a shrug. "We're just putting money in the bank." Then she stopped, looked at Nick. "Aren't we?"

"Yes, that's all we're doing," he confirmed. "Just putting money in the bank."

Mack looked at her. "Do you want any for … running around?"

"No," she said quickly. "Do you even need running-around money at this level?"

His grin widened. "I don't know. You don't seem to spend money as it is."

"True," she admitted, "but I didn't have money to spend before."

"That's okay," Mack replied. "You've been without for so long that you've forgotten that you need to spend money too."

"Do I?" she asked, giving him a sideways glance.

"Yes, you deserve to have peace of mind and to know you can get what you need at any time, not just what you need. You should get what you want as well. Besides, it's part of the economy, Doreen. If you spend it, other people can eat too."

She frowned at that and shrugged. "You'll have to explain that a little more later," she muttered. "Right about now, I really just want to be done with this banking stuff."

Next, they were led into a small room, and the safe deposit boxes were brought in. She looked at him and sighed. "Yeah, I can't even remember this process."

"Any idea what's inside?"

"Nope," she muttered, "not at all."

When the woman left, she opened the first one, and Mack whistled. "Good God."

"Yeah," she agreed. "I don't remember this part, not at all."

And inside were guns, … three small handguns.

Chapter 16

THE THREE WEAPONS lay in the drawer, a silent threat of a world she hadn't known with Mathew. She looked over at Mack and asked, "What do we do with them?"

He took photos, wrote down the registration numbers on each of them, and stated, "We'll check into this, but, for now, they'll stay here."

Under the guns were wads of cash … again.

She frowned at it. "I understand paranoia when you are doing shady things, but this is over-the-top."

"It is, and this is what I would consider more escape money. He may have had guns and cash stashed everywhere."

"He did in the house, as we know," she said pointedly. "I just hadn't expected so much of it."

"Neither did I." He looked over at his brother, who was shaking his head as he stared at it.

She suggested, "Let's leave it here because it's safe, right?" Both men nodded at her, as she looked for reassurance. "I mean, as long as you're telling me it's safe."

"It is safe," Nick confirmed.

Mack added, "These are secure banks, so short of anybody breaking into the bank—which isn't as easy as the movies make it sound—this cash is safe."

"Or, while we have the opportunity to deposit chunks like this without anybody asking more questions, should we add this money to the pile on deposit here?" she asked.

"I like that even better," Mack replied. "I don't know where this money came from, but considering it's here, and it's part of Mathew's estate …"

"Exactly, especially if my name is technically on all this."

And, with that decision done, he pulled out the cash and stacked it on the counter, then pointed to the second box. "Next."

"Wow," she muttered, with a slight shiver. "Who knew it was Christmas?" She opened it and looked inside. "I don't know about this one. It's all paperwork."

With that, Nick stepped up and reached inside and pulled it out. He started to laugh.

"What is it?" she asked.

"These are deeds to his properties," he shared shuffling the papers, "As you said, four in the Vancouver area and one in France," he noted, staring at it, "and another one over in England."

"At least he didn't purchase anymore." Doreen shook her head. "Oh, I get it now. Remember what he told me, how he had something better than money? He had another whole life in France he could run to. Along with the money, they represent his retaining his freedom, right?"

Nick nodded, staring at her. "That would make a whole lot of sense. He could come in here, take the cash, grab all his deeds, if he needed them. He probably had multiple copies of all this stashed at his other homes."

She turned back to Mack, who had a resigned look on

his face. "I'm sorry. I didn't know."

"I know you didn't, sweetie."

"Then don't look at me as if I'm to blame."

He started to laugh and explained, "Nobody is to blame, but I don't know that Mathew would be particularly happy right now."

"Nope, he sure wouldn't."

With all the paperwork collected, she asked, "How about we take those stocks and bonds and all this paperwork back to Kelowna with us?"

Mack asked, "So, you don't want to leave it here?"

"No, let's close this safe deposit box." She stopped to look at the weapons and shook her head. "I don't know what to do with those."

Mack nodded. "Let's take them with us too. None of these have been fired recently. We'll use one of these duffel bags."

And with that, they loaded up all the paperwork and the guns in one duffel bag and put the cash in the other bag and walked back out to the manager, who brought them back to his office.

"Anything else I can help you with today?" he asked.

She shared, "Let's close the two safe deposit boxes. We'll take the contents home, but we have more cash for you to add to my account."

"More cash?" he repeated, staring at her.

She nodded. "He was always so paranoid."

He quickly had the money counted, and she swallowed when she realized just that little bit was $75,000. Minutes later it had been added to her new account. She looked down at the numbers on deposit, and they were just so large that it was hard for her to make sense out of any of it. Yet she kept her cool and didn't say anything as the transactions were finalized. Then she looked over at Mack and asked, "Are we done now?"

"Almost," he whispered.

And, with that, they said their goodbyes to the bank manager, thanked him profusely, and walked outside.

She whispered to Mack, "What on earth will we do with the weapons?"

"I'll take them back to Kelowna, and we'll get them analyzed to confirm they haven't been involved in any crimes."

"Oh, that's a good idea," she stated, with a nod. "Mathew, ... you sure left me a mess."

"He also left you a very wealthy woman," Nick pointed out.

As he pointed to Mack's truck in the parking lot, she asked Nick, "Now where?"

"We have a second bank and a third, each with another safe deposit box." She groaned, yet Nick laughed. "Just think of it as treasure hunting."

"Yeah, and what if it's got more weapons in it?"

Nick shrugged. "You did say that Mathew liked to collect weapons, so it's quite possible that these are all legal."

"It may be quite possible," she noted, "but that's not exactly something I want to own."

"I'll handle these. We can turn them in to law enforcement office to be destroyed." He smiled at her and added, "Unless you want to keep any."

She shuddered. "Nope, I sure don't."

The manager in charge of the second bank was able to hide his surprise and awe much better as to her entourage of animals. Plus, they were faster at counting the cash in Mathew's sole safe deposit box, closing that down, as well as changing over any accounts in Mathew's name to new accounts in her name. She got another debit card too.

The manager of the third and final bank was nowhere near as welcoming to their furry and feathered friends, so Mack had to stay in the vehicle with the animals. She took a dislike to the manager and to the bank because of it.

Nick nudged her forward and whispered, "I know you're not happy about it, but let's go in, take care of the business that needs to be done, and get out."

She didn't argue about it, thinking she would transfer the funds from this account to the first bank, where they were nicer about her animals. They were allowed inside the private viewing room, after revealing the two legal documents with them. Once the safe deposit box had been brought over to her, she asked Nick, "Is this the last of them?"

"That we know of, yes," he muttered, "but obviously we'll continue to look for more. For now, this appears to be it." She opened it up. He groaned. "Good God."

It was stuffed with cash.

Doreen muttered, "This will be a problem because we don't have a nice bank manager to work with here."

"No, but we can take it to the nice bank, if you want." He nodded at the duffel bag with him and quickly loaded up the wads of cash.

She just stared at it. "It's just so unreal."

"At this point," Nick shared, looking a bit grim, "I'm thinking it's all just play money."

"It's an unbelievable amount, Nick."

"It sure is," he agreed, "but it also reveals the very deep level of psychosis Mathew had."

"I had no idea," she admitted, frowning at Nick, "but

Mathew needed help, didn't he?"

Nick smiled. "But would he ever accept help?"

She immediately shook her head. "No. Even though he never really got sick, anytime he had even a hint of a cold or something coming on, if I suggested anything, he got angry. I couldn't tell him anything."

"So, hang on to that thought. This was who he was, what he did, how he behaved, and all about the choices he made—again and again. There was nothing you could have done about it."

"I didn't try."

"Did you have much opportunity to try?"

"No, I got butted out of everything very quickly."

"So, keep that in mind," he reminded her. "As soon as he was ready to let you go, he—don't take it the wrong way—but he dumped you on the street like a sack of garbage. Sorry, that was a little too graphic."

"No, it's perfect because it's pretty well what it was."

"It blows me away that he had all this money and still he wouldn't share a penny of it with you."

"I don't think he ever thought he had enough," she explained.

After they had emptied all the cash from the safe deposit box into the duffel bag, they left the private room and asked that the bank close that box in that name. Then Nick and Doreen approached the manager again and asked to see if any accounts were in Mathew's name. The manager balked, until Nick explained the situation, showing him legal documents supporting Nick's presence here in his legal capacity and Doreen in hers as executrix and sole heir.

The manager searched through the bank's records. "I find no accounts in that name." Then he did a double take.

"There is, however, one under the name of Doreen Merriweather."

Nick nodded. "We would like access to that account, please, and to make a deposit. This is Doreen Merriweather. She goes by her maiden name now as Doreen Montgomery."

It took a bit more to sort through the identification process, but, with Nick hanging on to the duffel bag in his arms, the bank manager let her see the account balance before her deposit today. She didn't want to use this bank, but she went ahead and deposited the money here, while requesting an address change on the account and a debit card, so she could transfer this money elsewhere.

She got a printed copy of her current statement, updated to show her Kelowna address, plus a notice of closure as to the bank box. She thanked the helpful clerks and headed back to Mack's vehicle, Nick right beside her.

Just as they got outside, he whispered, "Just out of curiosity, how much money is in there?"

"A freaking ton," she muttered, "especially for an account in my name. The final balance is over $250,000."

He just nodded and didn't say anything.

"Are you okay?" she asked.

"Sure," he said. "I'm just thinking about how different your life will be."

"Incredibly different. Yet the good news is," she added, as they walked up to Mack, "that *I* won't be any different at all."

Chapter 17

DOREEN HUDDLED OVER her coffee the next morning, an exhausted Goliath curled up in her arms, Mugs at her feet, and Thaddeus tucked up under her hair. She heard his breath moving in and out in the softest of snores. She looked over at Mack and Nick, both busy on their laptops. "Is it just me," she said, with a scoff, "or do you guys need a holiday after this … holiday?"

Both men snorted.

She nodded. "Is this what holidays are supposed to be like?"

"Nope," Mack declared, with a laugh. "Yet often they do end up that way."

Nick agreed. "People take holidays to do big projects, like landscaping and home renovations and stuff," Nick noted, "and they basically say the same thing. They go back to work, exhausted."

"I have to admit that's how I feel right now," she muttered. Mugs gave a hefty sigh and rolled over onto his side. "Even the animals appear to be completely out of sorts here."

"I don't know that they're out of sorts as much as they appear to be tuckered out," Mack said, as he looked down at

Mugs. "It's been quite the adventure for them."

"For Mugs, at least, this is familiar turf," she noted, "although I don't know that it's a good memory for him."

"And that's a good point," Mack said. "I wonder if animals have nightmares about places where they used to live."

"Nightmares, dreams, who knows what else," she muttered. "I'm sure a lot of times that Mugs's life wasn't as nice as it could have been."

He chuckled. "I think you've been making up for any suffering he may have had to go through."

She smiled. "He was always my dog, and the two of us were inseparable. Most of the gardeners didn't even want him around because, of course, he was a dog and liked to dig in the gardens and cause all kinds of chaos. It wasn't that they particularly cared. At least I don't think they did, but Mathew did, and that caused problems in their world, since it was on them to make sure everything was perfect."

"Mathew really did have a problem with perfection, didn't he?"

"I think it was his way of controlling his environment." She yawned again and slumped lower in her chair, making Thaddeus shift on her shoulder.

"Thaddeus has been really quiet on this trip," Mack pointed out.

"I know, and I think, like the rest of us, he just wants to go home."

Mack nodded. "It would help if we were getting somewhere here."

"Yeah, and what about Daniel?" she muttered. "The detective who told us we couldn't leave without permission?"

Mack shook his head. "I'm pretty sure I can get that reversed if the captain knows where we're going and that I have a job to go home to," he pointed out.

"I don't know about that," Nick countered. "Still, I think Daniel just liked being able to tell you that."

Mack smiled and added, "It's definitely an interesting experience being on the other side of the law."

She looked at him with amusement. "Yeah," she said, with a smirk. "Not so nice sometimes, is it?"

He smiled at her, got up to give her a kiss on her temple, then headed to the fridge and pulled out some eggs.

"You really are a lifesaver, you know that?" she muttered.

He laughed. "Because I can scramble eggs?" he asked in a teasing voice.

"Yeah, plus you don't expect me to do it."

"Nope. I want to get fed today."

At that, Nick burst out laughing.

She glared at him and stated, "I'm pretty good with eggs, you know?"

"I'm glad to hear it," Nick noted. "I think we've all had enough to deal with these last few days."

"You're not kidding."

Just then, Scott called out from the side kitchen door, bypassing the greenhouse. Mack opened it and let him in.

"Hey," he greeted everyone in his usual bright, jovial mood. "How's everyone this morning?"

She stared at him and grumbled, "You do know I could hate you."

He looked at her in surprise, almost hurt. "What did I do?"

"You're bright and cheerful this morning, while I feel absolutely done in."

He smiled at her. "For me, this is all about treasure hunting. I'm excited about what I'm finding here. But, for you, it's exhausting, tiring, emotional, and all that other stuff, so you have my sincerest apologies for all of it. On the other hand," he added, hesitating a moment, "I woke up in the middle of the night, wondering about something." He held up his hands, pleading. "Please feel free to tell me that this has nothing to do with me. I'm just asking."

She smiled over at him. "Spit it out, Scott," she said encouragingly. "I'm sure at this point we have no more secrets anyway."

Scott asked, "Do you have any idea what is happening here with these murders?"

"Because of the second murder," she muttered, nodding.

Mack chuckled. "If you feel uneasy, Scott, that is normal. However, we seem to have safety in numbers."

"And you don't know anything?" Scott asked.

"Nope, nobody tells us anything," she said. "And, of course, the more of these things that I remove from the property, the more suspicious it looks to the officers out there."

"But you're entitled to all of it," Scott pointed out, "so it really doesn't matter."

"Maybe not to us, but to them?" She left her question hanging.

Scott thanked them for putting his mind at ease.

Doreen offered him some coffee and to stay for breakfast. He smiled and helped himself to a cup.

Mack looped his arms behind Doreen and just tugged her back so she rested against his chest. Thaddeus squawked from her shoulder, realized Mack was behind him, and immediately moved to higher ground.

She chuckled. "He really does prefer to be as high as possible."

"It's the only reason he likes me," Mack teased, with a smirk. "I'm just the next step up in life."

At that, Thaddeus ruffled his feathers and crooned, "Thaddeus loves Mack. Thaddeus loves Mack."

She smiled at him, as Mack looked down at his feathered friend. "Hey, buddy, that's a really nice thing for you to say."

Thaddeus didn't say anything more, just settled into his new roosting spot.

Nick looked over at him and nodded. "The animals really do accept you as their own, don't they?"

"Yeah," Mack confirmed. "Mostly because I'm always there to help out when they are saving Doreen," he added, with an eye roll.

Scott listened and watched with avid interest and noted, "Seems there's quite the story in that."

"An awful lot of stories," she clarified, with a headshake. "I have to admit that Mack's right. The animals have saved my life on numerous occasions."

Nick added, "Hopefully after this, you won't end up in the position where anybody has to save you."

"I would love that," she stated, "and it would be nice to think I'm not in danger all the time."

"If you would just stay out of trouble," Mack muttered.

She looked over at him and gave him an eye roll. "What he really means," she said to Scott, "is, if I would stay out of his cases."

Scott chuckled. "And yet it seems as if the two of you have quite the relationship."

"That we do," she murmured.

Soon a breakfast of pancakes and eggs and some fresh fruit was plated before everyone. After they all had their fill, Doreen asked Scott, "How are we doing on the furniture?"

"All the bedrooms are cleaned out. The larger pieces from the living room are gone. The two dining room sets have to be packaged a little bit differently, but we'll get to that."

"Is something like a used dining room set even worth selling?" Nick asked.

Scott shrugged. "It depends on the set. These are easily worth over one-quarter of a million dollars each."

The instant disappearance of all color from Nick's cheeks was enough to make his brother laugh.

Mack said, "See? You're just stepping into this world. I've been dealing with Doreen for a whole lot longer, and I can tell you that, at this point in time, one-quarter of a million for a dining room set makes me shake my head but doesn't faze me because I know she would never want it."

Doreen nodded. "People would just freak out when I let Thaddeus here walk across it with his claws."

Scott looked at her in horror.

"Exactly," she said. "I don't need furniture in that category."

"Anyway," Scott began, staring from her to Mack, "the packers and movers should get another good day in today. I think we're probably close to 80 percent wrapped up."

"For all three floors?" she asked. Scott nodded. "So what else is there?" Doreen asked him.

"The trailers for the cars are coming today," he shared, "and I believe we have two of them booked, so that will go pretty quickly, and it will be a big relief."

"You're not kidding," she muttered. "And to think there's that kind of money sitting in the garage."

He looked at her and laughed. "There's that kind of money sitting here in most rooms."

She shrugged. "I don't care about this stuff. Honestly, I don't care about the cars either. That was definitely a Mathew thing."

"Is there anything here you do care about?"

"Yes," she declared, "the painting of Mugs in the master bedroom."

Mack stared at her. "There is?"

"Yes, I saw it earlier in that little alcove. I thought for sure Mathew would have gotten rid of it, but it's not in a prominent position, so maybe he just didn't notice." With that, she led them all to the master suite, around the corner to where the alcove led to one of the seating areas. "We should take this downstairs with us and put it in my bedroom. I don't want to forget it."

Mack nodded, still staring at it. "Look at that." Mugs came up beside him, sat down, looked up at the painting, and woofed. "That's right, big guy. That's you."

Thaddeus poked his head out and squawked, "Big Guy. Big Guy. Big Guy."

"Ah, no," she murmured. She stroked Thaddeus on the cheek and said, "Sorry, Thaddeus. Big Guy isn't here."

He glared at her. "Big Guy. Big Guy. Big Guy."

"Nope, not here, but we'll go home soon, and then you can visit with Big Guy."

With Scott eyeing her curiously, she explained that Thaddeus liked to go for play dates with another friendly bird.

Scott shook his head. "Such a fascinating life you have."

"Maybe," she muttered.

"No *maybe* about it," Scott declared. "When you're ready, you should write a book."

"Write a book?" she repeated in astonishment.

"Yes, you have no idea how many people would be fascinated by everything that's gone on in your life."

She couldn't see it herself, but even Nick chuckled. "That's not a half-bad idea."

"It is a terrible idea," she argued, "and nobody would care about what I do or what I've done."

"Yes, they would," Nick countered, "all the more so because of the craziness in your world in terms of treasure."

She frowned.

"It's true," Scott agreed. "Everybody loves to hear about a good treasure hunt."

"Maybe *you* should write a book then. It's certainly nothing on my near horizon," she muttered.

"Just think," Mack added, turning to look at her, "with all those titles you assign to these cases, you could do a breakdown of each and every one of them in a book format."

She stared at him in astonishment. "Are you suggesting that I write a book too?" she asked.

"Why not?" he asked, and then he grinned. "Would it keep you out of my current cases?"

"No," she replied instantly. "It'll just have me coming back, looking for more. You already know that."

"Oh, in that case, maybe not then," he said, with an eye roll. "So, I'll get started on loading those breakfast dishes in the dishwasher."

"I can help you with that," Doreen replied, now facing Scott, raising one eyebrow.

He replied to her unasked question, "I'm busy and already distracted. It'll be another full day for me, and I still have more things to organize." He asked Doreen, "One last time …"

"The answer is no," she said crossly. "I do not want any of this."

"There are some uncut gems if you would like them instead."

She frowned at him. "Why would I care?"

He just stared at her for a long moment, wordless.

Mack wrapped his arms around her shoulders, nudging her toward the kitchen. "She really means it," he told Scott. "The Mathew stage of her life is over."

"Got it," Scott confirmed, sending a smile in her direction. "I guess whenever you want a piece of jewelry, you can find something you like and get it for yourself."

"Exactly," she replied, with a shrug. Then she held up the ring on her finger.

He gasped and asked, "May I see it?" She walked closer and showed it to him. "Now that is stunning... and absolutely wonderful."

Mack smiled, adding, "It's not worth even a tiny fraction of any of Mathew's jewelry collection."

"It's worth far more," Doreen declared, "because it's from someone who loves me, and it's from one of the cases I worked on with Mack, involving his family and some lost jewels."

Scott nodded and started to laugh. "In that case, I understand fully."

"Good. Now let's get this day started."

Chapter 18

DOREEN WOULDN'T EVEN have noticed when more moving trucks rolled down the driveway, except for the noise that they made, followed by Mugs's need to raise an even louder alarm. She groaned, then looked back over at Mack. "Hopefully those are the furniture trucks."

He got up and said, "Let me check." He headed to the front door as she waited until he returned. It didn't take long. He nodded. "Scott's bringing in the furniture trucks, and, as it turns out, the car trailers are here too. Do you want to watch as they get loaded?"

She thought about it, then shook her head. "Honestly, I want to find a quiet corner and just think about these crazy murders."

He grimaced. "We don't have any jurisdiction down here. You remember that, right?"

"I know that," she grumbled, "but I also know that, if we don't do something, we could end up on the chopping block."

He smiled at her. "I don't think it'll be that dire, not when we have Detective Clark and Captain Hawkins on this investigation now. Good riddance, Daniel."

She wasn't so sure, and, by the time she had made herself a cup of coffee and headed into Mathew's home office, a room she still hadn't gone completely through, she realized that, without Daniel around, she could think a little more clearly about all the events.

It made sense to her that somebody, somewhere, somehow, had told the criminals that this unoccupied house was a haul just waiting to be made. But it didn't change the fact that someone had killed somebody—two somebodies—and both on Mathew's property—now her property. And that estimated sales figure had not even been disclosed. She didn't know whether two dead bodies on the property would raise or lower the value of the estate. Because people, … well, they were just people.

It blew her away that people could have such a macabre interest in homes where murders happened. Yet being involved with these cold cases to the extent that Doreen was, in theory, it shouldn't be hard to figure out other people's interests too. Regardless, since no one was living permanently in Mathew's house, she would gladly leave it up to Nick and Mathew's probate lawyer and Scott to handle the disposal of all the assets, including the house itself.

With that thought, she started to go through his desk drawers, looking to see if anything could be an issue.

She wondered if Daniel had gone through these drawers on one of the earlier days before he had been escorted in and out of this main house. Regardless, she didn't know whether that was a good thing or a bad thing. As she worked her way through the desk, she opened up the two secret drawers and pulled out the file that she knew Mathew had always kept. Whether she was happy about the contents or not didn't matter and wasn't relevant.

As she sat there, she muttered, "Mathew, you sure were messed up. You left all this here for me to deal with, and I'm sure, in your own mind, that was never your intention. Yet something went wrong between you and Robin, and it went steadily downhill after that. More than downhill for Robin too."

They seemed to be a poisonous couple, and everything they touched turned to dust. It all had just blown up. The fact that Doreen still had to deal with Robin's house too was enough to make her groan, but, then again, maybe Robin's association with some of her shady people had brought Mathew's house to the attention of that element. And now they had all come to clean it out, which made a lot of sense to Doreen. As she thought about it, she realized how lucky she was that she and Mack and Nick had come down when they did. Otherwise, if they'd left this house vacant much longer, for all she knew, this would have been cleaned out already.

Sure, not the heavy bulky furniture probably, but, if anybody had found the safes, the jewelry, the bags of cash, and all those bearer's bonds, that would be gone for sure. There was just so much here that it was ridiculous. Most of it was gone, just with their day spent going to three different banks. The rest would be going soon, with Scott now responsible for a lot of it. A good deal more would be gone by the end of the day too. And that was something she couldn't wait for. She looked forward to some joy in knowing that all this would finally reach a certain amount of closure.

When Mack found her a little bit later, she was still here, going through the drawers.

"Anything?" he asked.

"Nothing," she said, "which is weird because he always

kept scratch pads to write stuff on, just bits and pieces, random thoughts. It wasn't even so much that he would keep notes of any value or importance, but notes to himself, notes about what he was working on."

"Did you find his notes?"

She shook her head. "I feel that's missing. A pad is here, … but the top sheet has been ripped off."

He came around, took a look, and asked, "So, what are you thinking?"

She shrugged. "I don't know, but there is the potential that somebody else removed that note."

He frowned. "Are you talking about an intruder, like here, right now?"

"Not right now, no, but I guess I'm considering that maybe an intruder came in over the last few weeks. I mean, we do have one dead person, and now a second one, so something is going on."

"Right," he agreed, "so in theory somebody could have been here in Mathew's office, but they wouldn't necessarily know what was important about his notes."

She frowned. "The indentations are here, so maybe we can read what was written on the previous page."

Mack nodded, coming closer to her. "Do you have a pencil in there?" She pulled out an old-style school pencil. He smiled. "To think that Mathew had a mundane pencil in there as well?" He shook his head. He dragged the pencil lead across the indented area in a smooth motion. Almost all the lettering came up. He stepped up behind her to read it and then frowned. "Good God."

"I know. He seemed to be making an inventory list."

He read it out softly. "*Move jewelry out of safe, relocate to safe deposit box, relocate cash into secondary safe deposit box.*"

There were a bunch of other notes, but Mack seemed stuck on these he had read.

"Do you think somebody saw this?" she murmured. "If they did and thought jewelry was in here, maybe they found something. That's a huge haul that we found, so maybe they found other jewelry elsewhere. Still, I doubt that anybody else would have found this note because it was in one of his hidden drawers. In fact, it was in the hidden drawer behind the hidden drawer."

She frowned, pondering that for a moment. "If anybody was looking for this, it could have only been an employee, someone who saw Mathew writing some notes like this. In other words, someone who stayed here for days or weeks on end, doing whatever work for Mathew, and, therefore, he may not have even noticed them around him, even in his office."

"Like his caretaker, outside his office window, working on the yard below."

"Exactly," she declared. "And what happened to the caretaker?"

Mack shrugged. "Mathew's probate attorney told Nick how the caretaker hired by the property management company was told *not* to come. There was some confusion as to whether the probate attorney did this on his own or whether the property management company told the probate attorney to do this. Heck, some third party may have called the true caretaker, lying about being a representative of either one of them."

"Regardless, what are the chances," she began, staring at him, "that Mathew's probate attorney, or the property management firm that he hired, who then hired a caretaker, found some of this when dealing with the estate claims or the property issues or whatnot and decided that he should be the one to find everything? He could have removed whatever he wanted before the place was sold, before we came down, and we would never have known."

Just then Nick walked into the room. "What's this about Mathew's local probate lawyer?"

She looked over at him and stated, "I know it's a far-fetched idea, but the probate lawyer that you've been dealing with …"

"Yeah, what about him?" he asked, as he walked over, took a look at the notepad with the scribbled message revealed, and frowned.

"Is there any chance that he would have come here to the house and maybe helped himself?"

He looked at her in astonishment. "Are you thinking more is missing?" he asked, as he glanced around.

"No, not so much missing, especially without some stranger being able to find the safes or even knowing about them," she clarified. "I'm not sure anybody would have been able to find everything, but I guess I'm just wondering …"

He turned to her and prodded, "*Wondering*?"

"Wondering if we had somebody who knew about all this stuff, potentially from this list of Mathew's, somebody who stayed close by, thinking they could dig up the goods themselves and remove them before anyone was the wiser. I'm not sure how we would know what was here and what wasn't."

"Let me answer this in parts," Nick began. "In theory, yes, we don't know what was here and what wasn't. After all, Robin was here and changed some things, it seems. As for any court documents revealing the treasures hidden in this house, the probate inventory does not do that. There should be full insurance paperwork and pictures of all the valuable items but that's not always the case. It is not a list so defined that thieves are ticking off items on their *Let's steal this* list. Nobody would know what was or wasn't here, not without a personal review of every square foot of this mansion. I mean, even you are still finding stuff," he pointed out. "Thank God we came when we did though."

She nodded. "I was just thinking that. Yet we found a dead man in the greenhouse within the first hour of our arrival here. So I'm wondering if maybe Mathew's probate lawyer knew about something, like bags of cash, for instance."

Mack asked Nick, "Would the estate lawyer have known about any of these particularities with Mathew's hoarding and hiding tendencies? His so-called collections?"

"It's hard to know what somebody would have known, versus what they wouldn't, especially in light of Mathew's tendency toward secrets," Nick pointed out, looking back and forth between Doreen and his brother. "Would Mathew really trust his own attorneys with this info? I sincerely doubt it. My vote is on a disgruntled employee. After all, a disgruntled employee was the one who killed Mathew, right? Plus, I know you've got this thing about lawyers, Doreen."

She smiled and nodded. "And about police detectives named Daniel. So I'm not saying that Mathew's probate attorney and this property management company are any more corrupt than any others. I'm just wondering who would have known about the hidden stashes in this house, because most of the players I had anything to do with are dead. And, if the local property management company hired this caretaker, then told him not to show up because he wasn't needed, what are the chances that was set up so the same property management company could be here, looking around for treasure?"

Nick shook his head at her. "I just went to see Mathew's probate attorney to drill down on the banks that Mathew used, and that attorney told me that he hadn't been in the house. Ever. Now it does make more sense for the local property management company to send a trusted employee to view the property, but the estate attorney couldn't confirm that."

"I know this will sound even weirder," she began, wincing as she looked over at him.

Nick crossed his arms and glared at her.

"Is the lawyer that you saw in person the other day the same lawyer that you've been talking to all the time on the phone?"

He just stared at her. "I don't get it."

"She's asking if it could be a different person, someone impersonating the local lawyer," Mack explained.

"I still don't get it." Nick looked from one to the other. "Are you saying the lawyer I just met with isn't a lawyer?"

"He might be. He might not be. However, it's also possible that whoever you were dealing with from the beginning on the phone isn't the same person you're dealing with now in person."

"As far as I know, it's exactly the same person I've been dealing with right from the beginning," Nick said in exasperation. "No offense, but the two of you have *conspiracy theory* written all over you."

"Maybe," she conceded. "However, most cons work because the targets are so honest that they cannot fathom someone acting in a dishonest way. Right? Even in theory?" She waited for Nick to begrudgingly nod. "We also have two dead people and a house full of money. Those are facts. They cannot be changed. So anybody who is thinking that Mathew may have owed them—or even that the world may have owed them—could very well see Mathew's house as a way to get out of the criminal life they've been leading and start fresh."

"You certainly can't go around accusing people," Nick noted.

"And I'm not. I'm just asking you because we have to consider that anybody and everybody connected to this mess *who had access to the house* is a potential murder suspect or just a plain thief."

"Even Mathew's local probate lawyer?" Nick asked, a note of humor in his voice.

She sighed. "I'm not accusing you. I'm not even accusing Mathew's probate attorney, but I wonder if they mentioned anything to anybody. I wonder if somebody contacted one of the two about showing this house. I wonder if somebody contacted the estate lawyer about the disposal of the assets, wondering if they were in the will or something."

"Ah," Nick said, settling down some, "now that's a different story. What if somebody did ask and then decided that, because they weren't in the will, they might just come help themselves to something here? What if someone of questionable wealth and a really bad credit score wanted a walk-through of this house, on the pretext of buying it? Okay. That is something I can ask Mathew's probate attorney and even the property management company," Nick confirmed. "Obviously, I won't ask if either came here and helped themselves."

She grinned at him. "I would, but … that's just me."

He stared at her, then turned to Mack. "Please tell me

that she wouldn't have done that."

Mack groaned. "You have no idea what this woman does. If she thinks she can get somebody to talk, if she can get some answers, she would not hold back one bit."

She chuckled. "I can't hold back because we have all kinds of things going on at this house. Plus, the bottom line is, two dead people were found here. We only just recently found proof that Butch killed Pete, but we have no murderer found for Butch, and I don't know how we're supposed to sell the house with that on the property record."

"Believe it or not, it won't be bad," Nick replied. "There's a certain amount of notoriety in owning a house like this, and it won't be cheap regardless. It's a massive property, and the pool of people who could both afford it and would want it will be fairly specific. Very wealthy *eccentric* people sometimes seek something unique, with a history, and this would certainly qualify."

She nodded.

"And if anybody thought there was still treasure to be found here, the future buyers would be all over that as well," Nick shared, with a headshake. "Including the realtors who want to check it out too. Those same realtors want to sell big-ticket properties. So telling people about murders and two dead bodies and hidden treasure may seal the deal. Regardless, the property will remain insured, while the realtors are all secured, bonded, restricted in terms of what people can take out of the house, but you know …"

"Once it's empty," Mack interjected, "we'll do another check."

Doreen shared, "Scott did say it would likely be empty soon, at least 80 to 90 percent of it."

"Hopefully he can make it a little higher than that,"

Mack said. "We still have a lot of stuff to deal with."

Doreen clarified, "I agree, but leaving some of the furniture is a good thing. Houses do sell faster if they have furniture in them, so people can envision how the rooms can be used. It would cost a fortune to hire someone to stage this place."

Mack added, "I don't think the lack of furniture will be a factor here. I would think these big old homes take a long time to sell anyway, going back to what Nick said about a limited number of people with the money and the fortitude to live where two men were murdered."

She nodded. "With the notoriety attached to it …"

"It could go either way," Nick noted. "It could sell faster because of the murders—or not."

"Right," she murmured. "All of it is just frustrating. … I don't know what's going on."

"No, but you raised an interesting point," Nick admitted, looking a bit unnerved. "I'll talk to the local probate lawyer. I didn't notice any change in his voice or anything to make me think he could be a different person than the one I spoke to on the phone for so long, but I'll admit I don't have the same naturally suspicious mind-set that you guys do. So, it's not something I would have looked for."

Doreen nodded. "I wouldn't have looked for it either, and I'm not saying I would have recognized if it was somebody different. So, if you could find out if he had anybody questioning him about the will, the provisions made, or anything related to all that, it would help a lot. Then ask the property management company or even Mathew's probate attorney if either of them knows of any realtors asking about the property possibly going up for sale."

Nick pulled out his phone, looked over at Mack, and

asked, "Are you sure you want to get involved in all this?"

Mack laughed. "You're forgetting something."

Nick eyed him questioningly.

Mack simply said, "I'm already involved. I'm totally in love with Doreen. Nothing will change that for me. Not even this."

Chapter 19

DOREEN NOTED IT was noon when Scott sought her out again. As he walked her through the upstairs bedrooms, she smiled with delight to see that 90 percent of the second floor had all been cleared out.

Scott pointed out, "You've got a few lamps and other things left in here and there."

Doreen suggested, "We'll gather them into one bedroom, so I can contact the local women's shelter and know where to direct them." She picked up two lamps from this room and carried them to the bedroom closest to the second-floor landing. Each time they went into a room, he picked up one or two of the remaining items, and so did she. Mack now trailed along with them, helping to gather it all together. Her animals made the trek with her to each room. She had to admire their loyalty to her.

When they got to the master, a little more was here, so she put all they had collected together in the one bedroom and went over everything with Scott. She looked at some electronics and found Mack eyeing them steadily. "If you want a TV," she suggested, "now is the time."

He looked at her and then grinned. "I may take you up on that."

"Hey, hey, hey, what about me?" Nick asked, from behind them.

"Oh, I'm pretty sure there are more than enough TVs in this house for the both of you," she stated, with an eye roll.

Both brothers grinned at her. Nick added, "*Finally* now we're talking about something we might want."

She turned to Scott and asked, "How much more is there to be done overall?"

"The vehicles are gone," he shared with a great big smile, counting on his fingers now. "The garage does need a bit of a cleaning. While it was in pretty immaculate condition to begin with, it probably still needs a quick sweep to take care of it. The bedrooms are done now, except for this donate pile and the last bits of stuff in the master closet," he added.

With that mention made, they all trooped into the master suite and opened up the massive walk-in closet. Again they all took an armful or two and dumped the remaining clothing in with the gathered decor to be donated, now in the one guest bedroom.

As they traipsed through the bedrooms again just to be sure that everything was gone, she noted, "You really don't like lamps, do you, Scott?"

"Those from the master suite are going. They just haven't been packed up yet." He sent off a text to somebody to remind them.

She laughed. "You can have the others from the guest bedrooms too, if you want them."

"We may take them yet," he muttered. "They just weren't on our priority list because there's a lot less value in them. But," he added, as he looked around at the ones she had gathered together from the different rooms, "one of the reasons I was less concerned with them was because they weren't part of a set. However, seeing them all together now, I can see that they are pairing up nicely."

She nodded. "Good. Take them too. After your guys are through with this second floor, I'll donate what's left."

He laughed. "I've lost count of how many truckloads we've already taken. So what's one more?"

"I know, and I'm happy to say that you're welcome to take even more."

As they wandered through, she realized that all the sitting rooms had been emptied, including the lamps and even paintings off the walls. She shook her head. "I can't even imagine the headache you'll have when you get to the other end."

"Not my headache there," Scott announced cheerfully, "and the unloading crew are all prepared and waiting to get started."

"Good to know."

"And you already know the drill. It'll take quite a while to get through all this and get it sold."

"I know, but hopefully there won't be quite as much repair or cleaning that needs to be done."

Nodding, he agreed. "No, everything is immaculate."

"Good, so that should move things along a little faster, plus keep the price up."

"The price will be whatever the highest bid is, but you're right. The condition of these pieces certainly won't detract from the price."

"Are you done now?"

"No, not quite yet," he said. "I've got to supervise the last few things."

"And what about the refrigerated paintings?"

"The temperature-controlled gallery room downstairs is empty."

"That's all good to know."

He hesitated, then just forged ahead, but in a whisper. "A really nice leather chair is down there, and I was thinking … I apologize if I'm being forward, but it's fairly tall and deep. So I thought it would be a really nice chair for Mack."

She looked at him, surprised. "Oh, wow, I hadn't even considered that." She turned back to Mack, but the two brothers were still fussing over their TV selections. She nodded. "I think that's an excellent idea. Could you guys bring anything that's left down there upstairs for me? Maybe just put it in the entry hallway?"

"We can do that," Scott confirmed.

"And add the chair and the matching footstool near the front door. We'll figure out how to get it home."

He beamed at her.

"Thank you, Scott. That was a nice thought. I honestly hadn't even considered such a thing."

"Mack's a big man, and I'm sure finding furniture that fits is a challenge."

"Again, not something I considered," she muttered, with a laugh. "Thankfully someone always seems to be around who can help me out."

Scott shrugged. "I would love to have a chair similar to that one myself."

"And yet you don't want to bring it all the way back to your place?" she asked.

"No," he replied, now laughing. "I will just get something locally, and now that I've seen it, I may just do that, in my size of course."

She smiled. "And, by all means, if there's anything left here that you want …"

"I'm flying," he added, "but thank you for the offer."

"Right," she agreed. "That flight really changes everything."

"It sure does," he noted, with a laugh. "Have you by any chance gone through the collection of books? We hadn't discussed them, but I did notice a lot of books in the library."

She blinked at him several times. "Oh, good Lord," she groaned, "I didn't even think of that either."

"I did, and I was thinking I might bring somebody in for that, if you don't mind."

"Of course."

"He's kind of tied up, but he wanted me to go into the library and send him some pictures and details. Would that be okay with you?"

She nodded and then smiled. "I think I better come along because I know the more valuable books are in a special case." He raised both eyebrows at her. "I know. I know. I'll be glad to be rid of this house because, for the life of me, I can't seem to remember all the bits and pieces of it."

Mack came up and asked, "Now what?"

"I forgot about the books," she muttered, as she led the way back down through the office into the library.

Mack glanced over the books and frowned. "I don't know anything about books. Are they valuable?"

"These here are valuable. Some of these"—Scott pointed to a glass case—"are collector items. If you wanted to, you could hang on to them, but Doreen mentioned a special cupboard."

She walked over to the bookshelves and frowned as she stood in front of them.

With excitement in his voice, Scott asked, "Does it open?"

She nodded. "It does open, but I don't remember how."

"Are you sure it opens?" Mack asked, frowning.

She snorted. "A whole room is back there."

"You've got to be kidding," Mack muttered, as he stepped back.

Scott immediately stepped forward and asked, "May I?"

"Please," she replied, as he went through the usual options.

When he went to pull out a book, as if maybe that would be the magic trick, she said, "Wait. Pull the one beside it."

He grabbed a huge maroon-colored leather-bound book and pulled it toward him. Immediately came some creaking, then barely a breath of air, and the whole wall pulled forward.

Both Mack and Nick stepped back, then forward into the hidden room, with Scott directly behind them. She walked in, having seen this room many times before.

The three men all sighed happily.

"Yeah, this was his man cave," she muttered. Then she walked over to a large glass wall and tapped the glass. "This is a wine cellar thingy."

And there, indeed, was a fully stocked cellar and bar. Mack looked at the bar and shook his head. "We will definitely take some of this home with us. You know that, right?"

She winced. "Scott, I don't know anything about booze. Would you happen to know anything?"

"About booze? Why?"

"He collected vintage. I don't even know these names. Some of the wine is very expensive, as is the whiskey and champagne."

He walked over to the glass wall then turned to look at the well-stocked bar and the bottles at the highest shelf, and not one of the bottles was opened, which Scott pointed out.

"Right. The ones Mathew drank all the time were on that shelf." She turned and pointed to a selection of open booze bottles. "That's the stuff he drank, and this is the stuff …" She shrugged and added, "served by him. All I can say is it was coveted."

Scott pulled out his phone and called somebody.

Nick noted behind her, "You really do have a huge asset in Scott, don't you?"

She nodded. "Oh gosh, yes. He's accomplished so much that it's amazing. I don't know anything about all these bottles," she muttered, "but I'm pretty sure Mathew spent a small fortune on them."

Scott looked at her and nodded. "So, we may have to pack up some more stuff if you don't want these."

She turned to Mack and Nick. "Do you guys want these?"

"No, I think we would be happy *making do* with these over here," Mack teased, as he pointed to the ones behind them, mostly open.

"Oh good," she said. "We have room in your truck to take those home." She looked at Scott and asked, "Anything valuable?"

The smile on his face was almost paternal with joy and pride. "My dear, all of them are valuable."

"Fine." Then she looked at the chair that Scott had mentioned. "This matches the one by the front door, doesn't it?"

"It does, indeed," he replied in delight.

Mack looked at the chair, walked over, and sat down. There was almost a groan of relief as he sat there, a big smile on his face. "Now *this* is a chair."

"That's good," she noted, "because we should bring it home for you." When he looked at her, she shrugged. "Remember that we don't have any furniture at my home."

"And you had Scott keep it aside for me?" he asked in shock.

"Sure. Scott pointed it out, to be honest. You are a big man, and these chairs were built for you."

At that, Nick walked over and ousted his brother, and stated, "I want a chance to sit in a real chair."

When he also collapsed into the chair, the groan and the expression of peace on his face made Doreen smile. "There are two of these chairs. So maybe Nick should have one of them." He opened his eyes, looked at her hopefully, and she nodded. "I mean, they're just chairs, right?"

"They are *just chairs*," Scott repeated, with a mix of envy in his tone, "but that pair is worth twenty thousand at least."

Nick hopped out, looked down at the chair, then back at her. "What? Ten thousand for *one* easy chair?"

She shrugged. "Yeah, that would be Mathew, and frankly they are probably some of the least expensive ones here."

"Is there a reason why you didn't take them with the rest of it?" Mack asked Scott.

"They're starting to show a little bit of wear," he admitted, "and the style isn't as over-the-top as a lot of it. So, when I mentioned to Doreen that they were about your size, she wanted to keep them."

Mack leaned over, kissed her with a loud buss on the cheek, and declared, "Thank you. This I will happily accept."

"And what about me?" Nick asked, his gaze going from one to the other in mock horror.

"The matching chair is already in the foyer, which I'm

saving for Doreen," Scott shared. "So there will be one for each of you."

The brothers just beamed.

"See? Now the chairs, the booze, and the TVs all made it worthwhile to come down with me, didn't it?" she teased. The two men just stared at her, and she added, "Pack up the booze that you two will drink because I sure won't."

They walked over and got into a discussion about that. "We'll need boxes for these," Mack said, rubbing his hands together.

She laughed. "There might be a box or two left around here. I don't know. Otherwise we'll have to go out and get some." When the doorbell rang, she groaned. "With our luck, that'll be the detective."

"Probably," Mack agreed. "At least it won't be Daniel coming here."

She told Scott, "You can leave the man cave using this lever on the side. I'll close it as we leave. Somehow it makes me happy to think of keeping the detective's nose out of at least *some* of my business."

And, with that, the three of them stepped out, leaving Scott still chuckling in the man cave. She headed to the front door, and, sure enough, it was Detective Clark.

"Sorry," she shrugged. "It's a huge house, and we are working in here. Thus it can take a while to get to the front door."

He shrugged and stepped inside.

"I presume you have more questions," she stated, standing in his way, so he couldn't just walk through the house.

"It's not that I have more questions but more observations. We've been canvassing the neighbors."

She looked at him with interest. "And?"

"Apparently, one of the neighbors saw a man and a woman around the house in the last couple days."

"That could well have been us," she stated, with a steady look.

"She also saw them here well before the timeline you provided."

She nodded. "Speak to Jefferson, the personal security guard for the Smithsons next door. He met us the first moment we arrived, telling us about a man and a woman seen trespassing on Mathew's property."

Clark made a notation of that.

Mack stepped up behind her and asked, "I know that Daniel didn't confirm our alibis, but have you had a chance to do so?"

Clark nodded. "Yes, we have. I'll follow up with Jefferson and the Smithsons."

Doreen nodded. "Thank you. After all it would make sense that these two dead guys have wives or girlfriends or moms or sisters. They might be in town, wondering how the investigation is going as well."

Clark nodded.

Nick interjected, "I spoke with the probate lawyer who's been handling Mathew's affairs. He did say a woman contacted him, asking when the estate would be settled. He told her it already was settled and if they hadn't been contacted, there was nothing for them. He shared with me that she appeared to be shocked and angry about it." He turned to Doreen. "That was a great idea of yours to check. Sorry, I got distracted and didn't fill you guys in."

"That's okay," she said. "At least you asked, and at least now we know somebody out there expected to be in the will."

"I'll need the name of that probate attorney, to get the name of that woman." Nick immediately handed him a card for the local one. "Any chance Mathew's will could be contested then?" Clark asked.

"Oh no, there won't be any contesting it," Nick declared. "We have a very locked-down case."

"But I understand Doreen and Mathew were separated and in the middle of a divorce."

"It was not a legal separation, and the divorce hadn't been finalized," Doreen cheerfully told him. He frowned at that, and she nodded. "Everything goes to me per Mathew's latest will. After the will was drafted, he never made any changes, not months later, not even replacing my name with Robin's, which surprised me."

"Who's Robin?" Detective Clark asked.

Doreen sighed. "She was my husband's girlfriend, the woman he hooked up with even *before* dumping me," she shared, "and thereafter they broke up in a very ugly way."

"Of course they did. Money seems to do that to people," he said, glancing around, frowning.

"What's the matter?" she asked.

"You already got everything moved out?"

"We sure did," she confirmed. "How am I supposed to sell the place when it's overstuffed with all that massive furniture?"

He didn't say anything, but his gaze sharpened. It seemed he didn't quite know what else to ask.

"Not to mention we did find a dead guy in the onion patch."

"Onion patch?" He now stared at her.

She nodded. "Yeah, the Vidalias in the greenhouse."

He stared at her suspiciously. "I know you lived here and

all, but how do you know it's onions?"

"Because I planted that garden bed, and I specifically chose Vidalias," she explained to the newest detective assigned to investigate these two murders. "I was married to Mathew for well over a decade, where we both lived in this house, his house. I enjoyed gardening, so the greenhouse was my happy place."

Mack instantly corrected her, "It is your house now."

"Right," she agreed, "thanks for the reminder." She smiled sweetly at Mack.

"What happened to the girlfriend?" Clark asked.

"She's dead," Doreen noted. "We explained it all to Daniel, but maybe we haven't mentioned it to you. Both my estranged husband and his girlfriend were killed, separately. Mathew was murdered in Kelowna. His murderer has been found and is in prison. I thought Daniel had requested those files, as additional insights into his investigation into these two latest murders?" Doreen asked, frowning.

Detective Clark shook his head. "No, … he did not." Clark noted, "An awful lot of dead people are found around you."

"Yeah, it goes with the territory." When he frowned at that, she sighed. "Oh, you probably don't know that either. I help the Kelowna police by solving cold cases. Thus I'm always dealing with people and murderers and dead bodies."

Clark's eyes widened in shock, and he turned to Mack for confirmation, who nodded.

Chapter 20

WITH DETECTIVE CLARK rushing off with his new information to double-check, Doreen leaned against the front door and stared down at Mugs, who was stretched out on the hallway tile. She looked back at Mack and Nick. "Will we ever be done with police investigations?"

Nick shook his head. "These detectives must think we are a ridiculous bunch. However, it's not us. It's Mathew and his kind. The amount of money Mathew put into his home is just insane."

Mack agreed. "Think of all the good he could have done for so many. Feeding the poor, healing sick children, clean water plants, regenerative farming co-ops in poor areas."

She snorted. "It's what happens when you have so much money that you don't even think about anything else anymore," she explained. "I mean, it's not even money in a way. It just becomes unbelievable figures on some bank account statement. Alternatively, what's that old saying? Something about *Enough money is never enough*? I just don't get it."

"Agreed," Mack conceded, as he smiled at her. "So now we need some boxes and maybe some packing materials for the stuff we want to take home, and Mugs probably needs a walk outside."

"Oh, that's a good idea," she noted. "We all could use some fresh air. A small park is up around the corner."

"Why don't we take them all out of this atmosphere, which appears to be fairly depressing to them?" He looked over at his brother. "Do you want to come?"

"No, I'll just stay here," Nick replied. "I've still got paperwork to do, and I'm dealing with the probate lawyer still."

"I wonder who the woman was?" Doreen asked thoughtfully. "Detective Clark said neighbors had spotted a woman here before we even arrived. Maybe she left that threatening note taped to the front door and thinks she's due some of Mathew's estate."

Mack shook his head. "I still think Butch left the first note, taped it to the front door, then ran off to hide in the garage apartment, until we found him the next day still in the garage apartment. However, you could be partially right, Doreen. That package delivered here, with its two notes inside, could very well have been sent by the woman asking if she were in Mathew's will."

Just then Nan phoned on a video call. Doreen answered it, while she was still in the entrance hallway.

Nan eyed her with lively curiosity. "How are things there?"

"You'll love this," she began, telling of the change in detectives assigned to investigate these two murders. "Did I tell you how Mugs peed on Daniel's pant leg?"

Nan went off in peals of delighted laughter. "Mugs has always been a great judge of character," she stated, chuckling madly.

"Yes, he is. I'll never be popular with Daniel no matter what." Then she added, "By the way, can you find out if, when Maisie talked to the inmates, were any women mentioned who may have known Pete or Butch or Sam?"

"I don't think she asked," Nan replied. So, Doreen told her about the woman who had contacted the probate attorney about the will. "Ooh, in that case, I am very interested to see the inmates' past employment records."

Doreen turned to Mack and asked, "Can we get those?"

Nick interrupted, "I'll get them. Daniel supposedly put in a request for them earlier, and I asked him to send a copy of them to me. I'll follow up with Detective Clark."

"I don't imagine Daniel was really up to sending you anything, even if you are a lawyer," she noted, a bit skeptical.

"Maybe not, and he certainly won't be cooperative now." He cast a meaningful look in Mack's direction.

Nan's laughter roared through the phone. "Oh my, and, once again, you've managed to have fun down there."

"I would love to be home right now," Doreen admitted, shivering as if to shake off a bad feeling. "This place is giving me a headache."

"Yeah, you used to get a lot of headaches when you were there, as I recall," Nan reminded her. "I'm pretty sure it was the stress of keeping that bright light of yours locked up inside."

"Maybe," she muttered. "We'll head out for a bit and take the animals for a romp in the park around the corner," she shared. "That reminds me, I should pick up more dog food for Mugs, who seems to feel as if he's been suffering lately. With any luck we can still be home in another day or two. I have no idea how many truckloads of items have been taken out of this house, but a lot more than I expected."

"You might need another week to do Robin's house," Nan suggested.

Doreen groaned. "I don't want to think about that one yet. I haven't even finished this one house of Mathew's. Plus, he has more in town, plus a couple overseas."

"Doesn't surprise me," Nan replied. "You'll still have to deal with it all."

"For Mathew's other homes here in Vancouver, Scott is in charge of getting rid of everything inside the homes and the houses themselves. I'm done being away from home. As for Robin's estate, I don't know that her house is ready or even out of probate. If I'm her executor, I guess I would have to deal with it personally. However, it's not my house yet, not in my name."

"Right," Nan muttered. "So, that will be another fun *holiday* down the road. I'm sure Mack will love that."

"Mack will not love that," Mack stated, speaking loudly so that Nan could hear him.

"On the other hand, dear," Nan replied dramatically, "maybe Robin wasn't a crazy collector, as Mathew apparently was."

Doreen muttered, "He certainly liked his *stuff*."

"That he did."

Mack leaned into the phone and asked Nan, "Did you realize just how much stuff he had in this house and how many millions he had sunk into this property?"

Nan asked, "You mean, in terms of furnishings, paintings, book collections, and jewelry?"

"All of it," he confirmed in exasperation. "Scott's having a heyday."

Nan burst out laughing. "I am really glad to hear that. At least Mathew invested in things that held their value, and, from the sounds of things, he was smart about it. So, I'm even more delighted that my granddaughter will be the beneficiary of it."

"She could do with a lot less," Mack muttered.

After a moment of silence, Nan, using a delicate tone, pointed out, "It won't change her, you know?"

"I know," he acknowledged. "It's just a lot for me to take in."

"No, it's not," she declared, "because she won't keep any of it. She'll let it all go, probably even all the jewelry, knowing her. She'll sell it all off, then turn it into cash for some charity. That much I know about my granddaughter."

He chuckled. "That's exactly what she's planning on doing."

"Exactly, so quit worrying and let her do her. It will make her happy, which she deserves. At the end of the day, there'll be plenty of money for the both of you to live on for the rest of your lives, without lifting a finger. But it's also not lost on me that neither one of you will care and that you'll both continue working your butts off."

"You are so right," he declared, his smile warming, even as Doreen hugged him.

"Because at the heart of all of it," Nan added, "you two are both who you are. Be proud of that, and don't let any of this get in the way." Then she called out, "Doreen, are you still there?"

"I'm here, Nan," she replied.

"Maisie is coming on over," she explained, "and we'll call the penitentiary again to see if we can roust out some female associates connected to this trio of criminals."

"I should have thought of that earlier," Doreen muttered.

"No, we all should have thought of that because wherever the males congregate," Nan suggested, "generally the females are right there too."

Doreen chuckled. "Let me know what you find."

Chapter 21

AFTER DOREEN ENDED the call, she looked down at Mugs. "I don't know why I thought Daniel was a friend, but he has certainly become much more of an enemy."

"We don't know exactly what he is at this time," Mack declared. "Let's see where the evidence takes us."

"He wasn't doing his job," she stated. "I would hate to think that he's part of this too."

"The problem was," Nick said, looking at her, "Daniel focused solely on the money angle. He probably thinks every rich person is scamming the system. And, when you have cash bonds, anybody and everybody is interested because it's not something that anybody declares. It's literally cash. They can take it and run. They don't have to sell expensive items, and not everybody has Scott with a network already in place to work on getting you the best price for all these things. Regardless, Daniel was hyper-focused on the money, in whatever form."

"And don't forget that Christie's takes a large percentage as well," she reminded him.

"Of course. That's how the world works."

Very quickly they had the animals loaded up, and Mack drove them to the nearby park.

"We could have walked," she muttered. "I didn't realize it was so close."

"Sure, but if we need to get dog food and packing boxes while we're out, it's best that we have a vehicle."

At the park she got out and saw no signs to keep the animals out of the park, although she found a sign that had been knocked down and beaten up by somebody who must not have liked the Keep Dogs Leashed message.

Taking a chance, she let Mugs off his leash and let him run. He ran and ran, doing zoomies all around the park, making her laugh. Thaddeus flew down to the ground, strutting around, exploring the new surroundings, and Goliath was already in the middle of the flower garden. She looked over at Mack. "This was a really good idea."

He smiled and nodded. "I think Mugs was feeling as tired and as restless as we were."

"No wonder," she noted, "it's been a pretty full day."

"Day?" he quipped.

She sighed. "Day seven here in Vancouver. One full week," she corrected. "I don't know what I was thinking."

He smiled. "The same as the rest of us, we're just taking it one day at a time and hoping to get through each one," he shared. "It's all good."

"Are you sure? You're not upset about the money, are you?"

Mack shrugged, then began, "I had no idea, no concept of anybody with *that … much … money.* I realize your grandmother is well off, sharing generously with you. Your good friend Bernard is well off and seems to be a good guy with good intentions. But Mathew's level of rich, wealthy, whatever, just defies a label. It doesn't seem possible. It certainly doesn't seem real. And to have this … *glut* of Mathew's assets growing, almost by the hour, right in front of me, was taxing, to say the least. My brain deals with facts, but this? *Taxing* as it is, I worry about money changing people, changing us. I don't want that. After all, we both saw what Mathew had become. Was he always like this before he got so rich? I don't know. Yet I've known you for not quite a year. Never have I seen any greed in you. Even when you didn't have money for food, you still were working these cold cases for free, never asking for money. So, no, I'm not worried that this money will change you—or me when we marry, as I benefit from all this coming to you. As Nan pointed out, it would be foolish to worry. You'll turn it into investment money and then give it away to good causes you care about."

"True, but that has to wait until somebody makes sure I don't give it all away, so I don't ever have to worry about money again," she stated. "I honestly think that's the best answer."

Seeing the grin on her face, he smiled.

"I know that look. That's your happy look. What are you thinking?" she asked him.

"I am thinking that it would probably piss off Mathew the most."

She laughed. "If we're considering Mathew's feelings, it probably really would."

Mack added, "And I'm all for it."

She smiled at him. "He is dead and gone, so he can't return and hurt me or others anymore."

"That's a good thing," Mack declared, "because I've never been so tempted to hurt a man as I am that one."

"Somebody already did the job for you," she reminded him, as if he could forget. "And somebody else may be *very* upset at not getting a piece of the pie. Somebody who probably has been inside this house and may have overheard something about Mathew's stashes. Whether they thought they deserved it or were just prepared to take it, regardless," she explained, "I can't imagine it has to do with anything else but greed."

She was quiet for a moment, then burst out with a confession. "I didn't even realize there was such thing as bags full of cash," she said, with a snort. "That's obscene, but that's so Mathew."

"It seems … he had an awful lot of problems."

She smiled at him. "Hang on a second. Am I hearing a hint of some sympathy for him?"

"No," he declared, "but it doesn't hurt to understand him better."

"As long as you realize he's not an enemy anymore. He's dead and gone."

"And that," he stated, as he looped an arm around her shoulders, tucked her up closer, and gave her a kiss on the cheek, "is another reason why I don't care so much about his money. He abused you, treated you badly, didn't love and respect you. So I can understand how you could transfer those feelings toward him onto his assets. However, if he were still around, it would be a different story for me."

She patted his cheek. "And the good news is that he's not around. We don't have to worry about him anymore, and our life is completely different now. If you wanted to, you could retire," she suggested. When he frowned at her, she shrugged. "As it's been pointed out to me, a ton of money is here. I don't think we would have to work again, … not ever."

He gazed at her, and his lips twitched. He added, "We might not have to, but I would want to."

"And would you want to do it just because you're worried about what somebody might say about being a *kept man*?" she asked, finally voicing a worry that had been plaguing her.

He shook his head. "It's your money, and I'm confident you will spend it wisely. However, I don't need you taking care of me financially or any such thing," he shared. "So, take that right out of your mind."

She smiled at him. "I wasn't thinking that at all. I just … I didn't want you to back away from me because of the money or because of what others might say."

"Nope," he said. "I was willing to take you on poor, so I think I should be willing to take you on when rich."

She smirked. "Yeah, and just think, at least this way, if I never learn to cook, we can always hire one if you don't want to. I mean, you say *rich*, but I think now it might be more like … *filthy rich*."

"God help us," he muttered. "And no hiring of a cook is needed. That just will not happen."

"Good," she admitted. "I really don't want people in my house all the time."

"It wasn't *your* house though, not here, and that was the problem. Mathew never gave you a chance for that mansion to be your house. It was always only *his*."

She nodded. "That's a good way to look at it too," she muttered.

"You two didn't share much."

"Ya *think*? You did see how only one chair was in that man cave."

Mack sighed. "Believe me that I understand a whole lot more about him now, after seeing his house and realizing to what degree he was all about himself. That man was one selfish jerk," he noted. "The best thing you ever did was leave."

"Even if I didn't leave on my own?" she asked, eyeing him sadly.

"Does that bother you?" he asked. "Thinking that you were supposed to leave before it got to that point?"

"I probably was supposed to leave before it got to that, and the good news is that he did kick me out, and it did help me get to where I am today," she shared, now deep in thought. "Without it, … well, I don't know where I would be."

"I think you would have come to your senses eventually," he suggested, "and it doesn't matter because that stage of your life is over. There is no more worrying about Mathew, not for you or for me."

"Good." She studied him for a brief moment. "Did you ever give any thought to psychics?"

He frowned at her. "No. … Why?"

"It's just that sometimes I get the feeling that he's around."

"Mathew?" he asked, turning to her in astonishment.

She shrugged. "Yeah, Mathew."

"And how much of that," he began hesitantly, "is because you're back in Vancouver, back in his house?"

She smiled. "I like the way you say, *his house*."

"No way that was ever your house," he declared, "and you may have lived there, but it wasn't anything that you were a part of, and he made that very clear."

She smiled. "I hadn't considered it in that way." She

called for Mugs, who was roaming a little too far off the pathway for her to be comfortable. When he raced back and collapsed on the ground beside her, she bent down and cuddled him. "Obviously you are enjoying this run," she muttered. Then Thaddeus flew up to her shoulder. She stroked his feathers as he seemed happy to stay here for now. "You okay, Thaddeus?"

"Thaddeus is here. Thaddeus is here," he squawked. She had to smile at that.

Goliath joined her soon afterward, and she looked back at Mack. "Thank you for thinking of this."

"I should have done it before," he noted. "We were all feeling pretty penned in. Amazing how that works in a mansion the size of a small planet."

She nodded. "I just … Is it wrong that I just want to go home?"

"I can't see that it's wrong," he stated, laughing, "because I want to leave too."

"Can we pack everything in your truck that we're taking back with us?"

"I don't know. How much are you planning on bringing home?" he asked warily.

"The two chairs for you and Nick."

"Are you sure you're okay if we take those chairs?" he asked. "I mean, it's just furniture. We're okay to leave them if it'll cause you trouble, if it will bring on bad memories."

She frowned at him in surprise. "The man is dead. He won't cause me trouble ever again."

"Good," Then he smiled and admitted, "I really do like that chair."

"And it didn't even occur to me to save it for you. Sorry. Thankfully Scott suggested it."

"I'm glad he did," Mack replied, still with a big smile, "because I'll enjoy it. I appreciate you thinking of Nick for the other one."

"I wondered about giving you one for your place, so you'd have one at both our houses, but honestly, if you have one at your place, it can just move to my place whenever we get there."

"Yeah, whenever we get there," he agreed, with an eyebrow waggle.

She smiled. "This trip is helping me clear up an awful lot of my history," she shared. "Even though I didn't really think about it, I needed to let go of it."

"Of course, and, if this is helping, I'm all for it."

She pointed her finger at him. "That doesn't mean I'm ready to set a date yet."

"I get it," he said, raising both hands in mock surrender. "By the time we're done with all this, you'll just be so grateful that I'm helping you, I'm sure you'll jump at a date."

She laughed. "I'm not refusing to choose a date on purpose. You know that, right?"

"I do know that." He brushed his finger along her lips. "When you get there, you'll get there."

She groaned. "How come you're always so reasonable?"

He burst out laughing. "Because I promised you no pressure, and so there's no pressure."

"Some people would say that you didn't care enough."

He chuckled. "Good thing we don't listen to some people then, isn't it?"

She smiled. "Absolutely."

"And as long as you're okay to not listen to people," he clarified, "I'm okay to not listen to people too."

She smiled. "I wasn't really thinking about it, but I

know some would be upset about that."

"Forget about other people. We have nothing to do with any other people. We have plenty to do just looking after ourselves."

"Yeah, you got that right."

Nan phoned again. Doreen put it on Speakerphone, then realized it would be another video call.

"She seems to really miss you," Mack whispered, as the call finally connected.

"Hi, Nan," Doreen answered.

"The girlfriend's name is Nancy."

"Nancy," Doreen repeated, frowning. "That name hasn't been mentioned so far."

"Yes, apparently she did some work for Mathew in the house."

"Like, housekeeping?"

"I think it was more secretarial or administrative, you know? Cleaning up his office and organizing stuff and filing that he needed a hand with because his main person was away doing other work."

"Oh, that could be," Doreen replied. "I do remember his right-hand man had to go away every once in a while, depending on what jobs Mathew sent him on."

"She was there for a while, and I guess at one point in time he got a little loquacious about his fortune and was showing off."

"Ah," Doreen muttered. "That would certainly have gotten the word out that Mathew had all this stuff stashed. The questions I have are, who she might have told and was she involved in trying to take some of this or not? Oh, which dead man was she the girlfriend of?"

"Sam," Nan declared. "Got it straight from the prison

guard, who confirmed Nancy also often visited Pete in prison. The prison grapevine says—and they make bets on this gossip. Isn't that glorious? Anyway, the prison pipeline states that Sam was Nancy's sweetheart and that Pete was Nancy's brother."

"We definitely need to track down her current whereabouts," Mack snapped.

"She lives down there," Nan told him, with a bright smile. "And I wouldn't be at all surprised if she didn't know exactly where some of those goodies were."

"She might have known, but she didn't get to them fast enough because we have emptied all the safes here," Mack stated abruptly.

"Good to know," Nan said. "You need to track her down because we have no clue how to do that from here."

"Not a problem," Mack noted. "Have you guys contacted Darren?"

Nan hesitated and then warily replied, "Maybe."

Mack rolled his eyes. "In that case, I'll contact him and see if I can get his help because he'll already be briefed on this, right?"

Another moment of silence followed before Nan spoke. "Maybe. Ritchie was trying to get information on Daniel so went to Darren, although I don't believe he came back with anything helpful. Darren wasn't happy about looking into another police officer."

"What about his family?" Doreen asked Nan.

"As far as we could tell, his parents are gone and brother lives in England. No one close."

"You and the crew gave us some great leads," Doreen said warmly. "Tell everyone we appreciate their help."

Mack nodded.

"That's good to hear," Nan exclaimed. "Darren has been pretty helpful."

"And he probably has been pretty helpful *because* …" Mack left it at that.

"Yes," Nan finally admitted, "because we told him that you were asking us to get information and that the internet down there was really bad and that you guys were swamped with work and that problems and things were dire."

"Oh, good God," Mack said. "Did you say, *dire*? Like, does he think we're down here being preyed upon and in major trouble?"

"Maybe," Nan muttered hesitantly.

Mack just glared into the phone.

Doreen chuckled. "I told you before, Mack. Just let 'em loose for five minutes, and they will run with it. That's what being a freethinker is all about. Right, Nan?"

"Exactly," Nan cried out triumphantly. "See? Doreen understands."

Mack now just glared at Doreen.

She shrugged and noted, "Don't know what you expected otherwise, Mack. Thanks, Nan. We'll get back to you."

"Okay, honey." And Nan ended the call.

Doreen turned to Mack, who was already phoning Darren. "You can't get mad at Darren either, Mack. You know that group can be very convincing."

"Probably too convincing," he muttered, his lips pursed. "No way Darren should have fallen for any of it."

"But that doesn't mean he didn't want to help willingly and allowed that to be part of the excuse." Mack stopped mid-dial to consider her and her statement. She nodded. "Yes. A lot of people have had fun getting involved in these cases," she shared, with a smile. "Maybe Darren just finds it easier to go with the flow than to buck his granddad."

Mack rolled his eyes at that. "You could be right, and I certainly know what a force that group can be. They're a hazard."

"Perhaps, but they're also funny and happy and excited to be involved."

"That's not exactly a reason to be doing this."

"Of course not," she conceded, her gaze still lit with amusement. "But you also know that it's engaging and fun for them, and, if they can rope Darren into doing something, they will."

"Darren knows better."

"Sure he does, and maybe he thought that helping might get him somewhere, knowing it also might get him in trouble. Plus, you don't know that he hasn't already contacted your captain for clearance."

"I hope so," he muttered.

She did too, but she didn't say that to him. When he finally connected with Darren, she decided to walk away a little bit farther into the park, so she didn't have to hear him yell at Darren. So she was surprised when no yelling came. She walked closer to hear Mack agreeing on a couple issues.

Finally, when he ended the call, he looked at her and shared, "I didn't yell at him."

"I know," she confirmed, staring at him with a warm smile. "I'm really glad you didn't."

He groaned. "You're just making me nuts. You do know that, right?"

"No, I'm not making you nuts at all," she argued.

"What? I was already nuts to begin with?"

"You were," she agreed. Then she burst out into peals of

laughter. "You have to be nuts if you're hanging out with me."

"Good point," he muttered. "Darren will look up this Nancy person and will pull her employment records."

"Good enough." Doreen looked around, watching for Mugs and Goliath. "Shall we head back?"

"Yeah, and we'll run by the store and grab some dog food, pick up some treats, and check if they have some boxes in the back we can have. Then I suggest we pick up some dinner too."

"I'm definitely looking forward to being home and eating your home-cooked meals again."

"Me too," he agreed, "but, on the bright side, we're getting much higher-end takeout these days because of you."

"The least I can do is pay for the food. Plus, I have my new accounts available to me now," she muttered. "You're all down here because of me, after all."

"We are." He frowned at her and added, "You do know my brother still has to charge you for his hours, right?"

She smiled at him and nodded. "I do know that, and I am just beginning to come into a whole lot of money, so I can definitely pay him."

"Him and everybody else in your world," Mack quipped.

She nodded. "Besides, I was planning to give him a bonus for doing all this when the deal is done."

He looked at her and asked, "Were you?"

"Yes," she replied, "not something ridiculous, but he's been so patient and wonderful all this time, and for him the work will continue for quite some time yet, it seems. And, well, we'll have so much, and I just thought maybe he should be rewarded well too."

The expression on his face changed, and he leaned over

and gave her a resoundingly passionate kiss that left her sagging against him. When he could speak again, he said, "You really are a good person. You know that, right?"

She sighed. "And you need to stop kissing me senseless like that," she muttered. "I can't think straight."

He grinned at her, looped an arm around her shoulders, and with the critters in tow, led her back to his truck. Every step along the way he whistled.

She grinned at her life. Having Mack with her really would make for an exciting life together. As long as he could see her point of view and let her do what she wanted, things would be great.

Chapter 22

BY THE TIME Doreen and Mack and the animals returned to Mathew's home again, they had picked up fresh sandwiches from the local deli as well.

Nick grinned when he saw the sandwiches. "At least you're feeding me," he muttered. "I forget the time when I'm working. Plus, pickings are slim here, at least for snacking."

"It's the least I can do," she noted, with a chuckle. "How are things going?"

He shrugged. "Can't really say they're going great but better than expected," he muttered.

Doreen added, "We did talk to Nan and came up with some answers in terms of a female, connected to both of our dead guys, plus a cellmate to another criminal named Sam," she shared. "She is the sister to Pete Singer and was a girlfriend to Sam and knew Butch too. Plus, she worked here in this house for my ex at some point." She gave him the name. "Nancy. Don't know if her last name is Singer, like her brother, or not."

He nodded. "Okay, so that's a name we need to follow up on."

"Exactly. And you already know that Detective Clark is

trying to get up to speed, taking over for Daniel. So we can go to Captain Hawkins directly, if need be. He is sharing some info with us, but it is usually delayed a couple days. So if you follow up on Nancy too, that would be great," Doreen suggested. "Plus, Mathew's employment records. Any luck there?"

"I'm hoping Mathew's probate attorney will come through, but it's hard to know at this point. I've called him three times so far."

Doreen sighed. "All you can do is ask. Tell him Daniel hasn't provided that to you. Now with this newest info, Mathew's employment records could help ID the man and the woman seen at Mathew's house before we ever got here. How many agree with me that it was probably Pete and Nancy?"

"Too soon to tell, Doreen," Mack warned her. "Her boyfriend Sam may have been here, for all we know."

Doreen frowned. "True."

Nick seemed to agree with both of them. "Right, let's hope that, if Clark won't do it, Captain Hawkins will follow up, then fill us in."

"And that is where the challenge comes in," Mack replied. "Just because all this is going on, that doesn't mean Clark or Hawkins will share. Still, Nan has beat Hawkins to the punch, a time or two." Mack shook his head at that.

"Exactly," Doreen agreed. "However, if we can get some of these answers ourselves, from Nan or wherever," she noted, "it won't matter what Clark does—or does not do."

"It will matter," Mack pointed out, "because we'll still have to deal with him. Trust me. It will matter in the end."

She winced and nodded. "I do understand that, as much as I don't really want to. At least Detective Clark doesn't seem to take sides. Daniel's point of view was polarizing," she muttered.

Mack chuckled. "Just do what I do. Ignore people like him."

She rolled her eyes. "It's a little hard for me because Daniel was always intent on my being found guilty of three murders, maybe four."

"What three? What four?" Mack asked.

"Pete Singer, Butch Weldon, Mathew, *and* Robin."

"Wow," Nick interjected. "You do have a problem with him—or he has a problem with you. Maybe he's busy. We are in Vancouver after all. It's not Kelowna."

"I keep reminding myself of that," she admitted, with a sigh. "You and your brother are far more generous than I am."

Mack laughed and added, "He's also a fellow colleague, so I was hoping he was on the up-and-up."

"Until proven differently," Doreen reminded him. "Yet … I get that. I really do. From your perspective, he's supposed to be suspicious and focused on just us as his suspects, while being on the up-and-up."

He rolled his eyes at that. "Thank you. I appreciate that you trust my judgment."

She groaned. "I didn't mean it that way."

"I know," he replied, "but let's give the new detective time to do his job. I hope that he eventually does what's right and that it will all come out fairly soon."

"And yet we do know how investigations can take forever," she muttered.

"Sure," Mack agreed. "They definitely can, and this one is not an open-and-shut case. Plus, we have no real suspects, just some names to check out."

"Because they're all dead or hiding somewhere," she snapped. "The fact of the matter is, Butch killed Pete—or at least Butch's gun was used to kill Pete. Both had access to some portion of Mathew's property—the attached greenhouse and the garage apartment. The note taped to the main house delivered a threat, a warning, wanting something from Mathew, maybe. Then the delivery had two more threats in it, both addressed to Daniel. So Pete and Butch and maybe Daniel were searching for treasure, hoping they could find it, or were they looking for something very specific and didn't know where it was?"

Mack nodded. "I agree with your premise. In this case, most people intent on stealing stuff wouldn't be here trying to remove fancy heavy furniture or even paintings," Mack pointed out, "because they wouldn't necessarily know the value of that. However, they could surely strip what's available and what's easily carried out of here—like TVs and jewels—but they would still need a fence to sell it, if they even found the safes where the jewels were. Plus, we can't confirm anything was taken from the main house."

"Many of these guys, even those fresh out of prison," Doreen noted, "could already have a fence available because of their other criminal experience and contacts."

"Yes, that's certainly possible," Mack pointed out. "A lot of other things could be happening too, including involving the actual caretaker, who we have yet to find."

"I was wondering about that. Even though Butch said he was the caretaker hired by Mathew, we have another caretaker hired by the property management firm who was then told *not* to come, right?" She turned to Nick. "You want to call back the probate lawyer, or just call the property management firm directly, and ask either of them for the name of that caretaker? It could have been Pete Singer, since he was the first to die. Also ask the local probate attorney if he knows the woman's name who thought she would get some of Mathew's estate."

While they stood here, Nick phoned him back.

The lawyer apologized for not getting back to him sooner. "I've been tied up with nonstop probates in court all week." He didn't know anything about the hired caretaker. He mentioned how the property management firm doesn't know how he was suddenly fired, after they had just hired him. Then he told Nick that the woman in question was somebody Mathew had hired at some point in time. "I have a short list of former employees, including Nancy. I'll send that text to you in about five minutes. Why are you asking about her?"

"If her name is Nancy, maybe last name Singer, she's associated with our two dead men."

"Oh my, really?"

"Yes."

Doreen tried hard to listen for any deceit in his voice. But it was hard to tell if anything was going on there. She shrugged as she glanced at Mack and Nick, before asking the probate attorney herself, "Can you tell us when Nancy Singer worked for Mathew and in what capacity?"

"Not quite a year ago," he replied, with no hesitation, "as a secretary. She only lasted a few months."

"Did he say why he got rid of her?"

"Yes, she was hired in between you leaving the house and Robin moving in. Mathew needed help with a bunch of paperwork, filing, and stuff for him. He was getting a little more organized, and then Robin came along and had a problem with Nancy. She was getting a little too, … shall we say, comfortable in the house. A little too pushy and making the moves on Mathew, but he wasn't interested."

"Ah," Doreen muttered. "So, in Nancy's mind, she expected some money coming to her."

"She probably did think that but had hardly worked long enough to even be a twinkle in Mathew's eye. Employees remembered in the wills of their bosses are rare in my experience, and, at best, only those with many decades of service."

"True, but people do have strange expectations. Did you ever get a feeling of disgruntlement from her?"

"I didn't have anything to do with her except the one inquiry about the will. Robin would be the one with the lowdown on her." Then he winced and added, "Sorry, I guess that's not an option."

"Nope, it sure isn't," Doreen said. "Yet we'll have to ponder that."

Silence came from the other end.

"Anybody else contact you over the will?" she asked.

"Nope, it's been pretty calm and quiet, but then again Mathew didn't have much in the way of friends."

"Right, and we have received two more threatening notes," she shared. "Did Mathew ever say that he owed somebody or that he was expected to give somebody something?"

He snorted. "Mathew wasn't the kind to give anything to anybody."

"I know that all too well. I just wonder where the threatening notes are coming from." The two men looked at her, and she shrugged. "I mean, handing out money wasn't really a thing that he did."

"No, it wasn't. I'm not trying to say anything against the

guy—he's dead after all—but any sense of philanthropy was sadly missing," the probate attorney shared.

Doreen continued. "And you don't know of anything he owed or anybody he screwed over when it came to the property or to work?"

"No, nothing I know of," he replied, "and again anybody could make that claim when doing business with Mathew, just hoping to get some of his money. But, for purposes of the probate of his estate, those debts must be proven and then submitted for approval to be paid. I've received no such notices nor any inheritance claims from anyone."

"What about workmen who did jobs on his various homes in Vancouver? Do you know if all the bills were paid?"

"Nothing's been done or was commissioned to be done in several years that I know of, so I don't know what it would be."

"Right," she muttered, "so that's not really helpful. How about keys to the main house? Would Nancy have had keys to the place?"

"No, absolutely not. Ah, wait." He groaned. "I think there was an issue with her, now that you mentioned *keys*. Mathew did get something re-keyed because of her."

"Interesting," she murmured.

"You might need to talk with her."

"We definitely need to talk with her," Mack interjected, "but we'll need a way to find her."

"Do you have an address for her?" Doreen asked the probate attorney. "Obviously we have to get to the bottom of this."

"I'm not sure that I can legally give it to you."

"Why not? Wasn't she Mathew's employee?"

"Yes."

But he sounded pretty hesitant about it. She looked at the other men with an eyebrow raised, urging them to say something.

Nick suggested, "With Doreen as Mathew's legal representative for his estate, I think, under these circumstances, it's fine to release that info. We have to get to the bottom of two murders."

"Oh gosh, that's right. Okay, hang on a moment, while I look it up." And very quickly he had an address for Nancy.

Doreen thanked him profusely and added, "Hopefully, we can get to the bottom of this before things get any uglier."

"Two dead people is already ugly enough," the probate attorney noted. "Two dead people on top of the fact that Mathew himself is dead, not to mention Robin, makes it worse."

"I know," she murmured, "and I'm pretty sure it's all connected to the fortune he kept here in the house."

"Yes, and I often told him that he should move it all. I presume you've found even more."

"Yes, I think so," she told him, "although I don't know if we found all of it. I mean, the furniture alone is worth a fortune, plus the cars, the paintings, the rare books, the jewelry. There's just so much of it."

"And again that's why I kept telling him to get it appraised."

"If you have copies of appraisals or insurance riders, that would be most helpful," she pointed out, "when it comes to dealing with the people who will sell it all."

"I can send that to you as well," he replied, "as we kept it as part of his asset documentation."

"Good enough," she said. "And what about the weapons? Do you know how many he had?"

"Five handguns for sure, but I don't know if that was all of them."

"Five?" she repeated, turning to look at Mack. "We found five. One in his office, one in the dresser in the master suite, and three in one of the safe deposit boxes."

Nick interjected, "But I see paperwork for six, based on the licenses found with the first gun."

"Oh, that's not good," the probate attorney replied.

She announced, "Hang on a minute, here's Mack." She handed the phone over to Mack and the conversation went to registrations and serial numbers on the weapons.

He explained to the probate attorney, "If they all haven't been found, we do need to report the one as missing and possibly stolen. The fact that weapons could be out there somewhere and associated with this estate … is bad news."

"That's true," Nick confirmed.

"Oh goodness, let's get it sorted soon," Doreen added, staring at Nick. "Especially after having a couple dead men found here, it will reflect on all of us."

"Exactly," Nick stated. Mack nodded in agreement.

The probate lawyer added, his voice rising in a mild panic, "Oh my, I had no idea when I took this on that it would be such a big job."

"I presume you're being well paid for it," Doreen asked.

"Yes, it's all laid out in the will itself." He laughed. "It's not that I didn't trust Mathew, but I knew he was stingy. So, I refused to do it unless the actual amount was laid out. So don't worry. I am getting paid."

"Good enough," she said.

"Of course, you could always top it up if you want to," he added cheerfully. And, with that, he ended the call.

She frowned at Nick. "Is that a common thing for people to do with lawyers?"

He shook his head. "No, not necessarily. But, in this case, when you have this kind of money involved, I guess maybe it makes sense."

She shrugged. "Maybe, I don't know." She looked at Mack and noted, "The missing weapon is an issue, isn't it?"

Mack nodded. "Yep, sure is. Particularly when no break-ins have been reported to the local police, as per Daniel anyway. Yet further confirmation through Captain Hawkins differed, finding a couple neighborhood reports."

Doreen snorted. "Just like Jefferson told us about the Smithsons." She shook her head.

"So I'll call Captain Hawkins and tell him about the missing gun, but I really don't like this."

"What about the security system on the house?" she asked. "Did anybody look at the security tapes?"

"Of course," Mack snapped, "but, gee, what a surprise, it hasn't been working since, oh, somewhere around the time that Mathew was killed."

She groaned. "Of course, and that would have been his own right-hand man's doings, right before he murdered Mathew."

"Probably so." Mack asked her, "Do you want to speak with any of Mathew's past employees?"

"Nope. None of them had any respect for me because Mathew treated me like the furniture, so that's how they treated me too."

He groaned. "In that case we won't worry about them expecting anything from you either."

"No, surely not."

They sat down and ate their dinners. When she felt better now that her stomach was full, she said, "The thing that I don't understand is the threat on that note. *Give it to me.* That could be nearly anything."

Mack nodded. "Exactly."

Doreen continued. "And that's my problem. It's not as if Mathew would ever give someone anything, whatever it is. He would refuse, and, if it was his—legally owned—then no way. Unless somebody took it forcefully. Of course somebody could do that still. … I'm getting a little scared here."

"Easy now. We'll sort this out," Mack said.

She shook her head. "We know it's somebody connected to this place. We know it must somebody who knew about a lot of the goings-on here, and, chances are, it's a disgruntled person, perhaps somebody involved in Mathew's business, even some part-time employee, like this Nancy woman." She looked at the guys and suggested, "Maybe we should go for a ride and find her."

"Maybe so." Mack immediately looked down at the animals.

"They're coming too," Doreen declared.

He just nodded, as if knowing it would be useless to argue. He looked at his brother, who held up his hands and said, "You guys go ahead. She keeps making more work for me, so now I've got to sort out a missing gun, among other stuff."

"Yes, please do that," she said. "And while you are at it, contact Detective Clark too and tell him there could be a weapon missing, and that we're still trying to sort our way through it."

"If the missing weapon from this house was used to kill

our dead guy number two, and we don't have it, then whoever took it is most likely to be the killer. However, the real question here is, how did they get in? How did they get the keys? I do know that Mathew had every exterior door set with a different lock than all the others. So he had different keys for several doors to enter the main house, like that double French door leading from the back of the house to the greenhouse. Plus, if people worked for Mathew and had a house key, he would rekey the lock to that particular house key. Just like Mathew's probate attorney told us about this Nancy woman. So, we need to find her and to sort out some things."

She added, "We also have two dead men and one missing convict, all who have been recently released from prison, and all who apparently knew one another. However, we don't have any contact information for Sam, if that's his real name."

"I'll contact the parole board too," Nick offered. "Come to think of it, we should have done that already."

"I thought you did," Mack clarified, "and they just hadn't got back to you yet."

His brother looked at him and sighed. "I think you're right. Let me do a follow-up. You guys go off and do whatever you're handling," Nick urged them. "I need a desk and a few hours to deal with this stuff."

"Go for it," she said, with a smile in his direction. "Use Mathew's office."

He grumbled about all the work she was giving him.

She chuckled. "Considering you'll be my brother-in-law, I'll get the family rate now too, won't I?" When he stared at her in horror, she burst into uproarious laughter. "I have no problem paying your bill. You've been as helpful as Scott has been."

Nick smiled. "I do like being appreciated—and paid."

"Right now we need to find whoever has decided to help themselves to part of Mathew's estate—claiming whatever to be theirs alone and not sharing it with their friends, who they killed to avoid sharing the goodies."

"You think it's one or two?" Nick asked.

"I think it was at least three partners to begin with—Pete, Butch, and Sam. Unfortunately two different people killed Pete and Butch, since Butch's gun killed Pete, even if Butch didn't pull the trigger himself. Nobody found the gun that killed Butch to date, right?"

Mack nodded, grimacing. "Sure hope it's not Mathew's missing gun."

Doreen grimaced, then continued. "So now we have Sam unaccounted for, plus Nancy. We have Jefferson's report of the Smithsons seeing a man and woman trespassing on this property. Could have been Sam with Nancy. However, who knows who else these people told about Mathew's house filled with treasures. That's what triggered the first murder."

Mack noted, "Yet these prisoners seem to tell all, once in a cell. So we have no idea how many criminals are truly involved. So keep an open mind, Doreen."

She sighed.

Nick stared at her and asked, "Do you just pull that stuff out of your head?"

"Yep, basically I do."

He grimaced. "But you do know what Mack will say."

Since Mack was standing right there, she groaned and nodded. "Yeah, he'll say facts and evidence first, suppositions and guesswork later."

Chapter 23

DOREEN AND MACK approached Nancy's address that they'd gotten from the probate attorney's files regarding Mathew's former employees. Doreen looked around at the area and sighed. "This apartment building and its surroundings certainly have seen better days. No wonder she was majorly hoping for something out of Mathew's will."

"Yep. And she has no record, at least not under Nancy Singer. But, on the plus side, Mathew's list of former employees was short. I've got Darren running them through the department's database, since we expect Mathew to hire criminals. Once Darren reports back to me, we'll know what else to put on our to-do list."

The neighborhood was rundown, so anybody who lived here was probably chronically short of cash.

As they parked, Mack looked around hesitantly, and she asked, "Are you afraid it won't be safe here?"

"It's definitely that kind of a neighborhood," he muttered.

"Let's go see if she's home. If not, it'll be a fast trip."

"Good, because it's not my home turf. I don't know anyone here, and I'm not familiar with the area. I don't have backup."

As they drove around trying to find a place to park, she gasped, then grabbed his hand. "Look."

He stopped and asked, "What? Look at what?"

"There."

Right in front of them, a block away, was Daniel, only he wasn't in a cop car. He was in a private unmarked vehicle.

"Now that is interesting," Mack whispered beside her.

"What do you want to bet that he knows exactly who Nancy is?"

"We don't know anything just yet," Mack noted. "It could be that he's just doing some investigation, as we are."

"But he's in a personal vehicle," she commented.

"As am I."

She frowned and nodded. "*Fine.* Maybe it isn't a suspicious visit."

"No," Mack noted, "maybe it isn't."

"Or you could let him see you, and then we'll watch for his reaction," Doreen suggested, keeping an eye on the wayward detective.

Mack offered, "Or we go talk to Nancy first, and then we see what his *and* her reactions are."

"Good point," she muttered.

He sighed.

"I know. I know," she grumbled, raising a hand. "You're way better at this than I am."

"I'm not so sure of that," he noted. "You certainly have made us look like idiots back home."

"Ouch," she murmured. "You know I don't try to, right?"

He muttered, "That makes it even worse."

He quickly parked, and they unloaded the animals. She walked up to the main entryway for the apartment building, still looking around. "It really is a struggling area, isn't it?"

"Yes, it is," he muttered.

As they walked closer, she kept glancing around.

"Problems?" he asked.

"It's just a little unnerving."

"Is it you affecting Mugs or Mugs affecting you?"

Mack was holding the dog's leash, and Mugs was acting in the exact same way as Doreen was. The dog was alert, glancing around at each of the apartment buildings.

"I don't know," she admitted, "but something feels … off somehow."

"I don't know if it's off as much as odd."

"*Odd* works," she replied.

The main entrance was not guarded, not locked, and required no code to get inside. So they stepped inside and took the stairs. When they found the right apartment, she knocked on the door. When no answer came, she knocked again, harder. The door popped open, but no one was there.

"Ah, darn," she whispered, looking over at Mack.

He nodded, his face grim. "You stay here." Leaving her outside with the animals, he stepped inside, then immediately yelled to Doreen, "Call for the cops and an ambulance. She's still alive."

Doreen immediately pulled out her phone and called, giving the address. Then she stepped near the open doorway and asked, "Can we come in?"

"No," he yelled, "you stay there. Do not come inside. You and the animals need to stay out there. Did you call for an ambulance?"

"Yes." She looked at him as he stepped back. "How bad is it?

"Looks to be a drug overdose, but I don't know for sure."

So they waited, but it wasn't very long before the ambulance showed up. The EMTs took charge, and, when she turned around, an official-looking man in a suit stared at the two of them. Probably a Vancouver detective.

She pointed to Mack. "He'll explain."

Mack snorted, but he pulled out his ID and explained who they were first. The officer pulled out his badge as well, which Mack regarded.

When the officer wanted to know what they were doing here, she gave an explanation but knew it was a little garbled because he didn't have any of the backstory.

The officer stared at her. "So, you're interfering in an investigation?"

"No," she stated. "I'm trying to figure out what happened, and this person, Nancy, was apparently employed by my late husband and had contacted Mathew's probate lawyer to see if she was in the will," she explained. "So, I wanted to meet with her personally and see why she had that expectation. Considering the fact that I've had threatening notes left on my doorstep, I wanted to know if it was her, wanted to find out if my husband had done something wrong."

"Why go there at all if he's passed on?" the officer asked suspiciously.

"To consider a wrongdoing? To right a wrong? My late husband was not a nice person," she shared, "and I wanted to know if Nancy had been wronged."

The detective frowned, unsure whether he believed her or not, so he looked to Mack, who just nodded.

"I know it sounds convoluted, but it is, indeed, the truth."

"And you can always talk to your colleague," she suggested. "Detective Daniel Sherwood." He looked at her in surprise, so she added, "He just left here a few minutes before us. We saw him drive away." When he stared at her for a long moment, she pulled out her phone and displayed a clear picture of Daniel driving off.

"I didn't know you took that," Mack noted.

"Yeah, I wanted you to notify Daniel that we were here, but he was already pulling away, so I just snapped the picture," she explained.

"Surely you're not thinking he had something to do with this?" the detective asked her.

"I have no idea, but, if he got the same information we did, then I presume he was here to talk to Nancy Singer, or whatever her last name may be now. Maybe I'll give him a pass and assume the door didn't pop open when he knocked, getting here before us," she shared. "But the door did pop open for us, and definitely nobody else was here except Nancy."

The detective didn't say anything, just took notes.

She groaned, turned to Mack, and asked, "Why don't you call Daniel now?"

"Yeah, I can do that." He pulled out his phone and contacted Daniel, who sounded snappy and short-tempered.

"Now what do you want?" he bellowed.

"Well," Mack began, glancing over at Detective Davis nearby, "were you following up on the woman who had contacted the probate lawyer about being in the Mathew's will?"

"No, of course not," he snapped, still sounding brusque. "And I wouldn't tell you even if I was."

Mack didn't have the call on Speaker, yet Daniel was practically yelling. Therefore, all three of them on the other end heard Daniel clearly. "So, you weren't at Nancy's place today?"

"No, I wasn't," he spat in an aggrieved tone. "What are you doing questioning me?"

"We waved at you, but apparently you didn't see us."

"When?" he asked, his voice suddenly sour but very, very quiet.

"When you drove away from her apartment just now," Doreen interjected.

In an ugly tone of voice, he snapped at her, "Are you following me now? Because I will rain down so much trouble in your life, you have no idea."

In shock, Detective Davis listened to Daniel railing at them, staring at the phone in Mack's hand.

Doreen explained, "We weren't following you, Daniel. You can rest easy on that. We came to talk to Nancy, and the door opened when we knocked. The poor woman was down and in desperate need of medical attention," she told him. "So, considering that you were here too, we wondered what your role in all this was."

When Detective Davis glared at her sharply, she shrugged.

She continued. "Daniel, we saw *you*. I even took a picture. So, did you have something to do with this poor woman's condition?"

"Good God," he yelled. "Why are *you* questioning me?"

Doreen snorted. "Detective Davis is here, overhearing this conversation with all your yelling going on, so, if not me questioning you, Daniel, you can bet someone from your own department will be questioning you soon enough."

"They only have your word," Daniel retorted in a surly tone.

"No, that's not true. I just took a very clear photo of you in this very neighborhood with my phone camera, so it's got the time and date stamp on it."

Daniel's tone turned surly as he cussed a long streak of threatening words.

Detective Davis took the phone, further identified himself, and told Daniel to report to the station for questioning within the next two hours. She heard Daniel protesting, but Davis was strict and didn't budge.

Handing the phone back to Mack, Davis turned to Doreen and ordered, "Send me that photo right now." She sent it to the number he gave her. He stared at her and added, "I don't understand what your role is in all of this."

"That's all right," she said. "Nobody ever really understands my role in these things. I'm used to it."

Mack sighed beside her.

"And he struggles with me too," she muttered. "I am sorry. I'm not trying to be a trial, but sometimes …" Mugs barked at her several times. "And, of course, I have Mugs here with me too. He's quite the little sidekick."

"Good God," Detective Davis muttered.

Mack added, "We've also been dealing directly with your captain, Captain Hawkins, and Detective Clark."

"Why is that?" Davis asked.

"We are getting better cooperation out of them." Davis seemed to get the underlying message.

"When are you guys returning to Kelowna?"

"Detective Daniel Sherwood told us that we aren't allowed to leave town," she shared, with a sniff. "Even though we have homes and family and jobs to go back to."

"Right," he muttered, "and so Detective Daniel Sherwood seems to think that you guys are guilty of something, *huh*?"

"No," Doreen clarified. "Daniel knows we're not guilty

at all, but he doesn't have any other suspects. He also knew my late husband."

At that comment, Davis frowned at her, asking for Mathew's full name, which she provided.

She continued. "I asked Daniel if there had been any vandalism calls or other reported cases regarding my late husband's property. Daniel told me no, but, according to my lawyer, who contacted the local lawyer handling Mathew's estate, there had, indeed, been several calls of vandalism from the neighbors."

"From the neighbors though."

"Yes, saying that they had seen people on Mathew's property and knew the owner was now deceased, so they were concerned."

"And yet Daniel told you there were no such calls?"

"Yes, that's right."

"Maybe he just didn't want you to know."

"I'm sure that's what he'll tell you," Doreen replied. Davis just stared at her, and she nodded. "Then Mack checked in with your captain, who confirmed that there *were* reports of vandalism in the area."

Detective Davis frowned at that.

Doreen continued. "I know it's never a good idea to blame a cop, but he also failed to find a gun at the crime scene of dead body number two at my late husband's property. Plus, Daniel refused to share any progress he was making on these two deaths at my late husband's home, even though I am the legal owner of the property now and also the executrix of my late husband's estate. Daniel comes over alone, never with a partner. He was just here in an unmarked car. He seems to work alone all the time. Is that standard procedure in Vancouver? Maybe he knew Nancy personally, so he wasn't in his official vehicle. I don't know, but I'm sure you'll find out about all that. I'm just telling you that this woman, Nancy Singer, who thankfully we were in time to save, contacted Mathew's probate lawyer to see if she was named in my late husband's will. She wasn't. Maybe she thought she was due something from Mathew."

Detective Davis frowned. "So, maybe, when she found out she wasn't in the will, she tried to take her own life."

"I don't know," Doreen conceded. "I really don't know anything about her."

"Do you know why she's no longer in your husband's employment?"

"She wasn't employed by Mathew in the days leading up to his death because he had let her go already. I was told she apparently got a little too familiar, and my husband's girlfriend at the time didn't like Nancy. Mathew thought she still had one key to one particular exterior door to the main house and worried she was getting it copied and handing them out. I don't know for sure."

"Good God," Davis muttered.

Mack added, "I've got this contact information for Nancy Singer from both Mathew's probate lawyer and Doreen's personal lawyer, who handled her probate interests. And, to save you the confusion, her attorney happens to be my brother."

Detective Davis took down the contact information and shrugged. "Of course he is. Okay, thanks. I will attempt to get to the bottom of this."

"The bottom line right now," Doreen pointed out, "is this young woman needs help."

"She's on the way to the hospital," Davis noted, "and hopefully she'll wake up soon."

"I hope so," she muttered, looking back into the apartment that she wasn't allowed access to. "I really want to know if she had anything to do with the threatening notes I got."

Davis frowned at her.

Doreen added, "I didn't tell you about those, did I?"

"No, but I presume your lawyer can fill me in."

"Yes," she confirmed, beaming at him. "Nick certainly can. Then, of course, Daniel could as well."

And with that, Davis nodded to Mack and said, "Good luck," and he left.

"Why the good luck?" she asked, turning to look at him. His lips twitched. "I didn't even tell him that we were engaged," she muttered.

"No, but it's obvious we're together," he shared.

She frowned. "In other words, he's laughing at me, and he thinks you're crazy to be with me." Her shoulders slumped, and Thaddeus poked his head out of her hair. "Thaddeus loves Doreen. Thaddeus loves Doreen."

"I know, buddy."

Hearing that, Detective Davis, who had stopped in the hallway to speak to somebody else, turned to her. "Good God."

She frowned. "Now what?"

"That bird."

"*That bird*," she explained, "is Thaddeus, and he's done a wonderful job taking care of me."

Davis's lips twitched again, but he didn't say anything more. He looked back at Mack, who just nodded.

"Anytime you're up in Kelowna, you may want to check in with my department."

"*Sure*," he replied.

Doreen noted that his tone of voice alone said, *Absolutely no way he ever would.*

As soon as he was gone, she turned to Mack and declared, “I don’t like it down here.”

“And that’s fine.” Mack gave her a smile. “We won’t be here for long. Let’s just keep checking on what we’ve got.”

“We don’t have anybody else to check with.”

“Well, the hospital is a start,” he muttered. “We can call to ask about her status later.”

“And we’re still missing one known criminal, so we need a location on Sam.”

“Nick will contact the parole officer again, and we should get names of some of his associates.”

“Good.” She snorted. “I personally like Daniel for it.”

“Of course you do, but that doesn’t mean he’s guilty.”

“No, unfortunately it doesn’t. I have to find proof first.”

“And right about now you’re not getting any proof.”

“But it was the right thing to come here today,” she declared, “because that poor woman may not have survived.”

“No argument there,” Mack noted. “She’s alive. She’ll get treatment at the hospital. Whether it was an attempted suicide or something totally different, at least she’ll get help. Now can we go home to Kelowna?”

“I would love to go home,” she said, with an eye roll, “but we’re not done with the house nor with our own investigations here either.”

“True,” Mack acknowledged, “but the house should be pretty empty by the time we get there today, and I think tomorrow will be Scott’s last day. Oh, but what about the dower’s house?”

Doreen grimaced, while nodding. “We must do at least an initial run-through of that home before we leave, taking whatever we want now or it's gone. As usual, Scott will get to it when he's next in Vancouver, just so he can sell this property intact. He'll do there what he did with the main house, the garages, the garage apartment—gut it of all valuables, donate the rest to charity, toss the remainder, ready the property for sale."

Mack sighed. "Glad to hear you and I will not be needed here again."

"That's the plan," Doreen noted, "at least for *this* residence."

"Oh my God," Mack muttered, shaking his head.

When they arrived at Mathew's house, they followed the noise of others speaking into the smaller formal dining room and joined the meeting of Nick, Daniel, Detective Davis—with Scott standing around, listening to the proceedings with interest.

Nick looked at Mack and shared, "She really does know how to get into trouble."

"Maybe," Mack acknowledged, with a smile. "On the other hand, Nancy was in far greater trouble."

"And she is doing much better," Detective Davis shared, "but her stomach had to be pumped, and we're not exactly sure yet how or why she ingested the supposed drugs. A tox screen is pending."

Doreen just nodded and didn't say anything. She was too busy staring at Daniel, who glared back at her.

Daniel spoke up. "I can't believe you put another detective on me."

"Why not?" she asked, staring right back at him. "All you've done is ask us repeatedly the same questions, as if you can't possibly find other suspects."

He shook his head, his glare nonstop. "It's a murder investigation."

"I know, and that's why I didn't hold back. You're the one who was already down there in Nancy's neighborhood."

"Sure," he admitted, "but for a completely different reason."

"So it's purely coincidental that you happened to be in the exact same place as Nancy, a woman who had just been drugged, almost dead when we found her?"

"What has she got to do with anything?" Daniel asked. "I don't understand."

"She's a known associate of the two men who were released from prison recently and who you now have in the morgue."

He stared at her in shock. "I didn't know that."

"How is it you didn't know that?" she asked in exasperation. "You were supposedly the lead detective on those cases, until the captain replaced you with Detective Clark. You were supposedly *investigating* those two deaths on Mathew's property."

He groaned, glancing at Davis.

Detective Davis considered him, then turned to Doreen.

She could clearly see that Davis wanted to say more, but he didn't dare.

She glared at them both. "I need a cup of tea." And, with that, she left them and marched into the kitchen.

Nick was right beside her. "Are you okay?"

"Davis and Daniel both think I'm nuts, but we go to talk to this woman, Nancy, find out that she's in a bad way, and Daniel's pulling out of the parking lot as we get there, not even in a marked vehicle."

"But he is a detective, so it's not as if he has to drive a squad car," Nick noted.

"I know that," she grumbled, followed with an eye roll.

"However, his presence there is suspicious as hell."

"It is not suspicious," Daniel roared from the kitchen doorway.

"It is suspicious," she repeated, "and just as suspicious as we seem to be to you. You won't even let us go back to Kelowna." At that, he glared at her, and she nodded. "See? Just as suspicious as we are of you."

"Oh, give it a break," Daniel snapped.

"Why should I?" she asked. "You're trying to stop us from going home, when we had nothing to do with anything. I'm exhausted from the work I've got to do here, clearing out this property," she snapped. "We've got two dead bodies, and now we have a poor woman who's either traumatized or victimized," she declared, not slowing down at all. "I don't know what to think about *you* at this point."

He glared at her and muttered, "Okay, so I was knocking on her door." Davis joined them and eyed Daniel in shock. Daniel nodded. "She is somebody I know, and I wondered if she knew Mathew. I wanted to talk to her privately before it became official."

Mack groaned and shook his head, "That's never a good idea for an active-duty police detective."

"Tell me about it," Daniel muttered through gritted teeth.

Doreen shook her head. "And you're telling me that you didn't know she was in there and needed help? Didn't the door swing open when you knocked?"

"I didn't know she was in there and needed help," he snapped. "I don't know how the door popped open for you guys, but it didn't for me."

She stared at him, shaking her head, not sure if she believed him or not. She groaned. "That poor woman, … what if we hadn't been there at all?"

"There's a good chance she would be dead," Detective Davis declared.

"There's also a good chance that *somebody* knows something," she snapped.

"Somebody always knows something," Daniel bellowed, staring at her with fury in his gaze. Davis gave him a long glare.

She added, "It's not on me to sort out your investigation. It's on you. You *were* the *lead detective* after all, something you've reminded us of at every turn."

Mugs added in a low growl.

Chapter 24

DOREEN CONTINUED. "AS far as I'm concerned, *Detective* Sherwood, you shouldn't be speaking to anybody about this case at all," she reiterated as she crossed her arms.

"It doesn't matter what you think," Daniel spat in a hard tone.

"You're the one who was at Nancy's apartment just minutes before we were, and she's now in the hospital from an overdose. The question is whether you had anything to do with her getting those drugs."

"What?" he asked in astonishment.

"Think about it, *Detective*. You were there. You knocked at her door. Yet, when *I* knocked on her door, it swung open. Did you finally find out that she was connected to the two deaths at Mathew's home or that her name was on Mathew's short list of former employees? How did you find her connection amid whatever your investigation included? *Plus,* you *knew* her. You just told us all yourself that you went there to talk to her privately."

"Yeah, I did. I wanted to make sure she knew what was happening."

Detective Davis looked shocked. "Jesus, Daniel, that's complete BS."

"I knew she didn't have anything to do with it," he muttered. "I mean, she's told me all about how bad he was to her."

"How bad who was?" Davis asked Daniel.

"How bad her husband was," he clarified, pointed at Doreen as if she were the reason for everything wrong in his life.

Doreen snorted. "I see. So you've been harassing me because of something my husband did, long after he kicked me out of the home?" She watched as Davis took notes. So did Daniel. Doreen asked Daniel, "What did my husband do to Nancy?" she asked, staring him down. "Not to mention this contradicts what you just said about not knowing if Nancy knew Mathew."

Mack reached out a gentle hand in warning but still a warning. She refused to look away from Daniel and took a deep breath. "Let's get one thing straight, *Detective.* I have absolutely no problem seeing my late husband for the man he was. He was not a nice person, and he hurt a lot of people. He handled his business like the hard character he was, but I am unaware of anything he did to Nancy, so enlighten me."

"She told me how she worked there for ten years, and he never even paid her the last of her wages."

"I see," she noted primly, raising one eyebrow, instantly knowing that wasn't true. "And what is it that she did for Mathew?"

"She was all over the house, doing everything that he needed. After all, you weren't there." Then he stopped and frowned.

She smirked. "Yeah, you caught yourself in your own lie there, didn't you, Daniel? What do you mean, *I wasn't there*? I was married to the man. I lived in his house for many years—up until a little over one year ago. Therefore, I can assure you, if Nancy had been working here for ten years and *all over the house,* as you say, I would have known her, and I do not. After seeing her nearly dying earlier today, I can confirm that I've never seen her before either."

Daniel repeated, "She was working here."

"Not when I was still living here, she was not," Doreen declared. "She might have worked for him during the thirteen months or so after I was gone from his home, but that is definitely not the same thing as working for Mathew for ten years."

Daniel didn't like hearing that.

Doreen nodded. "So, the question really is, if *you* thought Mathew had promised her something, and she didn't get it, did *you* do something to remedy the situation for her?"

He glared at her and spat, "I had nothing to do with anything happening here."

"That's not what I asked you. If you really truly thought that my late husband had missed paying wages to Nancy, and she had been suffering over something that Mathew had supposedly done, what might you have done to redress that *oversight*?"

He just flushed and glared at her.

"Please tell me that you didn't," Detective Davis began, standing beside Daniel now. "Please tell me that you didn't do anything unlawful and get involved in this."

"I didn't do anything," Daniel muttered, "at least nothing bad."

Detective Davis groaned, and she glared at them both. "Yeah, we need to define *bad.* Because Nancy wasn't working for Mathew even one full year, much less ten years. You can contact Mathew's probate attorney, who has employment info documenting the exact months Nancy worked for and was paid in full for by Mathew. Yet Nancy called Mathew's probate attorney, asking if she was in his will. The probate attorney confirmed to Nancy and later to us that she has nothing to do with Mathew's estate, so Nancy's making all that up. And, if she made that up, what else did she make up? What lies did she tell you, Daniel? I know that some locks had to be changed at Mathew's home as soon as he fired her, and we have that from the probate attorney, who was also Mathew's estate planner, as confirmed by my personal lawyer as well," she shared as she pointed at Nick. "So, Nancy may have given you a completely fabricated story, Daniel."

He stared at her, then at Nick, back to Mack. "That's not fair. Nancy can't defend herself."

"Oh, I'm looking forward to talking to her," Doreen stated, "because I highly suspect that she's taken a whole bunch of people for a ride. The question is, what did *you* do in the name of love?" she asked Daniel, trying hard to keep her voice in control. All she really wanted to do was rail at him and let Mugs have a go at him.

As if reading her thoughts, he looked around to see where Mugs was, and found him lurking just a few steps behind Daniel.

Daniel took a few deep breaths, his shoulders slumping now. "Are you sure she didn't work here all that time?" he whispered.

Nick interjected, "Yes, we're sure. She was here for a few

months at most, and then she was fired. She inserted herself in things well beyond her assigned duties. Apparently she was also a bit too forward or familiar with Mathew, to the point of pissing off Robin, who was—"

"My replacement," Doreen cut in.

"*Right*," Daniel muttered, staring off in the distance. "Look. I didn't do anything."

"Did she tell you where the money was in the house?" Doreen asked, her tone pensive. "Did she tell you about any of that?" When he glared at her, she nodded. "Oh, I'm fully aware of what's here. Mathew's home was my home too for many long years."

"Yes, but he got rid of you."

She stared at him and nodded. "Yes, he did, and that's the kind of man he was, but that doesn't change the fact that everything in this house is now mine, per Mathew's Last Will and Testament, already court-approved and legally transferred solely into my name. So your girlfriend, or your wannabe girlfriend, has a reason for being in the hospital."

"Nancy didn't do anything," he yelled, glaring at her, then groaned. "I don't know what's going on here, but I need to talk to her."

"We all need to talk to her," Detective Davis corrected, "not you, Daniel. You stay away from her, or I will arrest you for interfering with an official police investigation, with Detective Clark already designated as the new lead detective on these cases, along with me reporting directly to Captain Hawkins as needed. Do you understand me, Detective Sherwood?"

Daniel gave a short clip of his head and lowered his head.

Nick and Mack both nodded. "That would be appreciated, considering we have had threats to this property, threats to ourselves, and two murdered men found on the premises."

"I had nothing to do with that," Daniel protested.

Doreen snapped, "That's a good thing. You might keep your badge at the end of all this, but I really wouldn't count on it."

He glared at her. "I didn't do anything."

"That's not what I'm hearing though," she replied, still staring him down. "You're trying to defend your position, but you aren't being very successful at it."

"It's got nothing to do with you," he snapped.

She looked at him and snorted. "And I get that you want us to believe that. I really do. But the reality is, you have crossed a line. You've been harassing me from day one regarding the Pete Singer death, and it continues to this day. The question is, where did you cross that line? So I don't know what the results of all this will be for you."

"Nothing," he muttered, "because I didn't do anything."

"I can agree that you didn't do anything constructive as far as your investigation." She stared at him for a long minute, turned to Detective Davis, and added, "I don't particularly believe him at all, but there are still things I need to know." With that, she focused on Daniel. "You did search Mathew's house for cash and cash bonds that Nancy told you were here, didn't you?"

He flushed at that.

She nodded. "I'll take that as a yes. That would make more sense because you had access to the house."

"But I would need a key to gain access," he pointed out.

"Not when you first appeared as the detective on the case, coming here alone to investigate the first murder. Even before the second murder, we were already questioning your ethics, escorting you around the property at that time, meanwhile communicating with your Captain Hawkins, unbeknownst to you. Whether you were supposed to be on that initial investigative team to begin with remains to be seen. Captain Hawkins already removed you from all investigations regarding this property, due to your obvious harassment of me and your blind loyalty to Nancy."

"There's no reason I shouldn't be on the team."

"I think, because of your *relationship* with Nancy, you knew the two dead guys found on my property, right? Both of them?" she asked. "And you know of Sam too, I presume, the most recently released inmate as well. So I'm not sure how that works for you guys down here, but it's definitely suspect up in my corner. But, of course, we're just random people from some *hick town*, as you mentioned, right, Daniel?"

Detective Davis's frown moved off her and onto Daniel. "You knew the two dead men?"

When Daniel refused to reply, Doreen snorted. "I think he did because Nancy knew them too. Plus, Daniel knew my late husband, Mathew, the previous owner of this house," she clarified.

"Yeah, hardly the deceased persons in question," Daniel snapped.

"You didn't know the two dead guys found there? Really?" As she read out the first name, *Pete Singer*, she watched Daniel's expression change. "Pete is Nancy's brother. You didn't think I knew about that? Butch and Pete and Sam were all cellmates. And what about Sam, your wannabe girlfriend's *special friend*?"

He stared at her and shook his head. "No she's not."

"Yes," Nick confirmed, backing her up. "Nancy is Sam's girlfriend and is also Pete Singer's sister, all documented by the prison's visitor logs. Whether Sam and Nancy still have an ongoing relationship, I don't know. But that's her connection to this place at this time, knowing both dead guys found here, aside from the fact that she worked here too."

Doreen smiled. "By the way, Daniel, the money Mathew stashed in this house is now safe and sound in my bank account."

"You found it?" Daniel asked, looking at her with an incredulous expression. "It was supposed to be really well-hidden."

"Yes, but this was my house for a long time," she reminded him, still working to stay calm. "I certainly know the locations of the safes and the hidden storage places Mathew liked to use."

He glared at her. "That doesn't mean you know about all of it."

"Maybe you should tell me about that."

"No, because then …" He stopped and looked around at the other people nearby. "Fine, whatever."

"Yeah, but you can't get it now," she taunted him. "We'll make sure you and your prison buddies don't have access to this house ever again. However, should we find you have any keys to Mathew's house on your person, that would completely change things."

He stiffened and his hands immediately went to his pockets.

Mack grabbed his hand and pulled a set of keys from them, as Detective Davis glared at Daniel in disgust.

Daniel shrugged. "*Bags full of cash are here*," he muttered, "and she told me that they were hers."

"Do you mean it *was hers*, or do you mean it was *supposedly* owed to her? Really?" Detective Davis looked pissed as hell. "You believed that?"

"I wanted to believe it, yeah, and, if it's cash, … nobody would know."

"That's true. Nobody would know, and, Daniel, you are in some big trouble here," Mack confirmed. "However, as Doreen already shared, we took all those bags full of cash to the bank, as Doreen's legal inheritance from Mathew's estate."

Daniel stared at him in shock, then his shoulders slumped, and he nodded. "Fine, so no point in looking for them."

"No, there isn't. So, what happened to the dead guy in the garden, Pete Singer?"

"I don't know anything about that," he muttered, with a shake of his head.

Doreen snorted. "Funny, Daniel. Captain Hawkins shared with us that Butch used his own gun and killed Pete, who was Nancy's brother. So did you know the dead guy in the apartment suite, Butch Weldon?" Doreen asked.

He stared at her and shrugged.

She knew that look meant he was about to lie again, so she asked him, "You do know about him."

"No, I don't."

Meanwhile, Mack was lining up Daniel's keys to the ones Doreen handed over to him to compare. When he found an exact match, he held it up for everybody to see.

Doreen nodded. "Funny that you now have a copy of the newest key to get into Mathew's house, where we had two murders on the same property," she shared, still watching him. "The first murder happened before we even arrived in town. We drove from Kelowna, Detective Davis, but Daniel here didn't search for Pete Singer's murderer nor for Butch Weldon's murderer. Daniel was pretty quick to try and pin both of those on us."

"You're the ones living here." Daniel spat.

"Not living. Just taking a week or so to clear out the property so it can be sold. Yet you're the one with a new key to the main house."

He glared at her and stated, "I didn't kill Pete. I didn't kill Butch."

"But you didn't come here alone though, did you, that visit before we arrived and hindered your treasure hunt?" He paled and she nodded. "I figured as much. The neighbors saw a couple around the unoccupied house, and it wasn't us, so … it had to be somebody. At first I thought it was Singer and Nancy. Now I think it was you, Daniel, and Nancy. Am I right?"

Detective Davis pulled out his handcuffs, and, flipping Daniel around, he muttered, "I don't know yet who is behind Butch's murder, but you've already admitted enough that you are in trouble." Then he read him his rights.

"I suspect he's covering his own criminality or covering Nancy's or both," Doreen suggested.

"You don't know anything," Daniel yelled. "I didn't do anything."

"Except break into Mathew's property and look for something to steal," she noted, "all while you were on duty."

"I wasn't on duty."

"You cased this property while you were on duty."

He flushed at that. "Fine, okay, so I'll get a slap on the hand."

"Whenever you and Nancy trespassed on my property, did you leave her here by herself at times?"

Daniel's face seemed to pale.

Doreen nodded. "Because somebody surprised Pete on the property. I seriously doubt that Nancy killed her brother. Ballistics prove Butch killed Pete, which probably brought the wrath of Nancy down on Butch, but we're awaiting evidence on that. I'm also concerned about Sam's whereabouts, since all three—Pete, Butch, Sam—wanted to hunt for treasure, didn't they, Daniel? Just like you, all on the word of Nancy, right? Your potential girlfriend? All four of them, plus you of course, were already casing the joint, ready to enter Mathew's home with Nancy's key, to right a wrong, to find treasure.

He stared at her and shook his head. "No way."

"You mean you hope there's no way because if it happened at the same time you were here, whether you knew it or not, you brought with you someone to commit murder. You're up to your neck in this as an accomplice to *both* murders."

At that, he paled and shook his head frantically. "I didn't have anything to do with it, nothing. … I didn't."

She looked over at Mack, who fully knew what would happen now. "Sounds to me as if you need to tell us exactly who you came here with."

"No way," he repeated. "You're not pinning that on me."

"I want to know about the second murder."

"I didn't have anything to do with that," he snapped. "I had nothing to do with either murder."

Chapter 25

DOREEN STARED AT him and shook her head. "I don't believe you."

He rounded on her. "I don't care if you believe me or not," he roared. "This has nothing to do with you. You need to go right back to whatever corner you crawled out from."

Mugs gave a bark and stepped closer to Doreen.

"It's okay, Mugs." She even smiled at Daniel. "I think Nancy killed Butch."

Daniel paled but shook his head. "She had nothing to do with this."

"You'll really take a murder rap for Nancy? *Two* murder raps, seeing as you're an accomplice?"

He blinked several times.

Doreen explained, "I'm pretty sure that Nancy came with you, and she killed the man in the servants' quarters, Butch Weldon. I don't know whether he was supposed to be there or not, but the murder happened while he was in bed, sound asleep. So, whether it was a fit of temper on her part or something else, I don't know," she shared. "But the real question is, if that's what happened, did you know about it, Daniel?" When he started to shake and quiver in front of her, she sighed. "All for the love of a woman."

"What do you know about love?" he cried out. "You were married to that miserable man, and you got all that money to leave him alone."

"I didn't get any money when he told me to leave," she corrected him, staring him down. "And, if he had signed the divorce papers, this would be a whole different story, but he didn't. He was being his usual controlling self about everything, refusing to share any money at all with me while he was alive," she muttered, staring at him.

"Did you really come here with Nancy looking for treasure?" Mack asked. "The neighbors can probably ID you two."

He slowly nodded. "Nancy was so sure. She told me how there were bags, bags full of money."

"There absolutely was a lot of cash on these premises," Mack confirmed, "but not anymore."

Daniel slumped in place. "Really, there were bags?"

Mack nodded. "Sure, but the bags of money were secured in hidden safes."

"In the safes, where cash is supposed to be," Doreen pointed out. "Mathew was arrogant and not a nice man, but he wasn't stupid, nor the type to leave his money lying around for you wannabe thieves to come steal. And I get that, for you, this probably isn't important, but the fact of the matter is that Mathew's money wasn't yours, and it wasn't Nancy's either."

"It was owed to her," he repeated desperately.

"No, it wasn't," she stated. "The probate attorney confirmed that she was paid in full for the hours of work she did here. I get that you listened to her, that you believed her excuses or whatever, and that you followed through in a way that'll have incredible consequences for you," she muttered. "But Nancy wasn't entitled to anything, and somewhere along the line Butch was killed. Why would you bring a weapon to a burglary anyway?"

"I didn't," he wailed. "She found it here."

"Where?"

"In the house. She found it, thought it was a joke, and carried it around. I told her to put it back, to not touch it, but she'd never had a gun before, and she liked it." He shrugged. "I was more concerned about trying to get her the money she had coming to her."

"Right, that all-important money," Doreen noted, with a sneer. "You all were so fixated on money, money that wasn't yours. Certainly money that was not owed to Nancy. I presume at some point you split up with Nancy."

"Yes, we did," he muttered.

"Why? Because Mathew's gun she found is probably the same one she used to kill Butch Weldon in bed in the servants' quarters? Is that what split you up?"

"No, no, no," he muttered. Yet he stared at her and his shoulders started to shake a little more, and then they slumped. "Please no."

"Yes," she repeated, "and you probably knew it too."

"No, I didn't."

"You would have recognized him when the body was brought out," Mack pointed out.

Daniel stared at Mack desperately and shook his head. "Not really, no."

"And did you know Butch was her friend?"

"No." And then he broke down and changed his story again. "Yes, I did, but she didn't do it."

"You mean you don't want her to have done it because it

would have been at the same time that you were involved in a burglary," Mack explained, staring at him in understanding. "And, if she did that—murdered somebody while you were here with her—that murder is on you too."

He shook his head, breathing faster now.

Doreen added, "And that's also why she took the drugs that she overdosed on, isn't it? Maybe she called you, discussing this. So you came over to check on her, supposedly missing her at her apartment," Doreen theorized. "Nancy wanted to take her life because she realized what she'd done and what it would mean. Right, Daniel?" He stared at her with tears in his eyes, and she nodded. "But we still have a couple holes in this story. What about the original murder?"

"That was on him, Butch Weldon, the dead guy squatting in the servants' quarters," he cried out, "and the victim was Nancy's brother. When she found out, I think she just … lost it."

"You knew about it?"

"Not beforehand, I didn't. I hadn't talked to her about it. I didn't ask her, and that's what I went there to talk to her about, once I realized who both of the dead guys were on your property. But I don't know what happened, not really. Pete and Butch were always fighting, got caught doing stupid stuff, landed in prison. They were friends but got into it all the time. I think maybe the second guy killed the first guy, after Pete told Butch about the bags of money, but I don't know for sure," he muttered, raising both hands. "I didn't kill anybody."

Mack looked at him and raised his eyebrows. "You know it won't matter, don't you? You are still an accessory to both murders."

He stared at him, and such sadness filled his expression.

"I loved her."

"That's nice," Doreen muttered, "but that won't make things any easier because I don't think she loved you. She loved Sam."

He started to cry silently.

Detective Davis decided to uncuff him, even giving him a handkerchief. In a last-ditch effort, Daniel bolted out the front door and raced down the driveway. Just as he went to take another step, something crossed paths with him, tripping him up, sending him flying. He wound up flat on the pavement, with a thoroughly pleased Mugs sitting on top of him, preventing him from going anywhere. Thaddeus, realizing that he had missed out on a very important part of a game that he absolutely loved, burst from Doreen's hair, flying as hard and as fast as he could flap his wings, screaming, "Thaddeus is here. Thaddeus is here."

He came to a complete halt on Daniel's head. And, with that, he struck the same pose that Doreen had commissioned to be painted for Nan, with one leg atop the victim's head, and the other in the commanding stance of a triumphant ruler. Even Goliath showed up, parading around, swishing his tail with his nose in the air, demonstrating the appropriate amount of distain for their prisoner. As they all gathered around, Mack and Nick started to snicker, while Detective Davis was stunned into silence.

He looked over at her and muttered, "Those animals are …"

Mack nodded when the detective couldn't come up with any words. "Yes, they absolutely are. You've got to understand they have gotten Doreen out of any number of really dangerous situations," he murmured.

"The animals?" Davis asked, looking at him.

Mack nodded. "Yes, these animals. They defend her at all times and have never ever let her down."

"And they won't," Doreen declared, standing beside him. "Because they look after me with love, and that is so very important."

"Not half as important as you looking after yourself," Mack added. "I keep hoping that one day we won't get into situations that require their special protective skills."

Beside him, Nick snorted and replied, "I don't see that day coming anytime soon, bro. I've never seen her in action quite like this, but I've got to tell you. She would make one heck of a prosecutor."

"She would at that, if she could ever get her evidence lined up first," Mack noted, with a sigh. "In the meantime, she's got those animals primed, and they don't let anybody get away with anything."

"And that's a good thing," she said, "because look at this, Detective Davis. We solved your two murder cases. I'm really sorry that Daniel was involved though."

"Not him technically," Nick clarified, beside her.

"No, but he's likely to get charged the same regardless."

At that comment, Detective Davis nodded. "For any murder that occurs during the commission of a crime," he recited, "that's automatic. He will most likely be charged with murder in the first degree or at the least manslaughter. Detective Daniel, care to tell us where we can find Sam?"

Daniel shook his head. "He may have been staying with Nancy, at her place."

Doreen sighed. "And Daniel did all this because he fell in love."

"I understand the sentiment," Mack admitted.

She looked over at him, one eyebrow raised. "I kind of

like hearing that. Yet I prefer to think you're a whole lot smarter than Daniel was."

"Well," he began, a big grin on his face, "at least I fell in love with a woman who solves crimes instead of committing them." And, with that, he tucked her up close and chuckled at the look on her face.

She patted him on the chest and noted, "Seems you made the right choice."

She looked back over at the two detectives, as one pulled the other to his feet and snapped on the handcuffs once more.

"Can we finally go home now?" she asked Detective Davis.

Epilogue

DOREEN AND MACK had been home for a few days, with Nick happy to stay in Vancouver for a few more, overseeing Mathew's property, while helping a few of his clients he still worked for, even with his move to Kelowna. Today Doreen was thoroughly enjoying having a cup of tea at Nan's apartment. The entire group of Doreen's Deputies was gathered here, and everybody had questions. They each needed to know how their assistance had been invaluable, and, since they had made some very useful connections, Doreen was more than happy to give credit where credit was due.

"And you got even more treasure out of that house?" Maisie asked.

Doreen chuckled. "Yes," she replied, yet shaking her head. "An unbelievable amount of it."

"But you don't even care about that, do you?" Richie asked, with a knowing nod.

She shrugged. "I care for what money can do," she clarified. "And, therefore, all these items can be sold and will create more money that I can do things with to help others. But I don't particularly care about money itself, and I really,

really don't care about things."

She patted Mugs and Goliath, then stroked Thaddeus, who was on her shoulder. Afterward she reached for her grandmother's hand and shared, "It's really all about the people and the pets I love and has nothing to do with stuff. People are important, and it didn't take me long to learn that at all."

"What about Mack?" Maisie asked, rather delicately.

She chuckled. "Mack is doing just fine. I think he's resigned himself to the fact that, no matter what we do, this will be our life, and I, for one, don't mind," she stated. "It keeps things exciting."

Maisie grinned. "And what about the wedding?"

Immediately Doreen glared. "Nobody is allowed to ask me about when the wedding will be."

"But we need to know, dear," Nan replied. "Everybody has plans."

"Plans?" Doreen repeated, frowning at her in shock. "What do you mean, *plans*?"

"All kinds of things have to happen before you get married."

Doreen shook her head. "No, I've been married before, and no big plans are allowed this time. Maybe a nice big party down at the lake or something afterward," she suggested, "but other than that? Nope, not interested."

Maisie sat back with a big smile on her face. "Maybe you'll just have to be surprised because life is all about accepting that you can't control everything."

Doreen stared at Maisie a little dismally and asked, "What are you guys up to? Aside from the fact that my grandmother is undoubtedly betting on which day I'll choose for the wedding."

Nan chuckled. "I wouldn't be me if I wasn't."

"Maybe not," Doreen muttered.

"But that doesn't mean I won't listen to your wishes," Nan added, with a repressive look over at Maisie. "We will honor your wishes, Doreen."

Maisie nodded. "Of course we will," she quipped, with a beaming smile. "Just know that everything happens for a reason, and it's all because we love you."

Doreen groaned at that.

"Doreen," Richie interrupted, turning her attention to something else, taking the subject away from her wedding, for which she was grateful.

"Did you hear about what went on in the underbrush down along the river? Underneath the bridge I think, where the trees used to be, and now all that underbrush grows there?"

Doreen frowned at him. "No. What's going on?"

He shrugged. "I'm not really sure. You'll have to find out from Mack."

"We haven't been home that long, and I don't know if he's been assigned to any cases or not," she noted, eyeing Richie curiously. "What do you know about it?"

He grinned. "Nothing really, just some chaos going on there. I don't have any details," he added, holding up a hand, "but something criminal may be happening there."

"Oh, that's interesting," she noted.

"That's what I thought you would say," Richie declared, with a smile. "Of course Mack has the details."

"I might have to ask him, but he probably thinks I need a break and I should be staying out of trouble for a while," she muttered, with an eyeroll.

He chuckled.

"Besides, it's about *underbrush*, not exactly a case where you could work with that into a title or anything," Nan teased her, with a smile.

Doreen asked her, "You mean, my naming convention?"

"Exactly, which is why everybody was saying you should write a book."

"I don't know about writing a book," she argued. Then she gasped and announced, "*Undone in the Underbrush.*"

They all stared at her in silence, until Richie started to chuckle, then laughed and laughed. "It's perfect. You don't even know what it's about, but you've already got a title for this case."

"That's just so I can claim it," she murmured, as she gave him a big grin. "After all, if I point out to the universe that it's already mine, surely Mack won't stop me from working on it, will he?"

"Oh yes he will, dear," Nan countered, chuckling too. "He absolutely will."

"*If* he can," Richie clarified, with another chortle.

At that Mugs barked, and Goliath, who'd been sleeping beside him, took a swipe at him for waking him up. On cue, Thaddeus poked his head out from underneath Doreen's hair and cried out, "Thaddeus is here. Thaddeus is here."

Doreen burst into laughter, never happier to be home and to be with those whom she loved more than anything in this world.

This concludes Book 5 of Lovely Lethal Gardens Rewind: Vandals in the Vidalias.

Read about Undone in the Underbrush: Lovely Lethal Gardens Rewind, Book 6

Lovely Lethal Gardens Rewind: Undone in the Underbrush (Book 6)

Doreen and Mack and their animal entourage are home from their crazy trip to Vancouver—yet not long enough for boredom to set in. A new murder case appears, clearly defined as Mack's, not hers. Until …

The latest victim is connected to a little old lady living in Rosemoor, who has a lot of connections that she's more than willing to yank on to get the *best detective not on the force* to work this case.

Under these circumstances, Doreen steps up to help Mack—together with her loyal menagerie of animals—and digs deep into the mystery surrounding this latest murder. Her investigation involves unraveling local criminals, a shadowy crime boss, unexpected twists and turns, even one no one saw coming …

Find Undone in the Underbrush here!

To find out more visit Dale Mayer's website.

https://geni.us/DMSUndone

Author's Note

Thank you for reading Vandals in the Vidalias: Lovely Lethal Gardens Rewind, Book 5! If you enjoyed the book, please take a moment and leave a short review.

Dear reader,

I love to hear from readers, and you can contact me at my website: www.dalemayer.com or at my Facebook author page. To be informed of new releases and special offers, sign up for my newsletter or follow me on BookBub. And if you are interested in joining Dale Mayer's Reader Group, here is the Facebook sign up page.
http://geni.us/DaleMayerFBGroup

Cheers,
Dale Mayer

About the Author

Dale Mayer is a *USA Today* best-selling author, best known for her SEALs military romances, her Psychic Visions series, and her Lovely Lethal Garden cozy series. Her contemporary romances are raw and full of passion and emotion (Broken But … Mending, Hathaway House series). Her thrillers will keep you guessing (Kate Morgan, By Death series), and her romantic comedies will keep you giggling (*It's a Dog's Life*, a stand-alone novella; and the Broken Protocols series, starring Charming Marvin, the cat).

Dale honors the stories that come to her—and some of them are crazy, break all the rules and cross multiple genres!

To go with her fiction, she also writes nonfiction in many different fields, with books available on résumé writing, companion gardening, and the US mortgage system. All her books are available in print and ebook format.

Connect with Dale Mayer Online

Dale's Website – www.dalemayer.com

Twitter – @DaleMayer

Facebook Page – geni.us/DaleMayerFBFanPage

Facebook Group – geni.us/DaleMayerFBGroup

BookBub – geni.us/DaleMayerBookbub

Instagram – geni.us/DaleMayerInstagram

Goodreads – geni.us/DaleMayerGoodreads

Newsletter – geni.us/DaleNews

Made in United States
North Haven, CT
19 March 2026

90111531R00173